A HOME IN PERCIVAL

Paula Berman

Rowell Press

ISBN-13: 979-8-9997463-1-3

Cover design by: Arsalan Ali

Library of Congress Control Number: 2025917819

Printed in the United States of America

To Ted, for …. well, pretty much everything

CONTENTS

CHAPTER ONE: LIFE IN PERCIVAL

"'Oh, damn!'" said Lord Peter Wimsey at Piccadilly Circus.

"Damn it!" I echoed, putting the book down. Much as I loved Lord Peter Wimsey, I couldn't bring myself to read through the series one more time. I didn't want to read anything, in fact and for me, that is saying something. Reading is what I do unless I have to do something else – and sometimes even while I should be doing something else. But outside of work, and the bare necessities of daily life, I hadn't done much of anything else since I finished moving in.

I'd hardly talked to anyone in person in the months since we'd all been in quarantine – I hadn't touched anyone for so much as a handshake, hadn't traveled or eaten out, or, well, pretty much anything. The lack of touch was particularly annoying; my boyfriend Gil lived in Austin, Texas, and we hadn't seen each other in person since the start of the pandemic, though we talked every night.

On the positive side, I knew how lucky I was to be able to keep working, selling my spells online and doing some virtual consulting, and how privileged I was to be healthy even if it was a nuisance to do my grocery shopping masked and remotely order my spell ingredients.

I was also lucky to be here in Percival, Oregon, a couple of hours away from my former Portland condo. Percival was known for its covered bridge and not much else, but living by Orchard Lake was a continual delight. I'd never lived in a beautiful place before, where I could look out my own window at a view of water, trees and sky that was continually changing. I loved watching how it altered from hour to hour, as clouds moved by or the wind kicked up the lake, and also from season to season as the trees budded, flowered, grew leaves and then turned red and yellow in autumn.

I'd ended up here in a roundabout way. Meg, one of my favorite customers, lived on the East Coast where she worked for a company who made paints and varnishes with magical effects, but her grandfather, Ray Hobb, had lived here. He'd left her his house, but since COVID was at its height then, she couldn't travel across the country to see it. I'd surprised myself by volunteering to check it out for her and walk her through it on a video call. The house was small, but it sat right by the lake with its own private dock, and as soon as I walked through the front door I felt welcomed there.

Next thing I knew we'd set up a rent-to-own contract and I'd sold my old place, packed up my books, equipment, clothing, yarn, and kayaks, and moved in. The house was adorable: small and sunny, with just two bedrooms, and a nook in the living room that I used as a library. We'd had most of Grandpa Ray's furniture shipped to his granddaughter, but she'd allowed me to keep his bookshelves and some of his books. There was a cozy gas fireplace in the living room, and I set my favorite reading chair in front of it.

Even better, it appeared that Grandpa Ray might have had a roommate at one point, because though the main house was small, the attic had two rooms that might have once been a semi-separate apartment. Both rooms had windows so that I had plenty of light up here too, and one of them had been set up as a rudimentary kitchen, with running water. I used that room as a lab where I created spells and the other one as my office, leaving the entire main floor as living space. Until I moved into this house, I'd never had enough room to have completely distinct working and living quarters, and I loved the separation.

Really, the house was nearly perfect for me. It sometimes felt bigger and lonelier than such a small cozy house ought to be, but that was probably the effect of quarantine. It was sized just right for me, well-laid-out and comfortable. It would have been nice to have a garage, but there was a carport to provide some shelter for my car, and an alcove off my lab that I used for storage. That was one of the things I loved about the place; Grandpa Ray had built it by hand and there were niches and nooks and built-in storage everywhere. He'd built solid, and it was obvious he'd put a lot of thought into where everything would be most convenient.

I also appreciated that most of the land between me and the lake was owned by whichever government department controlled the dam on the lake, meaning I could look at it and walk through it to my dock but I didn't have to maintain it. I owned only the path from the house to the dock, plus a deck and just enough ground around the house to have a garden if I wanted one. Grandpa Ray evidently *hadn't* been much of a gardener, because there was just a covered patio, some grassy bits and some rocky bits.

I hadn't gotten around to it this past summer, but I kept trying to persuade myself that next year I should plant an herb garden, so I could grow some of my own ingredients for both cooking and my work. So far, my desire for a picturesque garden plot and fresh herbs had not managed to overcome my dislike of actually, you know, *gardening*.

The paradox was that things were loosening up now from the worst of the pandemic and if I had any local friends I could at least have gone hiking or kayaking with them. Or maybe even, daringly, eaten dinner at someone else's house. But because I'd moved here during some of the worst days of isolation, I hadn't had a chance to meet anyone local.

I didn't know my neighbors, either, because their houses weren't that close; mine was at the end of a dead-end street but set back on a long gravel driveway, so that it was a bit away from the others along the lakefront here. They all looked newer than mine, which I suspected had been the only house on the road when it was first built. Some of the other houses were just weekend cabins, too, though a few were lived in. I waved at my neighbors when I saw them and they waved back, but we hadn't gotten any farther than that.

I sometimes regretted moving to this small Oregon town, but then I'd never made any close friends in Portland either – the 'Northwest Freeze' is a real thing. I didn't need people anyway, did I? Not with a lake and mountains right outside my window. The lake view was so beautiful that my heart rose every time I looked outside, no matter what the weather was doing. I could just see the covered bridge and its white paint could be gray, golden, or sparkling, depending on the light and the lake's reflections. Oddly, the bridge extended only partway across the lake, with a modern bridge right beside taking cars all the way across, but it was a town landmark, and it was beautiful. I thought that the view sparked my creativity; even if I was lonely in my off hours, I'd created more new spells than ever in the past year.

I loved being in the kayak whenever it wasn't too rainy, windy or cold; I got to watch birds, small animals and the occasional people around the lake, and it was where I did my best creative thinking. It was probably not as effective an exercise regime as I liked to delude myself into believing, but at least I was moving. The best bit about working for myself was being able to get out on the water whenever I wanted, as long as I didn't actually have a meeting scheduled with suppliers or customers; the worst thing was that any work I postponed in order to get in the boat still had to be done later. On the other hand, part of my work was coming up with new ideas to try, and that part could be – and most often was – done in the boat, even if all the actual trial and error needed to happen back in the lab.

Anyway, if I didn't feel like reading and the weather wouldn't let me go paddling, I could at least do something useful. I glumly settled into writing some product documentation, hoping the weather would cooperate and let me take my kayak out later. With hardly anyone else out on the lake these days, going out paddling gave me a chance to experiment with some communication spells that seemed to work better over water than on land.

***

The next morning, I was doing my usual ten-minute pre-work morning scan – news, stocks, social media, a daily word game I liked, and a quick scan of personal email – and noticed an interesting post on a neighborhood community app:

> **Genna:** I'm new here, and would really like to make some local friends. I promise, I am not weird – well, not that weird – well, ok, just weird enough to be interesting – with no extremist views. I bathe regularly, swear too much, and don't do drugs other than alcohol. Looking for someone to do stuff with – hiking, visiting local points of interest, or just generally hanging out.

The original poster called herself Genna Genista, probably an online nom de keyboard, but her profile appeared genuine and the post seemed totally innocuous. However, when I focused on the words, I saw the sparkle behind them that meant they were written by someone in the Magical Community hoping to reach others. I couldn't tell anything else about who the writer was from those few lines; she could be a magic user like me, or someone born with magic. Looking at the lake and woods in the area, there had to be dryads and naiads, and there might be deep enough forest to attract elves or … well, who knew. I was under the impression that some of those terms like "fae" were just human labels, anyway, that might cover a host of groups who considered themselves separate peoples with unique features or cultures. I didn't want to presume – diversity and inclusion weren't only for the mundane world! That was why we used the term "MagiComms" or "MCs" for any community member, to avoid limiting terms like "magician" or pejorative ones like "creature". A few people, both magical and mundane, had already replied to show some interest. So I commented, cautiously,

> **Macrina:** I might be interested – were you thinking about starting with a meetup? The local coffee shop, From the Grounds Up, has some outdoor tables so those who are still doing social distancing can join too.

I focused my intent for a moment on the words I'd just typed, to make sure my reply would sparkle when read by any other MagiComms. Then I got to work, forcing myself not to check back on the post until the next morning because my hopes had surged and it would be too disappointing if this didn't work out – if nobody showed up, or worse, if lots of people did and I hated them all. Or worst of all, if lots of people were there and they all hated me.

When I did check back, during the next morning's social media rounds, there seemed to be a lot of local interest, and my suggestion of a coffee shop meetup had gained ground. Working from home allowed me a lot of flexibility, so I suggested a few time slots either around lunchtime or the end of the workday and waited to see what happened next.

***

Meanwhile, I reminded myself how lucky I was, if restlessness was my biggest problem at the moment. I luxuriated in the beauty around me, not to mention the quiet – there was no traffic to speak off on this dead-end street. If we heard sirens in this town, it was an event and everyone immediately checked the local emergency-services app, as opposed to my old city condo where the light rail rumbled by every fifteen minutes and I heard sirens multiple times a day. Living alone did get lonely though, especially with a long-distance relationship that had to *stay* long distance until travel became practical again. We'd decided years ago that we couldn't live together, but loved each other too much to break up. So Gil had his place and I had mine, and in normal times we visited each other or met up somewhere in the middle every month or two. It gave me all the stability of having someone I could talk to about anything plus the freedom to live my own way day to day. While I couldn't deny that it would be nice to get laid rather more regularly, or even just sleep snuggled up with another person, his job was in Austin, Texas now and I also couldn't live in the hot humid weather there.

I kept thinking about getting a couple of cats, but I was afraid I'd end up as one of those people who not only talk to their pets but voice the pet's reply. Instead, I ended up talking to my kayak whenever I took her out, and that couldn't be a good thing. At least, not when the kayak was the only one I talked to in person, most days. I really needed to get out more. (In my mind, the kayak replied, "Damn right you should!")

"I'm glad you said that," Gil told me when I made the same comment to him on our nightly call. "Your relationship with your kayak was beginning to get a little weird."

"Well, at least when I talk to myself I get interesting answers," I retorted. "What if I go meet these people and they're all really boring? What if they're all super-religious types who hate MagiComms and I have to live a lie?"

He replied reasonably, "You said the original post sparkled. So this Genna person who wrote it is MC, at least, and expects there to be some others around. And you've never cared if your friends had or used magic, as long as they knew enough about it that you didn't have to pretend with them."

I sighed. "True. It's just hard to force myself out to meet a completely new set of people, after being alone so long. How are you doing, now that you and Jimmy and Deepak and their families have decided to be a 'pod'?"

"Much better. It's nice to be able to go over other people's houses again, and they really needed to do it for the kids. Good thing their kids are all about the same age –

I'm just lucky they let me in too."

"You know you're the cool uncle. The kids probably all demanded they include you in the pod! Besides, those kids love to roughhouse with you – it gives the parents a break. And Jimmy and Deepak and their partners are smart enough to want their kids to have other adults in their lives they can talk to, for when they get a little older and their parents are too desperately uncool."

"You're right. Anyway, when are you meeting up with all of these local strangers?"

"Not sure yet, but I think it will be next week sometime."

"Well. You can vent your jitters at me some more before then. Miss you lots! I can't wait until travel is safer and I can see you again. I'm not sure I'm ready to start flying again yet either, but are you sure you don't want to road-trip down here?"

"I do, but it's a long way to drive for the amount of time I'd be able to stay – and a hell of a long drive to do solo."

"It is," he agreed sadly. "I need to go – got another of those calls with the India office. Goodnight, love you, Macrina-Meli!"

That was his nickname for me, because Gil liked multilevel wordplay. (Some would call it long-winded, needing so much explanation that it was tedious, but I shared his taste.) "Meli" meant honey in Greek; he called me that partly as an endearment, but also because he insisted my hair, eyes and skin were all golden-honey colored. (I'd have called my eyes light brown, my skin tan, and my hair a combination of brown and blonde, but whatever – if he liked the way they looked, I wasn't going to argue!) And he used the Greek word, because Macrina was a Greek name.

We hung up, but I had far too much extra energy to go to bed right away. I decided it was too late to rearrange the furniture (again), but that this small town was safe enough for me to go for a short walk, even this late in the evening. Fall was closing in and the air was getting chilly;

I'd need a light jacket.

I reminded myself that I needed to prep for my Samhain ritual on October 31, when tradition said that the veils between worlds were thinnest – even MagiComms like me who had no British or Irish background at all, tended to celebrate Samhain and Beltane, partly for the fun of it and partly because some spells just worked better at those times. No one had ever really figured out why. Anyhow, I didn't need to start my prep that night; I just enjoyed the quiet night with Orion rising in the dark skies and tried not to think about what it would be like to meet a bunch of strangers.

It was hard to begin peopling again after the solitude of the year when we were all in quarantine, but another reason I was a little reluctant to meet new people was the inevitable question, "What do you do?" Even MC types tend to expect magic users to do flashy spells, love potions (even though those were unethical) or healing or whatever, and I …. mostly didn't. I wrote background spells: some of mine might chain other spells together to make them work as one, or accelerate or decelerate their effects, or magnify or shrink them. (So far, my biggest success was the one that minimized the size of a healing spell, allowing healers who worked in genetics to do microsurgery on genes.) But try explaining all that in one sentence to someone who was only looking for casual conversation! Mostly I explained what I did by comparing it to software engineers who wrote firmware or operating systems, that stayed in the background and made everything else function. Or if they were still baffled, I'd say "I help people combine spells together or sometimes I make spells work better, whether that's faster, slower, bigger, smaller or whatever. Just better, however you define that." That was one reason Gil and I understood each other, since, like the majority of MC people, he had a nonmagical job and actually was a firmware engineer.

Over the next few days, I could feel my anxiety level rising. Part of that was the upcoming meeting – we'd decided to gather for a late-afternoon coffee. That made it possible for those who worked standard office hours to sneak out just a little early for our meetup, while those who had kids could pick them up from after school activities right afterward, especially as the town's sole coffee shop was right next to the grade school. The meeting wasn't the only thing that had me on edge, though – the coming of Samhain always unsettled me a little. In some traditions, that was when the Wild Hunt flew and prudent people kept their families and animals firmly inside on that night. I'd be outside during Trick or Treating hours, but after that I planned to have my doors locked and all shades firmly down. Not that I expected the Wild Hunt, but you never knew.

Fortunately, Samhain itself wasn't til Sunday, so I could put most of my prep for it off until after the meetup.

CHAPTER TWO: PEOPLING

On Tuesday, I had a couple conference calls with clients in the morning but managed to sneak in a quick paddle between them while the sun was out – luckily, the second call was voice-only so I was able to do the call as soon as I came in, and wait to shower after the meeting! After lunch I spent a little time writing up instructions for working with my spells in different use cases, until about an hour before the meetup – because I knew I'd change my mind about seventeen times on what to wear and I needed the time to decide. Did I want to look more professional, less intimidating, more earth-mother-granola-y, more stylish or what?

Eventually I decided that I needed to look as much like myself as possible, since what I needed here was for people to be able to tell if they liked me, and vice versa. If they took me for something I wasn't, we'd never make it as more than casual acquaintances.

I wet my hair and scrunched up my curls so my hair would look more like I meant to do that, but didn't put on any makeup over my everyday sunscreen that seemed so futile on this gray day. I wore an eggplant-colored oversized hoodie over straight jeans and my usual sturdy ankle boots. I added a small cowl I'd knitted, as a conversation starter in case any other knitters were there. Even though it had started raining again (because it's Oregon, and unless it's summer it's always raining) I decided to walk to the coffee-shop. I felt stupid driving three blocks, even though no matter how much I worked out, I still always got a little sweaty on the uphill walk to the end of my own block.

And of course I dithered again over the timing – I

didn't want to be the first there or the last, so I was careful to leave my house just five minutes before the meetup was scheduled to start. We'd agreed to grab the big table in the back of the shop, and since we had scheduled the meetup before the end of the school day, for once it was free of high-schoolers hanging out.

When I arrived, two gray-haired women were already there, one with shoulder-length hair who looked slightly lost, and the other with a stylish short cut, with a few purple locks, who had the air of someone running a meeting. I grabbed one of the more comfy chairs while they were still available. A few more people trickled in over the next few minutes – one 60ish woman with assertively-dyed blonde hair, two guys who sat together as if for protection against the estrogen level at the rest of the table, a young woman with many braids and a granola vibe, a confident-looking man in his early fifties who didn't seem to feel the need to cluster with the other men, a pretty woman with pale, pale skin and flowing bronze-colored hair who looked like the subject of a Pre-Raphaelite painting, and pinged my dryad-radar strongly and an edgier woman with a green buzzcut and pale brown skin almost the color of oak bark between numerous tattoos, who looked like she'd been designed to be the dryad's polar opposite. There were also a few others who didn't stand out from each other. At a guess, they were a nearly-even mixture of MCs and non-magical people, but I'd need to wait and see if those guesses were correct.

The woman with purple hair turned out to be Genna, who had posted the original message. At promptly ten minutes after the set time, she spoke up.

"Thanks for coming, everyone. Why don't we introduce ourselves? I can go first if you want." She looked around the table for approval, but of course no one argued. "I am Genna Genista, and I've recently transplanted here from Northern California. I'm an anthropologist studying traditional interactions between groups of Dryads and Naiads in the Northwest, so I've been coming out here for years to study this area. My husband has joined the university's faculty and I'll be semi-retired – teaching one section of Anthro 101 at the community college in addition to continuing my own research. I think it will work well, because I can still continue to collaborate with my team from our old university."

The woman with the green buzzcut spoke up next. "You did say you're looking for friends, not research subjects, right? Because I'm an evergreen dryad." Aaaand my radar for the various MC peoples was once again proven to be complete shit, though that did explain her oak-tree coloring.

Genna reassured her. "I study *traditional* interactions only, I promise. I realize modern dryads live where they want and hang out with who they want – if you have any information about your great-great-grandparents I might be interested, but I do know the difference between a person and a project! And I've got some dryad ancestry myself – that's where my name comes from, in fact. Genista is wild broom. But I have just a tiny bit of magic myself, just enough to let people know I'm part of the MC or run a few small boughten spells."

Green Buzzcut lowered her hackles a little, and even her hair seemed a bit less spiky. "Fair enough. I'm Menzy Douglas. I live in a house, not a tree, I work as a gardener because duh, and I thought it might be nice to get out a bit more, and meet some new people."

One of the young men said, "Um, hi, I'm Cayden Wycliffe. I work in the university library in Eugene. But haven't you been right around here all your life? I'd think you would know most of the town." He blushed. "Sorry, I don't know much about it, but I thought you people had to stay close to your tree." He blushed deeper and hurried back into speech. "Sorry again, that sounds awful! I didn't mean to call you 'you people'! I plead ignorance, not malice."

Menzy gave him a kinder smile than I'd expected. "That's OK. I don't mind people asking and that's something people always get wrong about us. As a dryad,

13

I am bound to a whole species, not an individual tree, so I can live anywhere within the range where Doug Firs grow. Thank goodness it works that way or every clearcut would be genocide. Although –" Her expression soured and she stopped talking for a moment, then resumed. "Anyway, I've pretty much bounced around the whole Pacific Northwest. What's the rest of your story, Cayden? Are you new in town?"

He seemed to have subdued his blush reflex, but still swallowed before speaking again. "Came for college and just stayed. I moved out here from Eugene because I grew up in a small town and liked it, but then I thought it might be nice to meet people right here instead of going into the city all the time."

Genna looked at the other young man and prompted, "And your buddy there?"

He spoke up in surprise. "Oh! No, we've never met before." The assessing look he gave Cayden suggested he was glad this omission had now been rectified, and I wondered if my gaydar was any more reliable than my dryad-dar. "I'm Rob Washington, a trainee at the fire station. I grew up in the Bay Area and always wanted to be a firefighter, but it's easier to get a starting job here and I always liked Oregon."

He paused for a minute and then said, "One quick question: if dryads and magic users are MagicComm, what are the rest of us? Muggles?"

Menzy, Genna, and I all laughed, while the others looked confused. I said, "Not unless you're a Harry Potter character! You can call us MCs, for short, that's not at all insulting, and people who are *not* MCs are NMCs. That's a lot quicker to say than "people who aren't part of the Magical Community!"

After that, Genna got us back on track for more introductions. A few more people spoke – and I don't remember what they said – then Genna nodded at the Pre-Raphaelite woman, who was next to me, to introduce herself. "Hi, I'm Brigid Priede, I teach the welding classes at the community college and do some art and commissions on the side. I moved here when I realized living in a smaller town meant I could manage without roommates – but that was right before the pandemic started, so even though I've been here for a while, I don't really know anyone."

I was on Brigid's left, so I introduced myself. "I'm Macrina Magid, and my story is similar. I moved here at almost the worst of the pandemic, so I haven't gotten to meet *anyone*. Before that I was in Portland for a while."

Genna prompted me. "And what do you do, Macrina? It doesn't have to be just a job – what are your hobbies, or what would you like a new friend to know about you? She looked around the circle. "That goes for all of you – maybe we should go around again. "

So much for hoping I didn't have to explain my job. "I'm a magic user and I work as an independent developer but don't get too excited – most of my products are background sort of things that just make other people's spells work better. Think of it like computer firmware, or an operating system. Other than that, I knit, I read, and I spend a lot of time in my kayak."

The older woman with blonde hair spoke next. "I didn't realize we had so many … is the right term MagiComms? … in town. I'm Deborah Johnson, but you can call me Deb. I've lived here since we moved from Idaho a decade ago. My grandchildren live nearby on my daughter and son-in-law's farm, so we stay to be close to them. I'm retired, so other than watching my grandchildren, I mostly volunteer at the church, as secretary and running the food bank."

The fifty-ish man closed out the intros. "I'm Andrew Carroll. Actually, my wife Nell asked me to come – she's the town mayor, so when she saw this meetup and realized a lot of you would be relatively new to town, she wanted to come and welcome you all. But she had a meeting, so I got volunteered. I'm a professor of logic at the university. I'm only teaching one remote class this semester, so I was able to sneak out after working on my next paper and before grading."

"What do you do for fun?" Genna prompted.

"Oh – we have a boat, and I like to fish, but other than that it's mostly research and writing. I'm in a fencing club for exercise and now and then I do a little weaving just to do something creative. And we have two kids, who are ten and twelve."

Genna continued asking people about their hobbies and passion projects – she was clearly skilled at the very kindest form of interrogation – but I had already forgotten almost all of their names. I am so not a people person! Still, a few of them sounded interesting and I hoped I might make a real friend or two.

Next, we moved on to discuss what sort of things we might like to do as a group. Deb invited people to join her church (predictably, I thought waspishly, then chided myself for being judgey). The mayor's husband mentioned the town's tree lighting in early December, which met with a good deal more interest. Regrettably, no one seemed all that interested in kayaking – or at least, they said they were but in that way that sounded more like "I like to think of myself as the person who loves kayaking but really you will never get me in any boat that doesn't have an engine!" – but I found out that the welding instructor – Brigid – was also a knitter when she admired my cowl.

Genna also commented on it, adding, "I'm a hooker, myself," which visibly confused Deb until she went on to explain, with slightly malicious amusement, "I crochet. We call ourselves 'hookers' because 'crochet-ers' is just too awkward to say."

We agreed to share our emails and set up a group on the same neighborhood app where Genna had originally posted, since clearly we were all on that one, so that anyone who wanted company for an activity could post it there. We discussed names for the group, but no one could come up with anything; various acronyms were mooted, but were shot down as being too clunky, too confusing or whatever, and names like Percival Social Club were deemed too boring or not inclusive of surrounding towns. I began to quietly despair of us ever agreeing on any actual activities, but held my peace.

Finally, I said, "Let's call it George."

"George?" Genna asked, bemusedly. "Does that stand for something, Macrina?"

"Not unless you can come up with anything. I was thinking 'What do we call it?' and what came to mind was that old Daffy Duck cartoon, you know." I put on a goofy monster voice "I will hug him and love him and squeeze him and call him George. George is my friend."

I got the distinct feeling that Genna had also been getting impatient with the drawn-out naming discussion, because she immediately chirped, "Sounds good to me!" She turned to the others. "Anyone object to calling our group George? Great, I'll set it up on the app!!"

We also (finally) agreed on a couple of additional meetups for anyone interested, and to my own bemusement I found myself offering to host anyone who wanted to join me on my deck that Friday evening. Soon after moving in, I'd invested in a propane heater that I'd been able to order online, which meant that I could use the covered deck for much of the year. In my opinion, one of the great pleasures in life was having a glass of wine on the deck in front of a sunset over a lake! Four or five people sounded interested, and fortunately they all suggested bringing wine and food, so all I would have to provide was a venue. We'd be outside for the whole thing so I wouldn't need to have strangers inside my space and we wouldn't need to wear masks. (I made a mental note to clean the bathroom nearest the deck, though.) Genna volunteered to set up the group, so we all gave her all our email addresses, then decided we were done for the day. As far as I could tell, everyone seemed happy with our first meetup. (In retrospect, most of the people whose names I couldn't remember were the ones we never saw again.)

***

That night on our usual call, I told Gil about the meetup, and that I was about to have real-live people physically in my house. Or at least, on my deck.

"No! The infamously misanthropic Macrina Magid is going to have company? Will you talk to them, too??"

"Oh, shut up," I said half-heartedly. "I am not misanthropic. I talk to people all day."

"Work doesn't count," he responded. "When was the last time you talked to anyone socially?"

"About ten seconds ago. I talk to you every night!"

"I'm not sure I count either. It's been so long since I've seen you that I'm beginning to think you think I'm a fictional character, or at best someone on the internet, only with the convenient ability to respond verbally instead of in print. Come to think of it...." He trailed off thoughtfully. "Meli ... what would you think about finally getting together in person? I think it's getting to be safe enough to travel now. And I have a ton of vacation time, seeing that I haven't taken any since the whole quarantine thing started – I could come and finally see that new house of yours."

My first gut reaction was to utterly reject the idea of having anyone other than me in my house (my house! My own bubble!!) but I realized that was probably just a relic of having spent so long all alone.

"Sure ... when were you thinking?"

"How fast is your internet? If I make it a working vacation, I could stay two weeks – say, starting in about two weeks from now?"

"Okay." My stomach fluttered some more at the idea of someone impinging in my space, but parts lower down warmed up at the idea of finally getting some action that didn't involve only my own fingers.

"Try not to sound so enthusiastic!" he responded, wryly.

"Sorry," I apologized. "It's just ... weird to think of being around other people again, of having other people *staying in my house*. But you are my *favorite* 'other people'!"

After that, the conversation got too mushy to write down here, until we reluctantly hung up to go to sleep.

CHAPTER THREE: STRANGERS IN THE HOUSE

I woke up the next morning with a feeling of dread hanging over me, and couldn't figure out why until I remembered that I'd unaccountably volunteered to host a group of near-strangers on Friday – and it was already Wednesday. But it was outside only, and people would bring food and drink, I reminded myself – that wasn't so bad.

Nonetheless, I spent that day alternating between working and getting the deck ready – sweeping it, putting out cushions on all my chairs, and even doing a little shopping so I could provide at least one kind of snack for whoever came over. I decided on little caprese skewers – one cherry tomato, one basil leaf, one mozzarella ball on each one, all on a toothpick and drizzled with olive oil and a sprinkle of salt – so each person could pick up their own food without touching anyone else's. I spared a nostalgic thought for pre-pandemic entertaining, when I'd have just put out a bowl of chips and another bowl with dip; presumably we'd get back to that at some point. I had wine on hand but might buy more if I had to shop anyway, and I should have enough wine glasses. Either I could pour wine for whoever wanted it, or I'd just let them pour their own and make sure I washed my hands after the gathering and didn't touch my face. I'd stock up on plastic bottles of water, too. On second thought, I would be very glad when we did get back to normal – entertaining in the waning days of a pandemic was just too complicated.

Posts drifted across the online George group over the next two days, people discussing whether they could or couldn't come on Friday and what they'd bring. I hoped that either no one would show and I could go back to my accustomed solitude, or else we'd get enough people to make our first real event an undoubted success. I also reminded myself of a handy truth I'd learned years before: if you are having people over and not enough people accept the invitation to make it feel like a real party, just change your branding and call it a "get-together". Somehow that lowers the expectations and makes a smaller gathering feel more like the proper size it was intended to be – the party planner's way of saying "I meant to do that!"

I also got an unexpected email from my quasi-landlord. I heard from Meg often, either on work matters or just to check in – there was a reason she was one of my favorite customers – but this time she was discussing a different matter. Working so much on my own, it could be hard to keep track of time passing, and I hadn't realized that I'd been in Percival and in this house for a whole year. Since we'd set up our original rent-to-own agreement in such an uncertain time, in the midst of the pandemic, we had specified that we'd check back in after a year, just in case she suddenly wanted to move into the house herself, or I'd found I hated small-town life and wanted to get out. If that happened, the money I'd paid her each month would just count as rent, and I'd have a couple months to decide what I wanted to do next. Or if I wanted to move and she didn't, she'd have that same period to find a new tenant or decide whether to sell.

She didn't want to take the house back though, writing "I love where I live now, in Maine – and I think I'm in love with more than the place. I met someone, online first and now we've been meeting in person, and he's firmly rooted here – he teaches at a local wilderness education program. So the house is yours at the agreed price if you still want it. Do you?"

I stopped and thought. Did I? Was it just a comfortable hole I'd dug myself into, or was it a place I could see myself thriving and growing for years ahead?

It was comfortable, certainly. It wasn't huge, but it was spacious for me, and even had enough room to have friends visit if we ever got back to normal. The workspace upstairs was ideal for my business, and I loved being right by the lake. I'd grown up reading books where kids were always going out exploring, over hills and woods and fields and they'd seemed like something from a foreign country to me, city girl as I was. Yet this location – and this decade – didn't have all the drawbacks I'd always expected from a more rural setting. I could shop in Eugene, only half an hour away, or order pretty much anything I wanted online. I could even get groceries delivered if I needed to, though I did miss having nearby restaurants that delivered. Now with the possibility of an actual social life thanks to 'my friend George', it wasn't a hard decision to make. Still, buying a house was always a big decision to make.

I was pretty sure what I wanted to do, but I forced myself to sleep on it rather than making an instant decision. Somewhere around 2:00 AM, I woke up, rolled over in bed, and realized this place was home to me – I didn't want to leave it any time soon.

First thing the next morning, I pulled up Meg's email and wrote back, "Yes!"

We'd agreed on a down payment when we set up the original contract – a percentage of the rent I'd paid over the past year would count toward that. The money I'd made from selling my Portland condo would more than cover the rest, with some left over in case I wanted to do any renovations or needed to cover any repairs. Meg promised to talk to a title company to see how we made it all happen.

I hadn't thought about making any changes to the house while I was more or less just a tenant, but now I probably should consider if I wanted any. I shoved that consideration aside for the moment though; nothing was leaking or breaking down, and the house had been comfortable enough for the past year, so there was no hurry, and meanwhile I had the gathering Friday night and then my Samhain preparations to make.

Another unexpected text arrived on Wednesday,

from Andrew, the mayor's husband, of all people. He wrote,

> **Andrew**: We try to make Percival a welcoming place for everyone, and so Nell and I host a Samhain feast every year. We hold it on the night before or after, so we don't interfere with people's own traditions or rituals.

> **Andrew:** This isn't a public town celebration like the Christmas tree lighting, just a dinner in our own house for anyone who might like to join us – we're inviting Menzy and Genna as well from the George group, so there will be at least a couple of people you know. We didn't have one last year, of course, but we didn't want to hold off on starting our dinners back up, so this will be in our courtyard – it's sheltered enough to stay warm and dry. Or warmish, anyway – bring a jacket just in case!"

Well, that was a nice surprise. I wrote back immediately:

> **Macrina**: Thanks for the invitation, I'd love to! Can I bring something?

> **Andrew**: Just yourself, unless you have something that is traditional for you, that you'd miss at the holiday feast.

Since my usual "holiday feast" for the last several years had been grabbing bites of a sandwich between the different parts of the rituals I needed to do to create my spells, I decided to bring a bottle of wine and call it good. I had to swing by the supermarket that afternoon anyway, for my weekly groceries and the ingredients for my caprese skewers, so I grabbed a couple nice boring bottles of Pinot Noir from a local winery. (Boring bottle, not boring wine – I'd generally noticed an inverse correlation between how cool the label on a bottle of wine was, and how good the wine itself was. I tended to prefer winemakers who saved their best creative efforts for their wine rather than their graphic arts, though there were definitely some exceptions.)

Since I lived alone the house never really got all that messy, but it still needed a little attention; for some reason, this house attracted more dust and spiderwebs than anywhere else I'd lived. I found time over the next couple of days to do a little vacuuming, run a damp mop quickly over the wood floors, and wipe down the bathroom. I also swept the deck and removed the latest batch of spiderwebs, then decided this would have to do. We'd all agreed that this would be a casual potluck, and if these were people who expected perfect housekeeping it was probably best they learned right away that they wouldn't find it at my house.

***

Finally, it was Friday. I had three conference calls that morning, but by noon I'd finished all the work I'd planned for the week. I usually liked knocking off early on Fridays, but that did me no favors this time. Of all the kinds of time there were, my least favorite was waiting time – it didn't even matter if I were waiting for something fun or something horrible, I just wanted that empty time to be done.

We'd agreed to meet around 4:30, wanting to have some time to hang out before the sun set, though I'd strung fairy lights around the deck. (The electronic kind; no actual Fae were harmed in the making of these lights!) I'd found some online that could be programmed to change their colors or even "dance" to music, and I'd promptly spent an hour creating different color schemes and gradients that I'd probably never use, and another half-hour creating a party playlist. I'd also set up a fire in the fire pit ready to be lighted and made sure I had plenty of propane for the heater, in case we were still out when it started getting either dark or cold.

The emails had been the usual confusing stream you get any time you are planning an activity with a bunch of people. As best I could tell, three people were definitely coming, one of whom might bring along a new person who hadn't been able to attend the original meetup, and a couple more were maybes. I wasn't worried either way; since it was a potluck, we'd have more food if more people came by. Worst case, nobody would show up and I'd go back inside and have caprese skewers and wine for dinner on my own. I made the caprese skewers and had them done by 4, in case anyone did show up early, and put a small sign on my front door directing people to just walk around the house and join us out back.

Luckily, it was a beautiful sunny day, with none of the usual Oregon fall drizzle, so I dragged the patio table and chairs out to the uncovered portion of my deck and set out the food, water and wine. In the unlikely event that too many people showed up to sit around the patio table, I'd bring out a table from inside the house and set up the food on it as a buffet table. The air was cool and crisp, so I brought out a box full of handknitted hats, scarves and even a few lap blankets, in case we got too cold sitting there.

I hoped no one would have trouble finding the house – the directions were simple, but there was a big willow tree in front that actually hid the house as you came up the street, so you couldn't see it until you'd passed the willow. That tree was annoying, anyway – it dropped a ton of leaves in fall, and dropped its long thin whip-like withies any time there was a high wind. One day I'd gotten bored and had fallen down a rabbit-hole of research, investigating whether I could make baskets of the withies, but apparently you had to cut fresh ones for that rather than picking up shed withies. I'd warned people about the tree, so hopefully no one would get lost on the way here.

Despite the many times I'd told myself it would be fine, though, I did breathe a sigh of relief when Genna showed up on the dot of 4:30. I was beginning to peg her as an organizer who was on time or early for everything. Menzy arrived a scant few minutes later, along with another woman she introduced as Sulis Badon. Sulis wore a sweater and jeans, but her short blue-black hair seemed to be dripping slightly. I turned on the patio heater and offered everyone a wine glass. Genna proffered a long platter with two long pastry rolls on it; I directed her to put it on the table and she busied herself arranging two small signs reading, respectively, "Pizza Rolls" and "Mushroom and Brie". Meanwhile, Menzy put out a bowl of what proved to be an artichoke dip and some pita chips.

Sulis asked, with a slight English accent, "Do you have a corkscrew?" holding up two bottles of wine.

"Of course," I answered, "Over there on the table by the other wine bottle. Do you want to open those right away, or wait and see if we need them?"

She looked at them, considering. "With four of us, we'll probably go through at least two bottles, more if other people show up. What's the bottle you have there? Pinot Noir? Let's open the Chardonnay to go with it, then if we run out, we can open the Rose. That one's a screw-top anyway."

"Sounds good to me. What was your name again? Sulis, like the old name for the city of Bath in England?"

She looked astounded. "That's right! How did you know that? Bath was originally Aquae Sulis, after a local goddess. I was named for her." She paused briefly, looking a bit embarrassed. "Family legend has it that she was an ancestor, but that's just an old story."

"I'm a bit of an Anglophile," I answered, "And I like history and languages, and the stories behind the old names. So you're not a dryad like Menzy?"

"Nope, but still a nymph. Naiad, to be specific, as you might expect from the water goddess story."

At this point I was 0 for 2 for unmet nymph expectations; next thing I knew, I'd be meeting a nereid – a water nymph like Sulis but associated with the sea rather than lakes or rivers – in the desert. Sulis sounded more like a professor or a writer than the airy pre-Raphaelite stereotype of a dryad or naiad I'd expected before I met Menzy. Speaking of which, someone called "Hello?" and the classic vision of a nymph appeared around the side of the house – Brigid, our local welding instructor, fully human as far as I could tell, though unexpectedly tall. I'd only seen her sitting down at the coffeehouse meetup, so I hadn't noticed her height before. It made her look even wispier, with her slimness and flowing hair, except that she wore combat boots with her flowing skirt. If she was a pre-Raphaelite painting, it had been modified in the 1990s/grunge era. I introduced her to Sulis, and she handed me a pie platter full of another dip, a bag of tortilla chips and a small cooler.

"That's a layer dip, and a six pack in case anyone prefers beer to wine."

At this point the table was getting crowded, so I put my cooler full of water bottles and Brigid's cooler with the beer on the deck nearby, poured myself a glass of Pinot, and sat down with everyone else around the table.

It sounded like Genna had already started grilling Sulis, though she was tactful enough not to make it sound like an interrogation this time.

"Sulis, nice to meet you. I remember seeing your name on the original discussion before our first meetup. Sorry you couldn't make it there. Did you already know Menzy before that?"

"Oh, yeah, we've been friends since she first moved to the area. I work for a local program that works on river cleanup, and she volunteered with us for a while. In fact, I couldn't make the original meetup because I was presenting at a grade school on the far side of Eugene that day, so I was happy to have another chance to meet everyone when she told me about this gathering."

Menzy and Brigid's conversation on my other side sounded a lot more animated, so I turned and tuned into them.

Brigid was saying, "And then my student said he wanted to weld without goggles on, because he wanted to record a video for his Instagram channel, and since one of his sponsors was a makeup company, he needed his eyeliner to show!"

Menzy howled with laughter. Genna looked over questioningly, Brigid repeated the story, and we were off to a much better start.

Well. I wish I could remember all the details of that evening – even at the time, I knew something special was happening. I do recall that I started a fire in the fire pit about an hour in, and I know we finished all the wine and most of the beer.

But also, even though the details are fuzzy, I remember Sulis recounting the truly epic tale of how she had ended up in Oregon from England by way of Alaska and Venezuela. Brigid told us why she switched from ballet to welding, and Menzy shared stories of the strangest things they'd found while cleaning up the river. Since Genna's admin at the community college had previously been a city administrator here, she had all the dirt on how this town worked, and who couldn't stand whom.

By the time another hour had gone by, we'd switched topics from work and travel to partners, and their annoying quirks. I found myself digging into my liquor stash and bringing out the bourbon, then telling them about Gil and how our long-term, long-distance relationship had been highjacked by a year of restricted travel. Menzy told tales of dating difficulties – who knew dryads had their own dating app? (Kindl*ng, if you were wondering.) And Sulis capped that with the story of her short marriage and speedy divorce from a nereid who lived in a beachfront house in Caracas. Brigid mentioned her late life partner, but avoided any details of what had happened to him. (Or her? She kept it so vague that I don't think she'd even used pronouns.) But it was Genna who had us falling over laughing – apparently when you have been married to the same man for thirty-five years, you have plenty of time to collect stories. The only one I recall now was about how she learned her husband was dyslexic the first time he put "beagles and cream cheese" on their grocery list. (Trust me, it was funnier with bourbon.)

My stomach muscles still hurt the next morning – no, I wasn't hung over, it had just been years since I'd laughed so hard! Sometimes the nights you'll never forget are also the ones you can't quite remember.

There had been one difference from similar evenings I'd spent with NMC friends or even other magic users. At the end of the night, as we were saying our goodbyes, Sulis looked over at Menzy and said, "Think we should take the back ways home tonight?"

Menzy answered, "Probably safer that way. Macrina, do you mind if I leave my car here and pick it up tomorrow morning?"

"Yes, you're not blocking my car, are you? Then it's fine. Are you going to walk?"

"Nope! See you tomorrow!" Eyes sparkling, she waved goodbye, stepped back a few paces, and just sort of leaned into a tree. All the way into, as in she disappeared into its bark.

Sulis called over, "Bye, and thanks again for having me over. I loved meeting you all – let's do this again!" Then she ran down and dived into the lake. As I half expected after seeing Menzy melt into the tree, she didn't come back up.

I looked over at Brigid and Genna. "How about you two? Are you OK to drive home?"

Brigid said, "They have the right idea. If I can leave my car here too, I'll walk home. It's safe around here and I'm only a block away."

Genna, on the other hand said, "I'll be fine. I just had a tiny taste of the bourbon, and haven't had anything else but water for the last hour. It's not far anyway. Thanks for checking!"

CHAPTER FOUR: DINNER WITH THE MAYOR

I love outdoor impromptu parties, where there is hardly any cleanup afterward. Once I'd made sure the fire was completely out and turned off the propane heater, all I had to do was bring in the empties and toss a few plates and glasses into the dishwasher. Easy. After that I brushed my teeth, fell into bed, and crawled under my duvet. I didn't even notice the scent of woodsmoke lingering in my hair until morning.

Since I didn't know how late people would stay, I'd warned Gil I might not be able to talk to him Friday night. We didn't really end up staying out all that late, but I fell into bed afterwards and didn't even think to call him. I called him Saturday morning and did try to give him a good run-down, but it was clearly one of those things better experienced than explained.

"So, you got drunk and talked girl-talk? Probably a good thing I wasn't there," was his verdict.

"Well, no, it felt more like a bunch of people who happened to be female talking people-talk. But I won't deny the drunk part!"

"And you're off to dinner with someone else tonight? You really have dropped into a giddy social whirl! Sure you won't break out in hives from being around so many people, all of a sudden?"

"I might, but so far we're keeping it pretty low key. I think tonight will be a lot calmer, anyway."

He asked, "So you're going to a Samhain dinner with people who don't celebrate Samhain? And you yourself mostly celebrate it, if you can call it that, for work purposes, as a time to do spells that have to happen then? Yup, sounds like a wild party."

29

"It's more than that to me, you know, even if I don't get all mystical about it," I answered. "If magic were that cut and dried, it would be science. I do still have to feel Samhain as a transition, the passing from summer half to winter half of the year and the time when – when – well, when the numinous is closer to us, or my Samhain rituals wouldn't work at all."

His voice gentled. Gil liked to needle me, but he really did get me. "I know. Sorry, I didn't mean to sound belittling. But you know I have to give you a hard time!"

"You really don't. Pretty sure that's not written anywhere in the Boyfriend Rules."

"No, it's specific to me. It's in the Gil Rules!" he said.

I sighed. "Right, the Gil Rules. Right along with "Every meal must contain meat" and "Don't expect Gil to answer you when he's reading.""

Once we got off the phone, I checked the online George group and saw a post from Genna, with comments from others:

> **Genna:** Our first real event, and it was wonderful! There is nothing better than hanging out with friends around a fire on a crisp fall night. Thanks, Macrina, for having us over. Nice to meet you, Sulis!
>
> **Sulis:** Glad to be here, and nice to meet you all last night!
>
> **Menzy:** Thanks, Macrina. And remember, all: what's said around the campfire, stays around the campfire!! 😄 😄 😄
> **Rob:** Sorry I missed it but glad you all had fun!
>
> **Cayden:** < = = what he said

***

After that night, I had high hopes for the next day's Samhain dinner, especially since Menzy and Genna had mentioned they'd be attending. And it was fun, though in a much quieter way. Luckily, I had remembered **not** to bring out the second bottle of Pinot when the previous one had run out, since this one was earmarked to bring along to Andrew's and Nell's house. I decided to walk there, since nothing in this town was more than a few blocks away, and found that they lived up on the hill where a lot of the larger houses in town were. Up here, they had beautiful views over the lake, though they'd have to walk or drive half a mile to the park if they actually wanted to go out in a boat; I decided I preferred my own little house with its path right to my dock.

Their house was gorgeous, though, with tall glass windows curving around the living room to take advantage of the views. Andrew, wearing a flour-spattered apron, opened the door and introduced me to Nell, his wife and Percival's mayor. Mayor Nell was a capable-looking person, who looked like she'd be more interested in feeding her constituents than making speeches. Her auburn hair – whose color must be natural, judging by the gray strands in it – was gathered in a low ponytail to keep it out of her cooking, and she wore an apron to match Andrew's, though his showed a front view of a fencer in full lunge, while hers said "Don't piss off the cook – she has sharp knives!"

Nell welcomed me into the living room, now glowing in the golden-hour light from the windows on both sides, and said, "Since this is your first time with us, let me explain a little. We want everyone to feel welcome in Percival, but the town doesn't have funds – or even enough people – to do celebrations for everyone's holidays. So we light candles and a tree in early December and bring everyone together to enjoy whatever holiday they celebrate around that time of year, and we ask different people to design the decorations every year. But

Andrew and I also do these dinners at our house, privately, a few times a year. It also helps us get to know more people in town. With the kids, there are four of us, and we have room for eight at the table, so we invite four different people each time. We've done dinners for Kwanzaa, Passover, Holi, you name it – we have the kids help with the research to make sure we got the foods more or less right for each one, though we have to depend on people giving us a bit of grace if we're not quite perfect."

I laughed. "I can just imagine. Did Andrew tell you I'm a magic user?"

"Yes, that's why he wanted to invite you tonight."

"Well, I celebrate Samhain and Beltane because some spells just have to be done then if they're going to work correctly, but my family is Jewish. One time a friend who was trying to be nice invited me over for Yom Kippur dinner!"

She laughed too. "Oh, no! On the day of the fast? What did you do?"

"I'm not observant, so I wasn't going to be fasting anyway, and I really appreciated the thought. I did have to explain to her afterward, though I really hated to! But I wouldn't have wanted her to invite some other Jewish friend later, who might keep the holidays more strictly, and then wonder why I didn't say anything."

"Wow. I hope people will let us know if we do something like that!" She ushered me to the courtyard behind the glass door on the other side of the living room. "Anyway, I know you already know Menzy and Genna – you can say hello to them and meet the kids and everyone else while we finish up in the kitchen. We'll be out in just a moment!"

The glassed-in courtyard was sheltered enough to be comfortable, though I wondered how they kept it from becoming an oven in summer. It was lush, with potted plants all around and a table for eight in the middle, as promised. Genna and Menzy were sitting there talking to two children, along with two other adults I didn't recognize. The seats at either end of the table were empty but I guessed those were for Andrew and Nell, so I took a seat at the side, between the younger child and one of the unknown adults.

"Hi, Macrina!" said Genna. "This is Macrina, everyone, she's been in town for around a year, and she's part of George, the new online local group we've started. Macrina, this is everyone. I'll let you introduce yourselves – Oliver, can you start, and tell them who you are?"

The smaller kid piped up, "Hi, I'm Oliver. I live here – Nell's my mom. I'm ten. Charli is my big sister."

Charli elbowed him, but companionably rather than angrily. "I can introduce myself, doofus. I'm Charli, like he said – really it's Charlotte but no one calls me that. I'm twelve. Our mom wants us to learn about different cultures, so we did the research on what to have for dinner. I hope you like it!" She rolled her eyes at the words "different cultures", but again I got the impression of tolerant amusement with her family rather than real annoyance.

The adult on her left spoke next. "Hi, I'm Rory. I'm a fiddler, Irish style, and I play a few other instruments as well – I've been playing around Eugene for years with my band O'Carolan, but I just moved out here when I was able to build a house on some friends' land."

"And I'm Eva," said the other adult. "I sometimes play second fiddle to Rory – literally – but mostly I'm an admin at the college. And we've got a hobby farm out here, so we are also his landlords. But my husband is out of town this week, so it's just me here tonight."

Genna added, "My husband is away too, off at a conference."

I would have shaken hands with everyone, but being in someone else's house felt exposed enough – touching strangers was definitely a step too far. (And elbow bumping was too silly!) So I just nodded at them all.

"I'm Macrina, as Genna said. I'm a magic user, and I've been living here about a year, but I really hadn't met anyone. Blasted pandemic!"

All the adults nodded, but Oliver burst out, "You do

magic? Can you do a spell for us?"

I knew that was coming. It's always the first thing NMC kids, and some adults, say. So I shook my head a little and said, "Sorry, I can't do anything very exciting. I do mostly back-end work, like to make other people's spells connect together, or make them work bigger or faster. But here's one of the first things we all learn."

I didn't need an invocation for this most basic spell; I just held out my hand, centered my breathing, felt for the warmth in my gut, and shaped a flame in my open palm. Not a huge one, for safety's sake, but bigger than a candle flame, about the height of a palm's width. Noticing unlit candles on the table, I casually reached over and lit them, then theatrically blew out my flame just as Nell and Andrew walked back into the courtyard.

The kids were wide-eyed. "Oh, I'm so glad you did that!" Nell applauded. "We really weren't sure whether there was supposed to be some kind of ritual around lighting the flames, and now you've saved us from worrying about it."

I wondered if I was blushing, but luckily, I mostly don't. I was embarrassed, though. "Sorry! Some people do that, but I mostly just do rituals for work on Samhain, so I didn't think about it." I looked around at the other guests. "I hope I didn't screw things up for anyone else."

Genna and Rory waved it off, while Menzy held up a hand and said, dryly, "No issue for me. Dryads aren't big on fires."

Eva grinned suddenly and said, "My family does do a ritual, but it's all sort of, "Marvel at the wonder of fire," so really, I think you caught the spirit of it."

"See?" said Nell, as she placed a brown loaf in front of me. "I told you, that was the perfect thing to do. Here, have some barmbrack."

"I made it!" Charli added, proudly. "And I found the colcannon recipe, then Mom and I made it together. Dad spatchcocked the chicken, though."

"Spatchcocked?" asked Menzy. "What's that?"

"My specialty!" answered Andrew, as proud of his

cooking as his daughter was of hers. "You cut out the backbone and spread the chicken flat. It roasts faster and more evenly that way. Looks a little different, though."

"It looks like it's sunbathing!" laughed Rory. "With its arms tucked behind where the head would be, and its legs splayed out like that. All it needs is a bikini!"

Oliver interjected, "I helped with the dessert!" He whispered, loudly enough for everyone to hear, "It's pumpkin ice cream!"

Nell said, "Ice cream isn't really the best dessert for this time of year, but there's nothing better than homemade ice cream, so we just make it in appropriate flavors."

The food and the conversation both were excellent, though at one point I found myself agreeing to think about volunteering in the school or the library. Nell was subtle, but implacable in enlisting people to volunteer in the town – I'm pretty sure that by the end of dinner, Rory and Eva had committed to creating a list of multicultural carols and holiday songs, as well as leading the singing at the tree-lighting. Charli made sure everyone took a large serving of her colcannon, which turned out to be potatoes mashed with kale and scallions, served with a knob of butter in the center, and instructed us to dip each forkful of the potatoes in the butter before eating it. It was clear she'd inherited her mom's implacability, though she hadn't developed the subtlety yet.

After dinner and more conversation, I walked home. It was a spectacularly clear night with no moon, and there were no streetlights on the quiet streets between Nell's and Andrew's house and mine. It was dark enough to be a little spooky this close to Samhain, and I used the flashlight on my phone to watch my steps and make sure I didn't trip over any curbs. When I looked up, though, the stars were crystalline and bright, and I was able to spot the Milky Way, Jupiter, Cassiopeia and the Big and Little Dippers. They kept me company the rest of the way home.

CHAPTER FIVE: RITUALS AND REVELATIONS

The dinner had been on the early side, and I got home by 8:30, which was convenient because I needed to be up before dawn the next morning. I set out my herbs, equipment and purified water before going to bed. Luckily, it was another beautifully clear day, the last one before the forecast said we were due to return to the normal gray drizzle of an Oregon autumn. Also, I could do the water-based rituals last, which would allow time for the day to warm up a bit before I headed out on the water – if there is a way to paddle a kayak without splashing yourself, I've yet to find it, and I haven't invested in a wetsuit or neoprene jacket yet.

The house rituals came first and were the reason for starting so early. I had to rededicate my lab space before I could do anything else in it, and then dedicate and imbue magical power into my lab equipment, which included my laptop, a spectrometer, a magnifying glass on a stand, various pliers and tweezers, and so on. Those all needed to be done before I imbued power into my ingredients and spell-stores. The important thing about ingredients was their symbolism to me, not their exact form, so mine were an odd mixture ranging anywhere from dried herbs to origami cranes to assorted other flotsam I'd picked up. I even used some swatches I'd knitted, mostly to unravel them when I needed to symbolize things coming apart. Whenever possible I preferred to store completed spells for delivery in a virtual format, in words or software code, but some spells needed a physical receptacle, and I preferred to use crystals for those. I found they helped the spells work better; magic depended on belief so while the placebo effect was a factor, there was also real added power from the fact that customers were often comfortable with the idea of power held in crystals.

The kayak was my secondary "office" for this kind of work; I liked to imbue power into ingredients and spell-stores on the water as much as possible since water holds power of its own, but some of them were best imbued with power right at dawn, or else were simply too bulky to take out in the kayak.

When I started the rededication ritual, though, and focused my intent, it felt more difficult than it should, like I was pushing through honey instead of water. I managed to finish, but I felt like I'd run a mile. And when I started imbuing power, it felt like I was trying to make it flow through too small a pipe. I finally finished, but I worried that some of the verses, especially, might have ended up less powerful than they were supposed to be. The physical objects like herbs and wires and stones were less of an issue, since their power levels were more measurable and I could just keep going until they were at full force.

The timing of my on-water rituals didn't matter as much, so once I was done with the morning rituals I went back to bed. I am generally terrible at napping and can't fall asleep during the day unless I'm exhausted or sick, but either I was more tired than I thought or else it was still early enough that my body viewed this as a continuation of the night's sleep. I fell soundly asleep and didn't wake up again until almost noon.

I was still tired, but the rituals had to be finished today. I ate a quick sandwich, then headed out, thanking past-me for pre-packing everything in advance so that I only had to grab a drybag, lifejacket and paddle and head out to the dock. The kayak was already there – during boating season I kept it on the dock, upside down and lashed down so it wouldn't blow away in storms. Soon I'd bring it into the garage for the winter, though I might carry it back out for an occasional paddle on unseasonably warm days.

Out on the water, everything flowed much more easily – in fact, when I started working on the first crystal, I unconsciously began by pushing power into it with the same force I'd had to use in the morning, and it exploded! I got a slight scratch on one cheek but fortunately none of the pieces holed the kayak. Once I dialed it back to normal levels, though, everything went smoothly.

Normally, I wouldn't even notice the energy drain from the afternoon's work, but on top of my unrecovered fatigue from the morning, I was completely exhausted as I pulled back into the dock. I unloaded my water bottle, crystals and whatever other small bits I hadn't stashed in the dry bag onto the dock, then put my paddle behind me and pushed myself up to sit on it and slide over onto the dock, as usual.

Only it wasn't "as usual" – I was so tired that as I pushed myself up, my elbow buckled, and I slid gracefully off the other side into the water. SPLASH!

***

The fall weather hadn't yet cooled the water to winter temperatures and it was shallow there close to the dock, so I didn't feel scared. I was so loopy, in fact, that I started giggling as I stood back up, with the water just above my waist. It was only once I started walking that I realized this situation might be a little tricky to get out of. The bottom was deep gluey mud and I was so *tired*. The rubber clogs I always wore kayaking had come off and were floating next to me; the oozing mud stuck to my feet and each time I lifted one, it felt like I had a bowling ball on the end of my leg and the other foot sank a little way into the soft bottom. The dry bag floated next to me. I would need to get between the kayak and the dock and hoist up the dry bag on to the dock, then hoist myself up with those bowling balls stuck to my ankles, all without letting the boat drift away. Or I could walk the longer way to shore towing the dry bag and kayak, somehow rinse the mud off while standing on the beachy area next to the dock to get rid of those bowling balls, then go get the rest of my gear.

Yuck. That was the downside to working alone. I was so worn out that I could feel tears starting to my eyes, when suddenly the water started to churn around me. Next thing I knew, it seemed to be pushing me toward the beach. As soon as I stepped out of the water, all the water and mud on me swirled once more, then flowed back into the lake and I was left standing there, dumbfounded and only mildly damp.

A voice behind me said, "That feel better?" I looked over my shoulder and there was Sulis, with her feet in the water by just a few inches but the rest of her completely dry except that her hair was dripping slightly, as usual.

"How did you...? Oh, right."

"Naiad!" she chirped. "Water is my native language. Do you need to get all that stuff back up the house? I'll give you a hand. Even dry, you look wrecked."

"Thanks," I said dryly. Or rather, not so dryly. "But yeah, you're right. For some reason, the rituals this morning were a horrible slog. It felt like I had to push three times the power to get anywhere."

Sulis frowned. "What were you doing?"

"Just my usual Samhain rituals – rededicating my lab and imbuing power into some ingredients and spell-stores."

She frowned again. "Hmmm. Can I walk through your lab? I won't touch anything, I promise. But I have some ideas on what might be happening."

I waved a hand vaguely upstairs-ward. "Sure, be my guest." I was too tired to argue and slightly desperate by now. Imbuing ingredients and equipment with power was a regular thing for me, Samhain being only the biggest of several times I did it each year, and I never wanted to go through today again. "You're right, I'm pretty wrecked. It's up in the attic; do you mind if I just flop on the sofa and let you go by yourself? Stairs are over there."

She disappeared upstairs. I flopped, as promised, and just laid there staring at the ceiling and watching dust motes dance in the beam of light from the window.

Some undefined time later she came back down and

sat on the other sofa, facing me. "Yup, I was right. I noticed it when we were here Friday, even though I was only ever on the deck. Your house is dead."

"My house is what?"

"Your house is dead. Well, mostly dead. Or at least, it's not alive."

"When you say 'alive', you don't mean it literally, do you? Is this a nymph thing? Because as a human, even with magic, I don't think I've ever met a living house."

"Well," she said, thoughtfully, "it is technically possible. But mostly I just mean that it doesn't think it's your house. And no, I don't even really mean it thinks, I just mean I don't sense it's yours when I walk around it."

"Well, technically I'm still renting, but we're about to sign the papers to make it mine…"

She shook her head. "No, I don't mean legally, I mean magically, in its essence. It doesn't feel like you when I walk through the rooms. It's not bonded to you. How long have you lived here?"

"I've been here a year, on a rent-to-own contract. My client's –" I stopped and corrected myself. "My friend's grandfather died and she lives out East, and I liked the idea of living on a lake so –"

"Have you made any changes to it in that time? Have you had any plants or pets, anything alive in it?"

"Nope, just me. And I didn't want to paint or anything, because I was just renting and we both had the option to withdraw if either of us changed our mind after I'd lived here a year."

She was nodding now. "Yeah, that matches what I feel. It was his house, and he died so it's just gone quiet. You haven't made it yours, so it's responding only sluggishly to your magic. You said you're about to sign papers to make it legally yours? So you're allowed to make changes in it now."

"Maybe, though I mostly like it the way it is. I might rearrange a little. Most of the furniture is mine, and when I moved it in, I just kind of put it in logical spots and left it there. The lab has all my work stuff, but even so, the table and shelves were already there and I just put stuff on them."

"Yes, that explains it. You said you'd lived in a condo before this, but I bet you spent more time thinking about it, setting everything up and making it your own."

"So what I do now?" I asked, plaintively. "And how fast do I have to do it?"

"You should at least get started before the next time you need to do anything that requires much power. Your equipment and spells will work fine for now, so you don't have to do everything tomorrow, or anything like that. As for what to do, stamp your personality on the place. Add colors you like. Move things around to suit yourself. And if you want a shortcut to adding life to the house, bring live things in. Get a pet, and maybe some plants."

"I was thinking of getting a couple of cats. Wrong time of year for kittens, though."

"Nah, you can get kittens any time of year. There are more of them in summer, but there are always some. Or you could get young cats, which is a little safer anyhow – they're starting to have their personalities established, not just indeterminate fluffballs."

"Are cats a naiad thing too? But a lot of them don't like the water."

She smiled. "No, not really a naiad thing. I just like them, is all. I volunteer to go cuddle them at a shelter every once in a while."

"So, you prescribe cats, plants, and colors, is that it?"

"Cats, plants, and home decoration, anyway. But not today, you still look exhausted. Maybe it's a good day to veg out and watch HGTV for ideas."

So that was what I did for the rest of the day. I gave thanks to past-me that in a burst of forethought a few weeks back, I'd made a big batch of chili and frozen it in portion size containers for days like this, so dinner was a bowl of chili (with corn chips I kept on hand for just this purpose) and a beer. Well, two beers, once I mustered the energy to get up off my ass and get a second one. And thank you, Josephine Cochran, for the invention of the dishwasher!

CHAPTER SIX: BRINGING THE HOUSE ALIVE

I took Sulis's words to heart – I'd missed having a cat anyway, and reworking the house to suit me could only be a good thing. I might hold off on the plants though; I have such a black thumb that I mostly buy my vegetables from the supermarket and my herbs already dried instead of trying to grow my own. If I did break down and get anything green, it would need to be a succulent. Or I could splurge on one of those self-watering hydroponic gardens. I'd need to wait and do some research – I didn't want to end up getting any plants that might be poisonous to kittens!

I sent a message out to the George group, asking if anyone had any kittens or young cats needing a home, or knew someone who did. Nobody did, but Genna recommended a local cat rescue network, so I checked out the list of adoptable cats on their webpage.

Scrolling through the photos, I found myself pinned by the most disapproving green eyes I'd ever seen. There were four of them – and they belonged to, not baby kittens but half-grown cats about six months old, brother and sister. One was black and one gray; the black cat had a small ruffled jabot of white fur at his neck while the gray one had a bigger white bandana and white paws. Their shared genes showed in the identical disdainful green gazes.

Clearly, I needed someone always on hand to judge everything I did and find me lacking, didn't I? The blurb under the kittens talked about how loving and cuddly they were, how Samantha loved treats and Darren would chase a ball, but those scornful eyes betrayed their real opinions.

I was smitten. Kitten smitten.

I filled out the form on the website, saying that I wanted to adopt a bonded pair of kittens or young cats and noting that I specifically wanted to be considered to adopt Darren and Samantha. (Ick, those names!) There were a lot of questions about where I lived, what animals I already had and whether I would commit to keeping the cats indoors, but that was generally the sign of a reliable rescue organization. (As a magic user, whether I kept the cats indoors or not would depend entirely on them and how communicative they were, but there wasn't room to explain that on the form, so I confess, I fibbed for the sake of simplicity and wrote "yes". If I let them out, they would be under my supervision or my instructions, at least.)

I took the next few days easy, regrouping from my strenuous Samhain rituals. There were a few spells I had to get started, but once they were set up, they could "rest" for a few days, strengthening their magical signature rather like the way bread dough rests while developing its gluten. I also made lists of everything I'd need to bring the cats home: a couple of litter boxes, bags of cat litter, food, toys, claw clippers, collars…There was a small storage area off my attic lab that would make a good spot for the litter boxes; I didn't keep anything there except some old boards that were leaning up against the wall when I moved in. I'd never gotten rid of it; you never know when you might need a bit of wood, and they weren't in my way. Luckily, as I knew from the last time I'd had a cat, there was a cheap spell I could buy that would keep all of the sand and dust within a small area around the little boxes. I'd put the cat food and water bowls in the kitchen, for easy cleanup.

The spell would probably count toward making the house more 'alive', as well. Since the house was small, I'd been living alone, I had more free time due to the pandemic, and I was at home all the time, I'd been doing all my cleaning the old-fashioned way. I hadn't bothered to install either any home spells or any automated means of cleaning, security, or anything. I hadn't even put in any automated lighting or anything like that; there's not much point saying "Alexa, turn on the kitchen light" when the switch is three steps away and you want to make sure you're not just sitting in one place all day. But if I was going to have cats living with me, it was time to consider both magical and mundane automated cleaning. For now, I dug out and set up the old robo-vacuums I'd used in my previous place and set up one on each floor, scheduling them to clean twice a week. I'd named them Curiosity and Perseverance, for the Mars rovers. I would implement the litter containment spell as soon as I was able to bring the cats home – no point in doing that until it was needed.

One other important thing happened during my recuperation: Meg, my client and former landlord, had worked with her title company and they sent me forms to sign digitally that would make the house mine – apparently yet another side effect of the pandemic had been that house-buying could now be done completely online, so I wouldn't have to go in to the title company's office. I signed the documents, had my bank send a check, and suddenly, I was a homeowner!

Clearly, the house was going to need a name, but I'd let that percolate in the back of my mind until I came up with the right thing.

Three days later, the cat rescue organization called me back. There was a phone interview, reiterating the questions I'd already answered on the form and adding a few new ones. This time I did specify that the cats might be allowed to go outside on a "leash", carefully not specifying that the leash might be made of magic rather than webbing. My interviewer seemed to be okay with that, and we made an appointment for me to come meet the cats in a few days, at a pet store in nearby Springfield that hosted pet adoption events in normal times. Right now, they weren't having big events, but did allow pet fosterers to use their small rooms to meet with prospective adopters.

***

This set-up was well organized – the store had a

small, quiet side room where I could meet the cats without traumatizing them with the noise of the main store. At least, not any more traumatized than they already were by being transported and meeting strangers. Still, when the fosterer opened their carrier, the black male kitten strutted right out, his extra-long tail making figure eights in the air. His sister emerged a few seconds later, after assessing the area more carefully. Neither seemed to be put off by the mask I was wearing – maybe because their foster-mom had one too. The male looked around, saw me kneeling by him, and came over to head-butt my knee. He allowed me to pet him, but wasn't quite ready to purr yet. His sister sat down in full cat-loaf position a few feet away. She didn't run when I petted her, so I gently picked her up – and she promptly flopped on her back to be carried like a baby, and angled her chin to be scratched.

I looked down at her quizzically, and carefully scratched her chin while keeping my hand well away from the inviting soft floof on her belly. "Is this where she lures me in and then attacks my hand?"

The fosterer smiled. "No, they both like belly rubs. I like to carry them that way from when they're tiny, so they're used to being on their backs."

I gently stroked the soft belly. She allowed this for a minute then squirmed to get down. I asked, "Is there anything more you can tell me about their personalities?"

"Well, Darren is a cocky little guy. He isn't scared of anything. I have two big dogs and he walked right up to them the first day. Didn't hiss or attack, just walked over and checked them out. Samantha is more of a diva; she gets a little jealous if you give him too much attention without petting her too. They both will jump up and sit on your lap – sometimes both at once – and then they get annoyed if you don't pet them. I work from home, so I disappoint them all the time."

"Good, then they'll be used to it. I work from home too, though I'm standing or on a high stool a lot of the time. Those names will need to change though – not a big fan of Bewitched!"

"That's OK. They're cats; it's not like they answer to their names anyway!"

I just smiled. Mine *might* answer to their names; we'd just have to wait and see. "Is there somewhere here where I can leave them for a little bit while I shop? I need to buy everything – carriers, litter boxes, food, bowls, and so on. It's been a while since I last had a pet."

"Sure, will half an hour be enough? I can stay here and keep them company, and say goodbye. I've enjoyed fostering these two!"

"Thanks. Also, what have you been feeding them? Since I have to buy food anyway, I may as well get what they're used to."

"They still should be fed kitten food until they're twelve months old. I mostly feed them dry food, with a spoonful each of canned food in the morning as a treat. Though the downside to that is that then they want it first thing in the morning and may wake you, so if you do treats or wet food you might want to do that later in the day!"

She told me the brands she used. I paid her the adoption fee, then loaded up a cart with everything I'd need, paid for it all, and took everything except the carriers to my car before returning to the kitten room.

I asked, "Since they're still so small, do you think it would be best if I put them both in one carrier for now? They might feel more secure that way."

"Good idea. Also, you can take this – they love playing with it, and it will smell like home to them." She handed me a small stuffed toy, shaped like an owl. I popped it into the carrier, then lowered the gray kitten in. She wasn't entirely thrilled about that, and it took both of us to get the other kitten into the carrier without letting the first one escape.

"Good thing I bought two carriers after all! This might be a good idea this time, but I don't think I will ever again be able to get them both into the same carrier unless I have a set of extra hands to help."

She held the carrier up and said goodbye to the

kittens. I took them to the car, placing the carrier on the front passenger seat where I'd be able to talk to them on the drive. Few cats liked riding in cars, and they tended to make their feelings known LOUDLY, so I used a two-pronged approach; I'd bought a cat-calming spray and sprayed it into the carrier before loading the kittens in, and now I invoked a tranquility spell I'd been smart enough to buy and download earlier that day. It worked; they slept all the way home. Sometimes it's good to be a magic user.

***

It is not a good idea to use that sort of spell too often on animals, especially young ones, or to make it too strong, so I'd just bought a light one-use version of the spell. By the time I pulled into my garage, the kittens were already stirring. Since they weren't yet fully awake, I took advantage of their sleepiness and left them in the car while I quickly set up food and water and one litter box in the spare bedroom – I'd keep them contained in one room for a few days to get used to the smell of the house, letting them out for longer and longer periods to learn their way around. I set out their stuffed owl and another of the new toys I'd bought – no point in putting out everything at once so they could get tired of it.

When I got back to the car, I was bemused to find the black male sitting calmly on the passenger seat, *outside* the carrier. I checked but couldn't find any open zippers, so it was a mystery how he'd escaped. His sister was seated inside, mirroring him in the same pose, sitting in the very center of the carrier's cushion as if on a throne. Still, self-possessed as they already were, they remained just a little groggy, and I was able to sneak him into the carrier without her escaping. I carried them to the spare room, closed the door, sat on the carpeted floor, and opened the carrier door.

In that last minute, all grogginess had completely worn off. As before, Darren strutted right out, while Samantha emerged a little more slowly. He took one look at the place and then went into a fit of the zoomies, circling the room three times at top speed, bouncing off the walls like a pinball. Apparently energized by his example, Samantha started zinging around the room in the opposite direction. Somehow, they managed to avoid head-on collisions and though both kittens used me as a launching pad a few times, they managed to rebound only off my legs – and I was wearing jeans, so their claws didn't get through to skin.

As if on a prearranged signal, they stopped racing around the room at the same second. Black Darren said, "Meh!" in a voice more like a young goat than a young cat, while gray Samantha walked to the closed door and meowed in a higher-pitched tone.

"So, you two are talkative kittens, huh?" I asked. "Good, then you can give me opinions. Those names cannot stay – you two don't look like a Darren or a Samantha, anyway. What do you want to be called?"

The black male head-butted my leg and said "Merl!" assertively.

"Merlin?" I asked.

"Merl!" he bleated again.

"Sounds like a yes to me. So if you're Merlin, we can call your sister…Nimue?"

"Nyeah" he answered again, seeming happy to enter into conversation.

"No, not Nimue or Vivian, too weird since you're siblings. How about Morgana? Merlin and Morgana sounds like a good pair of names."

At this, the gray cat gave up on getting through the door, came over and climbed into my lap. I petted her and she curled up as if she planned to stay put for a while.

"Right, then, Merlin and Morgana it is. Welcome home!"

CHAPTER SEVEN: GETTING READY FOR GIL

Obviously, I announced my new family members on George and posted photos of the kittens. (In my next life, I want to be as photogenic as a cat. Even when they're in the most ridiculous poses, they're still adorable. I, on the other hand, look completely ridiculous and not so adorable in 90% of the photos I'm in. Unfair!)

Everyone oohed and aahed at the kittens' photos. Genna reminded me that there are local coyotes and a few wildcats, not to mention hawks and eagles, so I needed to keep the kittens safe indoors (at least until and unless they could look after themselves, I amended to myself).

Cayden asked if I wanted a cat tower that his parents were getting rid of. When he sent a photo, it turned out to be glorious – over six feet tall and handmade by his father to look like a tree, with several levels for the cats to climb to and hang out, safely hidden by artfully arranged branches and "leaves". I accepted gratefully and he brought it over in his pickup and helped me to install it in a corner of the front room by a window, even screwing a brace on the back into the wall studs so that it couldn't shift or fall over.

Menzy saw the photo of it in place, told me I needed another tree to balance it, and brought over a small Schefflera tree to stand on the other side of the window. I objected to this, as the owner of two certified black thumbs, but she overruled my objections.

"It's in a self-watering pot. All you have to do is remember to top up the water level every month or so – as long as it doesn't get beneath this line, it will be fine. And anyway, are you or are you not a magic user? Use your magic! Put in a spell to either water the plant automatically or remind you to do it. Or at least use your phone and set up a regular reminder to fill up the water reservoir. I'm sure you can handle it."

So there I was, off to a good start in livening up my house: two small cats, one fake tree, one real tree. I realized I'd done it in entirely the wrong order, though: having the cats around was probably not going to make it easier to do whatever redecorating I decided on, but we'd manage. Meanwhile, I'd lost track of time, and Gil's impending visit was only a week away. Maybe I'd defer any decorating plans until he got here – he had a good eye for color and might have some ideas. Also, I didn't want to deal with having a houseguest, even one as familiar as Gil, while having furniture out of place or wet paint on the walls.

I did spend a little time working on the spare bedroom, though – not that he'd be sleeping there, but he would use it as an office. I'd let the cats out of the room, but had kept one litter box there to make sure they knew where to find it. Now they'd found the other one in its dedicated location, I moved this one next to it. I had remembered to use the containment spell, so there wasn't litter dust all over the room, but I vacuumed the floor and every surface to get rid of the hair they'd shed everywhere, especially in the anxiety of their first few days here. I also opened the window to air out the room.

The room already had a bed and desk, but the chair I'd shoved in with the desk had been one of Grandpa Ray's that was in the house when I got here. It looked like an old classroom chair – plain wood, straight lines, no wheels. I tried sitting and writing at the desk and realized it just wouldn't do; not being able to move or swivel would drive me mad if I had to work here, and the lack of lumbar support would do no favors to a middle-aged back. I went over to the local discount warehouse store and was pleased to find a chair on sale that was a knockoff of an expensive designer office-chair, with breathable mesh back and an adjustment system that would tax Gil's engineering skills to figure out. As a bonus, it was a soft blue that would look less industrial in a bedroom than the standard black. While

I was out, I picked up some pens, paper, paperclips and sticky notes to stock the desk. For a software engineer, Gil had a strange dependence on paper notes that he arrayed all over any desk he worked at. I had no idea how he kept track of them all, but it worked for him! I also picked up a whiteboard to mount on the wall beside the desk.

When I got home, I moved the desk to where it caught the best light and had a view of the lake, arranged the supplies, then moved the old desk chair to my bedroom where it would be more useful. That is, for values of "useful" that were supposed to mean "sitting on it to put on my shoes", but more realistically included "supporting a heap of clothing I meant to wear again but didn't or was simply too lazy to put away".

As Gil's visit got closer, I changed the sheets on my bed, wiped off the counters, vacuumed and mopped the rest of the floors. I hoped to be in this house for a long time, and since I expected *he'd* be in my life for a long time, I wanted him to love it. Also, even though he'd seen me (and my previous homes) at my best and worst, it had been a whole year since I'd seen him in person, so this visit felt like a Very Big Deal.

***

Two days before he was due, Brigid posted on George:

> **Brigid:** Planning to visit a couple of wineries tomorrow, anyone else want to go? Sorry for the short notice but I just saw that they've opened back up to outdoor tastings without reservations!

> **Sulis:** What time?

> **Brigid:** I figured on leaving around 11, since Diamond Point opens at noon and it's just about an hour away.

> **Rob:** I can go.

Cayden: Me too!

Brigid: Anyone else? I can drive and I've got room for one more in the car.

Macrina: Me please!

We arranged to meet at the local park, where we could leave our cars and all ride together in Brigid's vehicle. We all crammed into her Jeep, with Sulis in front and me, Rob and Cayden in the back. I offered to ride in the middle, since my legs were shortest, but Rob insisted on taking the middle spot. The two men leaned so close together that I had plenty of room; luckily it was a scenic drive despite the rain, so I didn't mind not joining their low-voiced conversation.

We headed up Highway 99 to Diamond Point Winery, where Sulis knew the owners and we were treated like old friends. Their Pinot Noir was excellent, a classic Oregon Pinot with cherry flavors up front and an earthy finish and I was pleased to see that they also had some bolder red wines, made with grapes sourced from up north in the Columbia Valley and down south in the Applegate region. I knew that I wanted to join a wine club or two, where you get shipments of two or three bottles at special discounts a few times a year, but decided to hold off until I'd sampled a few more wineries. For now, I just grabbed a wine club leaflet to keep for reference. We stayed there for an hour, the three of us women laughing and talking while Rob and Cayden tried to participate but seemed unable to tear their attention from each other.

Our second stop was at a winery that appeared to be run as a hobby from the owner's garage. The wine wasn't bad, but it was inconsistent; it was clear he'd experimented with different methods on every batch and was eager to have us taste all of them while he explained Every. Single. Detail. of his methodology and winemaking philosophy. We'd only planned to visit two places, but once we managed to escape from the winemaker's conversational clutches, we unanimously decided that we needed a palate cleanser, so to speak. There were a number of wineries off this highway, a bonus of living in a great wine region, so we just headed south and chose one that sounded good. As we drove by a big sign, Sulis yelped "There's Plaid! Let's go there, I love their wines!" so Brigid turned onto their road.

We were lucky here. Plaid was a relatively well-known place that specialized in sparkling wines but it happened to be fairly empty that day, probably due to the drizzly weather, so we were able to get in without a reservation. I'd already tasted six different Pinots so this time I opted for a wine flight featuring their bubblies. This tasting room was large, with an entire wall of glass panes that could be opened depending on weather. The panes were closed today to exclude the drizzle, except for a ventilation opening at the top that was shielded by the roof's overhang, so we got all the benefits of the long green views over vine covered hills, while staying dry.

Plaid's wines fully lived up to their reputation – I thought about getting a wine club membership with them, until I grabbed their club leaflet and saw the prices. The very, very pricy prices. Uh, nope, I could just get a bottle of bubbly here when I needed to celebrate without committing to a membership and giving them my nonexistent firstborn child. When Rob and Cayden went to the bar to get our next round of tasters, Brigid and Sulis and I discussed whether it would be in bad taste for us to set up a betting pool on George to place bets when they'd admit they were a couple. We were still sober enough to decide, with regret, that it would be rude, especially after Sulis pointed out that it wasn't clear whether they'd even admitted it to themselves yet, and we didn't want to scare them off each other!

***

And then I was back home, disinclined to do anything else that day and glad I'd finished getting the house in shape before heading out to drink wine. It felt like a popcorn-for-dinner night so that was what I did, fed the cats, cleaned up, and went to bed early so that the next day, and Gil's visit, would come sooner.

Of course I would have been happy to pick Gil up at the airport, but he'd decided to rent a car at the airport so he wouldn't have to borrow mine and leave me stranded if he wanted to sightsee or decided to work in a coffee shop for a few hours. So I waited in the living room, absentmindedly knitting a simple sock pattern and reading the same page of my book over and over. (Yes, I read and knit at the same time. Or at least, I normally do – but not that morning!) Finally, I heard a car pull up in front of the house, opened the door and there he was with a small suitcase, a big smile, and the overstuffed backpack he always carried his work computer in. He came inside, gently closed the door, put down the backpack, kissed me until I was panting for breath and my toes tingled, and said, "Where's your bedroom?"

So much for cleaning. I don't think he even looked at the rest of the house at all that day.

CHAPTER EIGHT: BOYFRIEND, MEET HOUSE

There was some controversy during the night, when the cats objected to having not one but two humans taking up space in "their" bed, but they adapted. Next morning I was amused to see Morgana snuggled into the bend of Gil's legs, with her chin resting on his knees and an unmistakably proprietary look on her fuzzy little face.

I stayed where I was for a moment, curled against Gil's back, smelling the combination of his usual rosemary shampoo, the same brand of deodorant he'd used for years and the underlying hint of male musk that said "Gil" to me, and luxuriated in the feeling that all was right with my world.

When I was finally able to get up, I had to extricate myself carefully, since Merlin was lodged into the bend of *my* legs. No wonder I'd been so warm!

I'm not normally a fan of big breakfasts – they leave me feeling weighted down all day. I usually just grab whatever's around – granola bar, leftovers, instant oatmeal, or even popcorn if I want to indulge myself. I'd shopped indulgently for Gil's visit, though, and for his first morning here, I went all out and cooked bacon, eggs and potatoes. I didn't need to go anywhere that day anyhow, and I always appreciate an excuse to eat bacon!

Gil doesn't share my opinions about big breakfasts, but he knows my ways, so he was surprised when he followed his nose to the kitchen.

"Wow, eggs, bacon *and* potatoes! I must have been a very good boy to deserve this spread!"

I smiled back and gave him an over-exaggerated once-over, from head to toe and halfway back up. "Oh, you were. And I figured we deserved a treat, for our first visit together in a year. I didn't get a chance to ask yesterday, how was the flight?"

"Uncomfortable. The airport was definitely less crowded than usual and there was even an empty middle seat next to me, but to balance that I wore a mask the whole way. Only about half the people there were wearing them, but I didn't want to come visit you and bring the plague with me!"

"Thanks, I appreciate that. Want the house tour after breakfast?"

"Why, are you afraid I'll get lost?"

"No, it's just that I want your opinion on some things."

"Well, you know me, I'm not short on opinions. Speaking of opinionated people, this cat seems strangely interested in my eggs. Do you give them people food?"

"Don't let her eat off your plate, or I'll have to be fending them off at every meal. If there are any eggs left, I'll give them a taste, but I'll put it over by their food bowl so they learn that's the only place they get fed. I hope they didn't keep you awake last night?"

"No, nothing keeps me awake after a day of dealing with airports and car rentals! Though one of your cats appears to have ambitions to become a night cap – it slept for a while on my pillow, above my head. At least it didn't try to knead my scalp, so it was actually kind of nice – it kept my bald spot warm."

"You don't have a bald spot!"

"Well, thinning, anyway. I can't complain, at least I've had all my hair this long. My younger brother started going bald at 19."

"Is that why he shaves his head?"

"Yup. At first, he tried wearing a ball cap everywhere, but Mom objected to him wearing a hat at meals. So I'm just happy to be in my forties with most of my hair still here!"

"Yes, you are definitely…genetically gifted." He laughed as I gave him an exaggerated leer to nail down the double entendre.

We finished breakfast, then sat around the table chatting amicably about the cats, his work projects, my clients, and everything else. We'd talked on the phone almost every night over the past year, but somehow it still felt like we needed to catch up.

Finally, I stood and loaded the plates into the dishwasher. "Want to see the rest of the house now?"

"Sure. What did you want my opinion on?"

"Nope. Tour first, opinions after."

He'd already seen the kitchen and my bedroom, so I toured him through the living room and spare room, then took him out to the deck and walked over to the dock to see the lake, which was currently brooding dramatically, under a layer of low clouds, with wisps of fog rising from the water, and then finally back to the house and up to the lab / office space.

"And that's all of it. What do you think?"

"It's tiny. Good for one person, though."

"You call it tiny, I say it's cozy and adorable. And it fits me and the cats perfectly. What else?"

"But it doesn't fit you really, does it? You told me about your friend Sulis said. I remember your old condo; you had interesting things everywhere that you'd collected along the way. This place has your furniture, but it sort of looks like you've just been camping out here. What happened to your old stuff?"

"When I was packing up, I noticed that a lot of pieces were falling apart or showing their age. So I decided to throw them all away, because I was sure I'd collect new things. But then I haven't gone anywhere for the past year, so..."

"Just looking at the place, I'd guess you spend most of your time in the lab and at your computer. In the house you cook and eat in the kitchen, and then in the living room you read and knit in one corner, because that has a light, your knitting bag, plus a table for your tea and a bookshelf nearby. I'd bet you only walk through the rest of that room, and you never go into the rest of the house. Am I right?"

"Well, yes. But there's only one of me! I can only sit in one place at a time, and I sit where it's comfortable. I've only used one chair at the dining table because I haven't had people over to eat. We'll eat there tonight, since it's too cold and drizzly to eat outside, but I think that might be the first time the rest of the table was used since I've been here – except occasionally when I let mail pile up there."

"Yes, you can only sit in one place at a time, but the rest of the house should still reflect you – otherwise you never will be comfortable in it, and neither will anyone else. The place is all white walls, brown leather and wood, and your gray stone counters – what about adding some colors?"

"I had a feeling you'd get it – that was exactly what I wanted your opinions on. What colors?"

"Hm. If it were for me, it would probably be all blue and gray, but for you ... what colors do you wear most?"

"Remember, I hardly go out of the house these days, so I mostly wear leggings and t-shirts with flannel shirts over that. So, black, white, and whatever is on sale."

"You could start with black and white, but I don't think monochrome works with the vibe of this house. But I have seen black-painted rooms that looked good – you could do the powder room in black, or maybe charcoal gray with white trim, and maybe even do your bedroom the same, with a fluffy white comforter to lighten it up and some pictures for more color?"

I squinted, trying to imagine it, and liking what I saw. "OK, what about the living room?"

"What color would you want to wear if you were to actually, you know, get dressed in the morning?"

"Red," I said decisively, thinking of my favorite dress. "Not crayon red, but a darker rosy red."

"There you go. That would be a whole lot of red if you painted the whole room, but what about just doing that back wall that goes the length of the house from the living room to the kitchen as an accent?"

Again, I tried to picture it. "You know what? I think I have an old illusion spell I never used. I bet I could tweak that to put those colors up, at least for a little while, so we could see how they look."

"That might be a good idea. I just realized we've settled on black, white and red for your house – it could end up looking like a vampire movie!"

***

Later that afternoon, while Gil spent a couple of hours catching up on work, I implemented the illusion spell in three areas: I didn't want stark black so I put up off-black walls the color of a used chalkboard in the powder room and main bedroom, with an accent wall in the red of a Tempranillo wine (just a little darker than a Merlot) along the back wall of the public areas.

This wasn't a permanent spell – that would have required a lot more power and been a lot more expensive – so I'd still need to paint if I wanted to keep the walls this color. But this would last for a week or more, and would give me the chance to live with the colors and see how I liked them on a daily basis. Even better, I could adjust them if I wanted a change. I'd only just changed the bed sheets right before Gil arrived (and making a king-sized bed is a non-trivial task!) so while I was at it, I also changed the sheets and duvet cover from a sprigged flower pattern to pure white.

I made a mental note to check where I'd bought this spell and to replace it from the same vendor. I liked this version a lot; it was easy to implement, took little energy from me, and was considerably more flexible than some others I'd used. If my backbrain was willing to do me a favor, I might think of some enhancements for this spell I could sell to its creator; then if they were willing, we might be able to barter, where I'd swap enhancements (say, a way to make this spell last longer, or to randomize it in case the user wasn't sure what colors they wanted) for more copies of the spell or even a licensed version that would allow me to use it regularly.

Once I was done, I walked around the rooms

considering the new look. I really liked the red in the living area; my dark brown leather sofa grounded it, the various colors of books on my shelves and implements in my kitchen broke it up so it wasn't too heavy. The side of the house facing the lake was mostly window, to capture the view, so it wasn't too dark despite the deeper color. I'd need to decide what to do with the window covers and maybe add some throw pillows, but this felt like a keeper.

The powder room looked like something out of a home-décor magazine, which was good – but so did the bedroom, and I wasn't so sure about that. On the one hand, the dark walls made it feel like a cave, which seemed like a good look for a restful bedroom; on the other hand, they were so on-trend that it didn't feel like me. Also, the chalkboard color combined with the overall cave feel made me want to get some chalk and create my own "cave-art" graffiti. I'd leave it for now, think about it some more, and see what Gil thought. After all, with luck he'd be sleeping here more often in future!

***

With all the fuss about getting ready to have a houseguest, I hadn't checked in with George for a few days. I did that now, seeing some of the usual chatter about what the weather was going to do and people getting their gardens ready for winter. Also, there was an invitation:

> **Genna:** Anyone want to go to Antlers tomorrow night? I made a pot roast yesterday and we have leftovers tonight, but I could use a break from cooking tomorrow.

> **Menzy:** Ooooooh, do we finally get to meet Mr. Genna?

> **Genna:** Yes, he'll be there. Be gentle.

> **Brigid:** Oh, we will ;-)

Antlers was the bar in the town across the lake (so, a whole ten minutes' drive away). I hadn't been there yet, but I'd heard they had a decent bar menu – hamburgers, fish & chips, and that sort of thing. I wasn't the only one who was still feeling iffy about the idea of eating in a restaurant where I'd need to be both indoors and unmasked, but when they reopened after the worst of the pandemic, they had set up a covered outdoor seating area with heaters, so that was where we planned to meet.

I was still in the mode of celebrating Gil's first visit to this house, so I'd planned steaks for dinner that night and even had a bottle of champagne chilled, but I didn't have any plans for the next night; bar food sounded perfect. Was it too soon to introduce him to my new friends?

The nice thing about Gil was, he was a competent adult. He could choose his own clothing, clean and cook, and in general take care of himself like a grownup. I'd had previous boyfriends who'd had to be babysat – if they were in a roomful of people they didn't know and weren't comfortable with, I had to stay nearby to introduce them and talk to them. Gil was an ambivert – neither a shy introvert nor a raging extrovert, but able to enjoy meeting new people and strike up conversations with them, then go home and hang out on the couch with a good book to recharge and soak up the silence. If he couldn't find anyone to talk to in a group, he'd go order another drink, or look at pictures on the walls or whatever. I really did want him to meet the local group, so I decided to check if this was a good time to ask.

I poked my head into the spare room. "Knock, knock. Is it OK to ask a question?"

"Yeah, go ahead. Just let me finish answering this email. And … there!"

He turned to face me, and I saw that Merlin was lying on the front edge of the desk, between Gil and his keyboard. He saw where I was looking and said, "Yup, he's been 'helping' me."

"How can you even type, with him in front of the

keyboard like that?"

"I d'know, he makes a good wrist rest. He's been purring, so he obviously doesn't mind it – and who knows, maybe the warmth and vibration help prevent carpal tunnel syndrome. If only he didn't keep trying to catch my fingers as I type, that would be helpful."

"Kittens. Gotta love them, even when they won't let you work. I wanted to ask, do you want to go out to the bar with some of my local friends tomorrow?"

"Sure, sounds like fun. Is this the infamous George group?"

"This is, indeed, the infamous George group."

"And does George have a last name?"

"George *is* his last name," I said, looking down my nose at his uncouth lack of knowledge. (I was sitting on the bed, and he was in the desk chair. As he's a fair bit taller than I am whether standing up or sitting down, this required some contortion.)

"Well, what's his first name then? Or should that be, 'What's its first name?'"

"Percival, of course, after the town!"

I went back to my laptop and pulled up the browser window with the George chat.

> **Macrina:** I'll be there! I'm bringing a +1

> **Sulis:** Ooh! We get to meet Mr. Genna and the infamous Gil!

> **Macrina:** Funny, that's what he said about you folks. 'The infamous George group'.

> **Menzy:** ⩊We can all be infamous together! That bar won't know what hit them.

> **Rob:** Cayden and I will be there!

I smiled at the clear implication that they were making plans together as a routine thing now.

***

I made Gil grill the steaks, guest or no guest, simply because he was better at it. Meanwhile, I assembled a salad, having put the baked potatoes in the oven earlier. The steaks were done perfectly, of course, a ribeye for him and a much smaller tenderloin for me – there are advantages of having been together long enough to know exactly what we each like. I'd put the dining table right in front of the biggest window; it was where I drank my morning tea, and I loved watching how the lake's color changed throughout the day depending on the weather and the angle of the sun.

Over dinner, I told Gil about my experience on Samhain, my fall into the lake and what Sulis had said. Though MC, Gil wasn't a magic user himself, but he'd been friends growing up with a neighbor kid whose parents created and sold cooking spells. Between that and what he'd learned from me over the years, he had a pretty good idea of how things worked – though it was occasionally confusing to both of us that my 'backend' spells and his firmware had so much in common – right up to the point where they didn't.

He said, "So, since she said that, you've gotten two cats, one plant (plus a fake plant), installed two robo-vacuums with their own names, put color on the walls even if it's temporary, and rearranged the guest bedroom to make it fit your needs better … did I miss anything?"

"I think I get double credit for the illusion spell – not just the added color, but also just doing magic to the house. Of course I've done magic in it for work the whole time I've lived here, but since it's so small I'd been cleaning by hand, and I hadn't really done any spells that affect the house itself til now. So that probably counts too."

"Does it seem to be working? Does it feel more alive?"

"I'd have to get Sulis over and ask her; I think she's a lot more sensitive to that kind of thing than I am. I can't tell any difference yet; maybe it just needs to settle in and absorb for a while. What I should really do is to infuse some power into a spell – not one of the big Samhain invocations, but just a routine one. That would tell me if I've gotten any further toward fixing the problem. Anyway, speaking of the illusion spell, what do you think of the colors?"

"Beautiful, but not quite right. They just don't feel like you."

"Got it. Beautiful equals not like me. Thanks a lot!"

He flicked his hand to disavow my words. "Yes, Meli, you are beautiful. Stunning. Gorgeous. And clearly completely secure in your attractiveness. Can we take that as read and just assume I mean beautiful in a different way?"

He went on, "I think it's a couple things. That off-black in the bedroom is cozy but cold – I know that sounds like a contradiction, so maybe 'cozy' is the wrong word. It's like a cave: it huddles around you but isn't actually warming or welcoming.

"Yeah, I think you might've nailed it. I do like that color in the half bath, though – powder rooms are a good place for a dramatic design and I like how stylish it is. What about the red wall?"

"I love that color and it is very you, in fact – but I noticed one thing. That wall is next to the lake wall, with all those windows and all that blue and gray and green. Their reflection cools that color, and it kind of fights with the colors in the view."

"What if I swapped them then, and put the red in the bedroom?"

"Yes! That would work. You could make the wall behind your headboard that dark red. I think that would work well. And you never open your bedroom window shades anyway. But when you say 'swap' do you mean you'd put the chalkboard black in the living area?"

"No, yuck, too dark. How about…" I thought about it, and remembered the way the Drama teacher had painted the stage I'd helped build for a class play back in high school. "How about sort of a pale gold, the kind of color that you don't really register as yellow because it just looks like it's got warm light on it?"

He smiled. "I think that could look really good. But if your end goal is not just to make things look better but to bring the house alive in magic terms, you've forgotten another obvious tactic."

I raised an eyebrow. "I have?"

"Yes, you need a name for your house!"

I sighed "I know. I'd already thought of that. But it has to be the perfect name. Any ideas?"

"Nope. I'll think about it."

CHAPTER NINE: BOYFRIEND, MEET FRIENDS

The next morning I tweaked the spell to change the wall colors. The pale gold looked warm and welcoming in the morning sun, but I hated the way the dark red wall in the bedroom looked – that is, I still liked the color, but I hated the contrast of the dark red with the other cream-colored walls in the room. I tried making all four walls Merlot red, and that was much better – warm and cozy, as I'd wanted. The illusion spell should be good for at least another week; I'd let this stay and see how it was to live with.

I realized I'd overlooked one small issue. I could change the colors however I wanted by making them a little lighter, darker, redder, bluer, and so forth, but eventually I would have to paint the walls if I wanted to keep the color scheme permanently – and how do you take a sample of an illusion to the paint counter to be duplicated? I could take a photo on my phone, but then you have the risk of the camera changing the color, and if I tried to print it out that would be another change.

The intersection of magic and technology did not always flow smoothly. I'd figure something out – but I took some pictures, just in case.

After breakfast I packed sandwiches and snacks, and we went for a drive along the back roads so he could get a better idea of the area. An hour away, we stopped for a short hike to Diamond Creek Falls waterfall, and I marveled again at how beautiful Oregon is. It was chilly but not cold, and was a changeable day, moving quickly from sun to beautiful cloudscapes to short periods of drizzle and back again; Gil seemed to enjoy it after the heat of Texas. We passed through the town of Oakridge, known for its mountain biking trails, and I stopped to pick up a trail map. It had been far too long since I'd ridden, though; if I wanted to try these trails, I'd need to get my bike overhauled. I also made a mental note to check whether any of the George group were cyclists.

We were home in plenty of time to relax, change and head out to Antlers. Gil put on a pair of cowboy boots I hadn't seen before, explaining that they were "protective coloration" where he lived in Texas.

"Well, not so much in Austin," he explained further. "Some people do dress cowboy there, but not everyone. I originally got these as kind of a joke, but then I got to liking them – they're comfortable, and keep my ankles warm in some of those over-air-conditioned offices. I wore them here because I can kick them off for airport security and put them back on without having to bend over and tie shoelaces. I figured you had your share of cowboys here in rural Oregon and I could fit right in. Plus, they make me two inches taller!" He winked at me.

***

The first thing we saw as we entered the bar was a trio of young men, all in cowboy hats and boots, playing pool (and wearing no masks).

Gil gave me a meaningful glance and drawled softly in my ear, "Need to get me a hat!" I bit my lip to keep from laughing. We continued through the bar and out to the open-air seating in back, where we saw our people.

Genna, a man who must be her husband, Menzy and Sulis were already at a table with drinks in front of them; Rob and Cayden came through just behind us. We took our seats and grabbed a chair from another table a few minutes later when Brigid joined us.

Once we were all seated, Genna said, "You must be Gil!"

"The infamous," he responded, laughing, and stood up, started to put his hand out to shake hers, then obviously remembered Covid was still a thing, pulled his hand back and gave her an awkward wave.

She continued, politely ignoring his embarrassment, "This is my husband, Duncan. He's an anthropologist too, but he tends to focus on the ancient Pictish tribes, in Scotland."

Duncan waved to everyone, and then said, "I think Genna has told me about all of you, but can you all please say your names, so I can put them to faces?" He went on, "It feels like the first day teaching a class, but I promise not to do a roll call and there will be no quiz!"

Menzy muttered audibly, "Damned good thing. NOT my favorite part of college."

I leaned over and asked her, "So what was your favorite part?"

"The drinking, of course!" She raised her glass and grinned. "So I'm all set."

I asked everyone, "Can I assume I'd be better off ordering beer or whiskey than wine here?"

Genna answered, "They do have wine, but it's not exactly a wine list – just one red and one white. It's usually not terrible."

" 'Not terrible' sounds like a good reason to stick to beer!" I answered, as the waitress came over. She handed out menus and took our drink orders.

After she left, Gil asked, "Is there anything we should avoid on the menu?"

"Nope," Menzy said. "Nothing fancy, but it's all good. Don't miss the fries, though – they're the kind where they start with a potato and a cutter, not with a bag out of the freezer."

She was right. The food came quickly, the burgers were juicy, and the sides of fries were ridiculously large. Conversation stopped as we all dived in.

Once the initial feeding frenzy had slowed down, I turned to Sulis. "I've taken your advice on bringing the house alive – I wasn't planning to dive in quite so quickly, but I think I've done just about everything you suggested – well, almost. I'm still testing out colors for the rooms."

She smiled, "I saw your kitten photos – they're

adorable!"

Hearing that, Cayden looked over and asked, "How are they liking the cat tower?"

I told him, "I love it – the way it's made to look like a tree growing out of the wall is brilliant. The kittens are still working out their territory – there's one branch that leans over to where they can see out the window, that they both love, and they keep squabbling over that spot. Yesterday I saw Morgana move so far out on the branch that she ended up falling off. Good thing kittens bounce; she just shook her head and walked off like 'I meant to do that!' "

He smiled and went back to his conversation with Rob and Gil about beer and how hard it was to find an ale that *wasn't* an IPA in Oregon.

Sulis went on to ask, "So did it work? Does the house feel more alive to you?"

"Well, with Gil visiting I haven't had the chance to do any spell testing, but they've definitely been good changes. I love having cats in the house again, especially when I'm there alone. The robotic vacuums are going to make it easier to not have cat fur coating every room, and the colors make the rooms feel homier. I'm going to have to paint the walls once Gil goes home, though – right now I'm just using an illusion spell to try out the colors and make sure I know what I want. So thanks for the advice; hopefully it will make my spells and magic infusions work better, but even if they don't, these are changes I should have made long ago."

She smiled. "I'm glad, then."

Brigid turned to say, "While you're redoing your house, let me know if you want any custom metalwork. My students are always looking for project ideas, and because they're still students, they have good rates. I supervise everything they do, though."

"Thanks! I'll have to think about it."

A bit later, I found myself talking to Genna and Duncan about his work. "I was just reading that we don't really know much about the Picts – but it was in some fantasy fiction, so I don't know how accurate that is. Is it true? And how do you learn about them?"

He answered, "No, we actually know quite a lot. The problem is that we don't have any writing by them, just writing about them from other groups. And some of those groups were their enemies, so we need to be careful in what we believe. The other problem is that "Pict" is just what other people called them, and there's some evidence that there were a lot of unconnected groups lumped under that name. But we do have some stone monuments and some remains of their brochs and crannogs – those are stone roundhouses and artificial islands. In fact, I've got a trip over to Scotland in a few months to excavate a newly discovered broch structure not too far from Aberdeen. We think it was a fort."

Genna put in, proudly, "Not just to excavate – he's been offered a visiting professorship at the University of Aberdeen for the spring semester. As you'd imagine, they have plenty of local experts so it's not often they invite an outside professor to talk about their own history."

He smiled down at her – it was hard to tell while they were sitting, but he looked to be a good foot or more taller than his wife. "Yes, I feel lucky to be invited."

"Lucky!" she objected. "They're the lucky ones, to get you, and it sounds like they know it."

"Are you going with him, Genna?" I asked.

"I'll go over with him and stay for a couple weeks, but not the whole semester," she told me. "I can't spare that much time from my own research."

When we left, I asked Gil what he thought.

"About the bar or the people?" he asked.

"Either."

"Good bar, and it's nice to have one that close. I like the people too – from what you've said, you've spent the last year as a hermit and even before you moved here, you didn't really have that many local friends in Portland. So it's probably good for you to have this group."

He went on, "I was talking to Rob and Cayden about mountain biking around Oakridge. Sounds like they're both pretty familiar with the trails there. Rob said he works twenty-four-hour shifts at the firehouse, but then he gets a bunch of days off, so he'd be happy to take you out riding."

"Did you tell him he'd have to ride at a sloth's pace so I could keep up?"

"You can tell him that. I did warn him it had been a few years since you'd ridden, and you'd have to get your bike tuned first."

***

For the rest of Gil's visit, we got into an easy routine: grabbing a quick breakfast together, then splitting up to work for most of the day, with lunches together if we could manage it and dinners that went late as we talked and talked, aside from a few times when one or the other of us had late meetings. I'd been sleeping alone so long that it was shockingly pleasant to have him there to snuggle up to when we went to bed, even aside from any other possible pleasures. We managed to get through the entire two weeks without any arguments, except for a few tiny squabbles as we discussed the best possible layout of my furniture. That was probably a record for us (there was a reason we didn't live together, after all). Either we were both on our best behavior after the long time apart, or we were finally growing up.

Once he left, the bed felt very big, and very cold. We'd tried living together once when we were in our late twenties and it had been a disaster, but right now I missed having him around all the time.

CHAPTER TEN: NOVEMBER IS THE MOST...

"November is the most disagreeable month in the whole year," said Margaret, standing at the window one dull afternoon, looking out at the frostbitten garden.
"That's the reason I was born in it," observed Jo pensively, quite unconscious of the blot on her nose."

After Gil left, the house felt empty and dull; I started my annual reread of Little Women, partly in honor of Jo March's birthday (and Louisa May Alcott's) and partly to start getting myself in a holiday mood, but Meg March's comment about November rang all too true.

I filled the gap by keeping myself very busy; with my equipment and ingredients freshly rededicated and imbued with magical energy from the Samhain rituals, this was a good time to build up my product stores. Sometimes there was a holiday rush as people prepared spells for their celebrations, and I'd spent a few too many holiday seasons going flat out until the last minute to get all my orders delivered in time. Gil was busy too, as people always seemed to schedule software projects to complete by the end of the year for fiscal reasons.

I kept busy with other tasks too; one day I took my bike to the shop in town and picked it up a few days later, ready to ride. And I decided, given the small size of my house and the reasonable ceiling height, that I would paint my rooms myself. I solved my color matching issue by pulling out a less powerful version of the same illusion spell and casting the colors I'd chosen on a few pieces of cardboard I could take with me to the paint store. I spent a couple of intensive evenings masking off the woodwork and covering my furniture and floor with tarps, but I had one unexpected issue: the color on my walls still hadn't faded. Apparently "livening" up the house actually had worked, and the result was unexpected longevity on the illusion spell. It wasn't a permanent spell, and I knew the effects would fade at some point; the question was just when. I decided to start by painting the bedroom, since that would take longer, so that the living room would have another few days to fade and I could use that time to see just how long the spell would last.

I also promised myself to test the strength of every spell I'd made in the past few weeks before sending it to a customer – if I'd accidentally put extra power into a spell I'd bought from someone else and only invoked myself, I might have done the same to spells I'd created for sale. A color illusion lasting longer than expected was no big deal, but accurate calibration mattered for some things. For one example, a spell meant to increase the power of a combustion spell had better not be any stronger than it was expected to be!

For the almost-black color in the powder room, I used a magical paint from my friend-and-former-landlord Meg's company. It had a twinkling effect that I thought would be fun in there, though it might be annoyingly distracting in a bigger room. It also had the advantage of drying quickly and not giving off any fumes. I used the same company's paint in colors with no special visual effects for the rest of the house for those reasons and because it covered more completely and evenly than nonmagical paint.

There was one possible problem with painting before the illusion's colors wore off: I was worried that, if I'd gotten my paint matched well enough, I wouldn't be able to tell which areas I'd painted and where I might have missed some spots. That turned out not to be a problem after all; wet paint is a little lighter than the color it will be when dry. As long as I checked carefully right after painting, I could see any areas I'd missed. The bedroom took two days to paint, and another day to do the white woodwork, so I slept on the living room couch for those days. The morning of the third day, I woke up and noticed that the warm gold of the walls had lost color saturation and turned to an unappealing beige. Good, the illusion was finally fading! By the time I was nearly finished painting the accent wall, the unpainted bits were back to their original cream color.

***

Genna and Duncan invited all of us to their house for Friendsgiving dinner, the day after Thanksgiving. My parents were gone and I'd been an only child, so I had no big holiday plans; I cooked myself a turkey breast and indulgent loaded mashed potatoes on the day itself and made two of my specialty flourless chocolate cakes – one small one for my own Thanksgiving dinner, and one full-sized one to take to Genna's. Menzy, Sulis and Brigid also attended, along with Nell, Andrew, their kids, and a few of Genna's neighbors.

It was only a few blocks but I drove over so I wouldn't have to carry the cake in the rain. Their house was warm and welcoming, with a big open area divided into different levels: a main level with steps down in one direction to the kitchen and in another direction to a seating area with couches and chairs facing a fireplace. At the back of the main level was a farmhouse table with places already set for dinner. Their two yellow Labs sat next to the table, carefully watching the kitchen to see if food was coming out yet.

Genna told us, "They won't bother you while you're eating, as long as you don't mind being watched. They know they're not allowed to eat food from the kitchen counters or dining table, but they like to keep watch just in case someone drops something!"

It was clear I'd been memorable to Oliver and Charli, Nell and Andrew's kids: after politely asking Genna for permission, they blew out the candles she'd set on the table and made me relight them. This made me instantly popular with all the kids, especially Laxmi, a neighbor child whose family were MC, at least by ancestry, and who wanted to be a magic user herself when she grew up.

I enjoyed that dinner, though I still felt a little awkward at being in an enclosed room with a bunch of other people – the 'social distancing' habits I'd acquired during a year and more of pandemic were hard to break! But the space was big and airy, and Genna kept a few windows open despite the late-November chill; the big wood fire in the fireplace across the room kept us from getting too cold.

The food was excellent: Duncan made a deep-fried turkey for which he is apparently locally famous. I'm not sure whether Sulis and Brigid had collaborated or if it was a coincidence, but they'd gone German, bringing beef rouladen and apple strudel respectively. Nell and Andrew provided a potato gratin, while the kids brought the green bean casserole without which no Thanksgiving potluck ever seems to be complete. They proudly announced that they'd made it entirely by themselves, with parental contributions limited to oversight and advice. Genna's neighbors had brought appetizers and salads; there was far more food than we could possibly eat. The food was set up along another long table behind the dining table, so we could all serve ourselves.

In addition to the wine that seemed to be a necessity at our group gatherings, Genna had also provided a non-alcoholic sangria punch, which was much appreciated. Not only did it give the adults an interesting alternative when we needed to cut off drinking wine for those of us who were driving, it also let the kids have a celebratory beverage along with us.

I was glad I'd made myself an extra chocolate cake because the one I'd taken to Genna's was completely devoured. Though that didn't stop me from snagging an additional piece of leftover strudel to take home with me. It would make a healthy breakfast, right? It had fruit in it, after all!

***

I told Gil about the dinner in our call that night, making sure to taunt him about the chocolate cake he'd missed. He loved that cake. He told me in turn about the dinner he'd gone to with his closest coworkers, who were longtime friends I'd also gotten to know over the years.

I asked, "So how were Jimmy and Deepak and their families?"

"Great! I hadn't seen the kids for a few weeks, so we roughhoused a bit – I think I have some new bruises, because those little elbows are *sharp*! And you missed out," he said smugly. "Jimmy's brother from New Orleans came, and made us a deep fried turkey. It was really, really good."

One of the few things I did like about Texas was the conglomeration of flavors in their cooking – Cajun food from neighboring Louisiana, different regional varieties of Mexican food including Tex-Mex, homemade venison sausages, German food from the Fredericksburg area – but this time I didn't feel I'd missed out. "Nope, I didn't miss anything! Genna's husband Duncan deep-fried a turkey too. I think he went to Tulane or somewhere down there for college, and now he likes to cook Cajun food. I even got to hang out with some kids while I was there. One of them, Laxmi, wants to be a magic user when she grows up. I told her and her parents that I'd be happy to meet with her one day soon, show her around my lab and answer all her questions. She was so excited, she was almost glowing with delight."

"Will you really have her over to your lab?"

"Oh, yeah, it'll be fun for me. And I like to do it to pay it forward for the people that mentored me when I was young."

"Cool. And I'm glad you had a good time, Meli. I know holidays have been lonely for you, and I feel bad when we aren't together for them."

"Me too, but we made choices on how to live our lives, and these are the consequences."

"I know, but sometimes I wonder if it's time to change our choices."

I asked him what he was thinking about, but he backed off and changed the subject. We talked about the possibility of getting together for the next holidays (Christmas for him, Yule and Chanukah for me, though Chanukah was soon after Thanksgiving this year), and we agreed to check our schedules but didn't come to any decisions.

***

Even aside from Friendsgiving, I was suddenly being a lot more social – not a hermit anymore. We started a tradition of going to Antlers on Wednesday nights – there was no band, and it was empty enough in the earlier part of the evenings that we could hear ourselves talk. We stayed in the outside seating area; as the weather grew colder, the bar put up tarped frame walls to keep wind out, and added more heaters, but there was still open space between the walls and the roof for ventilation. No one came down with the plague, so it seemed to be fairly safe – at least on these less crowded nights. An added advantage was that this space always had fewer people, as more regular customers gave up on social distancing and moved indoors. Given the impossibility of drinking beer through a mask, I was glad my George friends agreed on staying outside.

The number of us at the table varied each week; people showed up or didn't, depending on what they had going on. Some nights, the whole George group was there, while other nights there were only two or three of us.

One night, it was just me and Brigid there, because all the others had various things keeping them busy that night. I liked Brigid, but this time the conversation was heavy going. She seemed distracted (and honestly, I was getting a little bored). I decided if I wanted us to be real friends, rather than just drinking buddies, I needed to speak out.

"Brigid? Is anything wrong?"

She seemed startled. "No, I'm fine. Why?"

"You just seem distracted tonight. Something on your mind?"

"No, nothing really. Well, yes, there's something but it's stupid."

I tapped my glass on the table. "What happens at Antlers, stays at Antlers. Do you want to talk about it? I promise, I won't think you're stupid."

She said, "No, I don't think I'm stupid either...but I think of myself as a logical person and this isn't logical."

I pointed at myself. "Magic user, remember? We think almost like engineers...except that sometimes we have to take that intuitive jump beyond logic, or it wouldn't be magic. I'm guessing this is about feelings, right? They're closer to magic than to logic."

She sighed. "There's this guy..."

"And you're interested in him? What's the problem?"

"No, that's not it. Or not exactly."

I was pretty sure I knew where this was going – I knew she was a widow, and it can't be easy to date again after your partner has died. This is why I could never be a psychoanalyst; people never go quite where you expect them to.

She went on, "He just started working for the company that services some of the welding equipment we use in my classes, so I'll be seeing him every few months. But I would never want to date him."

I jumped to another conclusion – I should really know better by now. "Because you're a professor and he's –"

"NO. It's not that. I don't care what people do for a living, and anyway, those guys need to be pretty technical. He's hot, but I wouldn't want to actually date him. For one thing, what if we had an ugly break-up? Would he still come fix my equipment? And it would be too weird, in front of my students. Anyway, I just like him: I don't have, like, a burning passion to renounce the world for him. I can enjoy it for what it is without going any further."

"OK, then what's the problem?"

"Well, look, you know my partner Carrie died, right? I don't talk about her much because she was sick for a long time, and it's still painful. But she was wonderful, and I loved her with everything I am. It's not that I'll never want another romance in my life. It will be hard, and it will be weird at first, but I know that already. She knew that, even – even when she was so sick, she used to joke about who I could date that would measure up to her. And she made damned sure I knew she was joking, and that it wouldn't be disloyal to her if I fell in love again."

I restrained my urge to say, "So what's the problem already?" because even I could tell she was hurting and needed support, not prodding. So I only said, as gently as I could, "She sounds wonderful, and clearly she didn't want you to withdraw from life after she died."

"I know that! And the problem isn't that I have a crush, and it isn't what he does. It's just – it's who he is that feels so strange to me."

"Because he's a guy?"

"Not even that so much – well, maybe partly. I dated guys before my Carrie, but everything was so different with her, so much more, that I thought maybe I was a lesbian instead of bi after all. But it's mostly about the kind of person he is. She was a very cerebral, analytical, restrained sort of person – she had strong feelings, but you had to know her to be able to see them. She had a great sense of humor, but it was so dry that sometimes I was the only one who could tell she was joking. Her favorite book in the world was Gaudy Night, if that tells you anything."

"And he is?"

"Big, brash, and loud – everything he is, is right there to see. He probably doesn't have a favorite book at all – he's not stupid, but I can't see him sitting still long enough to read. From the conversations we've had, he likes hiking, rock climbing, and making stuff."

"Making stuff?"

"Welding, obviously, but also carpentry, 3D printing, building models – he likes figuring things out with his hands."

"And you like these things about him"

"Yeah, I do. I like looking at him, and I like talking to him, and maybe we can be friends even if we never date. "

I suppressed my comments about that last part, having seen more than a few "we're only friends" relationships turn into something much different (and several romantic couples who realized they were really better just as friends), and said, simply, "There you go then; it sounds like you can enjoy him as he is, and there isn't a problem with that."

"But it's not him! He's fine – it's what it says about me! Don't you see, it's not just that I thought I was a lesbian, but also, I thought I was the kind of person who needs a certain kind of partner. And now if I'm interested in this totally different sort of person, how does that change who I am?"

I said, firmly, "It doesn't change who you are. It only changes who you thought you were. It just says you are bigger than that, more than the person in that little box you made for yourself. And part of that is that you have added to yourself; you've had new experiences since you fell in love with Carrie, including loving her and losing her physical presence, though she'll always be part of you. But maybe you underestimated yourself all along; maybe you were always bigger than you thought, and more capable of wanting different kinds of people in your most important relationships."

She seemed struck by this. "You mean, maybe I could even have fallen in love with someone like him instead of someone like Carrie years ago?"

"Maybe. And who knows? You'll never regret having her in your life, but maybe if things had turned out differently, if you'd happened to go to different parties and met different people, your life would have been completely changed but still happy. I don't really believe that we all have one predestined perfect true love – there are lots of people who are wrong for us, or who are ok but not great, but maybe there are multiple people who are right, too. And then once you get there, it's about building a relationship together rather than falling into something that's already perfect."

She said, "Huh. Thanks. That helps. I'm still not dating him, but maybe I don't have to feel so weird about liking him. But there's still a problem."

"A different problem or part of the same one?"

She thought about it and waggled her hand in the air. "A little of both. Different aspect of the same problem. Maybe it's mostly stubbornness, though. It's about my family."

"Your family are stubborn?"

"No, I am. But they can be obnoxious. They definitely were, about me and Carrie. I had to fight so hard to get them to accept her. Now if I ever bring home a big hairy guy, I'm worried they'll think they were right all along."

"Is this back to the LGBTQ thing?"

"Not exactly. More of a species thing."

I was honestly shocked. I'd assumed Carrie was human and said so, apologizing for making assumptions again.

"Oh. No, she was human. But I'm not."

"You???" I looked at her more closely. I hadn't seen her doing any magic, which wasn't conclusive, but could mean she *was* magic. "You're a magic species? But you look completely human."

"I mostly am. Do you know what sexual dimorphism is?"

"Yeah, just means males and females of a species look different. Like peacocks."

"And did you ever wonder why Sasquatches – Bigfoot – are so rarely spotted?"

"Can't say that I have, because I just thought they were mythical. So you –"

I bit my cheek so I wouldn't laugh. Not at her

problem, but at the idea of Brigid as a Bigfoot, with her willowy build and ethereal looks. If someone had told me that we had one dryad and one Sasquatch in the group at our first meetup, I might have pegged Menzy as the Bigfoot, just as I'd thought Brigid might be a dryad. Oops.

"Yep. We're hardly ever spotted because the women do all the shopping, or anything that involves going into human communities, and we blend right in."

"So, back to your family problem. Your partner was a human woman, and you had to fight to be with her, and if you bring home a big hairy guy, your family will assume you're…returning to your roots, or something?"

"Or that I'm signaling that I want to come back home and be a good little wife, or even that I'm taking second best just so I can stay out in the human world, yes. They'll be more polite now that they've finally accepted I'm grown up, but I'll still know they're thinking it."

"Ouch. I can't help you with that one! Families can be a lot alike, no matter what species they are. Just, maybe, don't anticipate trouble before you have to? After all, who knows who you'll fall for, when you're really ready to date again."

"Good advice, thanks!" She drained her beer and stood up, taking a step back from both the table and the conversation. "I'd better head out, class is early tomorrow. But thank you, I really appreciate your listening ear."

We had a polite argument over whether I was paying for her drinks because she'd needed a friend, or she was paying for mine in thanks, agreed to each pay for our own, and cashed out at the bar.

CHAPTER ELEVEN: ON THE TRAIL

The first few days of December felt like they'd been borrowed from May: we had a few days with no rain in the forecast, and temperatures reaching up to almost 70°F. I'd gotten my mountain bike back from the shop, so I checked out the trail map Gil and I had gotten from Oakridge, then messaged Rob:

> **Macrina:** I was thinking about checking out the Lookout Loop bike trail near Oakridge. Any advice? And do you wanna go, if you think you can ride slow enough for me?

> **Rob:** I'd love to go riding with you, in this gorgeous weather! Wouldn't recommend that trail, though. It used to be great, but there was a fire near there a couple years ago and all the trees are just blackened ghosts now. What are you looking for in a trail?

I shuddered. The sites of old fires were sad places, until the trees started growing back, and from what I'd seen there were way too many of them out here.

> **Macrina:** Maybe five miles? Nothing too hard; I used to be a solid intermediate rider but it's been a while. I mean, a looooong while! I was serious about being slow.

> **Rob:** Great! My favorite trail is Greentrees, and after three miles you can turn off into a loop that takes you back to the parking area – that gets you off before the rougher part of the main trail,

but the loop back is still scenic. Does tomorrow work for you?

Rob: And don't worry, I've taken out a lot of new riders. You couldn't possibly be slower than some of them.

Macrina: Wanna bet?

It turned out that he'd done a lot of work with kids just learning to ride off-road, though, so he was probably right.

The next day was beautiful – cold in the early morning, but I knew it would warm up quickly. I spent the morning getting ready, finding my old cycling gloves and clip-in shoes, and packing water and snacks. Since it had been so many years, I'd bought a new helmet at the shop when I picked up my bike. Rob came to meet me at my house, since he had a truck with a rack that made it easy to load up both bikes.

I invited him inside while I gathered all my stuff, and he looked around appreciatively. "This place looks great! I love the new color you've added."

"Oh, had you been here before?"

"Yeah, when I was in high school, old Ray used to hire me to help with yardwork and some handyman stuff inside the house – he didn't like climbing ladders anymore. So I was in here all the time. It used to look kind of dated – lots of chintz curtains and sofa covers that I think were left over from before his wife died."

He added, thoughtfully, "He was the first MagiComm person I ever really got to know. As he got older, he had lots of spells working in the house – to open doors, to keep food from going bad, and I don't know what all. Once I swore I saw a whole big library room, and then that door was never there again and old Ray would never answer my questions about it. I don't really know how these things work, but you should check if any of those spells are still in place."

***

We loaded up my bike and headed out. Along the way, he pointed out trailheads for both hiking and biking trails, and told stories of some of his more epic wipeouts. I suddenly realized this was the first time I'd been in a car with anyone since before the pandemic, except of course for Gil, during his visit. But then, if Gil had been harboring any germs, I'd have been exposed to those anyhow.

Once we got to the trailhead, we unloaded and set out, and I was glad to find this trail was fairly level, without any really long climbs, and with nice soft dirt to fall on. I'd lived in Arizona back in the days when I rode more, and it was also nice not to have thorny cactus crowding both sides of the trail! There were a few sections of single-track where we wound between close-set trees, but other parts of the trail were wide enough to ride side by side. Rob proved to be very patient with my wobbly legs and rusty skills, and coaxed me into letting go a bit, rather than clamping down on my brakes on the downhills. After a while, I started to relax, and really enjoyed the middle part of the ride, after the nerves from being off a bike for so long had worn off, and before my butt started feeling sore.

On one wider section of trail, I turned my head toward Rob (for just a second, until I had to check the ground ahead again) and asked, "So, are you and Cayden an *official* item yet?"

His head swiveled around so fast his bike wobbled and he was in some danger of hitting one of the boulders widely spaced along the trail. "How did you know?!?"

I took my left hand off the handle for just a moment (it had to be the left one, because I could only ride one-handed with my right hand on the handlebars!), pointed at my eyes, and said, "These work."

He said, with chagrin, "I thought we were being subtle," and I laughed so hard I had to stop and put a foot down to keep from falling over.

"I promise you, everyone knows. The entire room

heats up ten degrees when you two look at each other."

He returned, "Hey! I'm not the only one! Menzy told me about you and Gil."

"What about me and Gil?" I asked, with real curiosity. "We've been together for years. We're old news. I don't think we're in danger of burning down any rooms."

"Funny, because that's exactly how she put it. Well, maybe not so odd, you know dryads are sensitive about fire, especially out here where so much forest has burned. Her exact words, if I remember them right, were 'Not like a campfire out of control, more like a fire that's been set up and banked with ashes to keep it burning a long, long time. And you know it's controlled and safe as it is, but it can flare up any time someone stirs it.' I think she meant it in a good way, not a forest-fire way!"

After that the trail narrowed, so we didn't talk for a while except for him to point out directions. I think we were both a little relieved to be off the personal topics.

It was a great ride, and aside from a slightly sore tailbone, I was feeling good – until, almost at the end of the trail, I hit a whoop-de-doo, a small dip with a quick down and then up, that my bike-handling skills were too rusty to manage. Luckily, I did manage to unclip my feet as I lost my grip, and then, though I'm sure it wasn't nearly so dramatic to look at, it felt like one of those falls you see replayed in slow motion, where gravity turns off for a moment and you fly over the handlebars end over end over end. (No, I don't know how that works either, but it's a known mountain bike thing. It probably just looked like I went skidding along the ground.)

Rob was off his bike and over to me in an instant and I could see his first-aid training kick in. "Are you OK?"

"I think so." I gingerly moved my arms and legs. "I mostly landed on my butt, and I hit my head, but the helmet handled that, it doesn't hurt at all." I looked down and saw a drop of blood on the ground. "Where's that from? Oh, there."

There was a good-sized cut on my right shin – long

but not too deep. Rob had his first aid kit out, cleaned it up, and was talking about stitches until I laughed at him.

"No, it's fine. Just stick a bandage over it so I don't bleed in your car. It's just shallow – I used to get worse than that all the time as a kid."

Still, his calm professionalism was relaxing – I'd always lived in big cities before, and it was a little unnerving to be in a small town with no doctors nearer than a half-hour drive. It was good to know our local firefighters were so well trained!

There was one other advantage to being in a small town; when we got home, Rob mentioned the ride and my injury on George, and I was inundated with offers to help. Sulis and Menzy both, separately, offered to bring dinner so I could stay off my feet, Genna told me to let her know if I decided that I wanted a doctor after all and needed a ride into town, and Brigid said to call her if I needed any help rebandaging it in a day or so. Apparently welding teachers also get a lot of training in first aid. Menzy also offered to try healing the cut, but it didn't work. Dryad healing only works on nymphs (dryads, naiads, nereids, and so on). Though I didn't have any of those genes in the more recent generations that I knew of, she'd volunteered to try her healing just in case I had nymph heritage farther back in my family tree. Apparently, I didn't.

CHAPTER TWELVE: A TREE IN A BRIDGE

It was a good thing we'd seized that glorious warm day for our ride, because the winter rains set in with a vengeance right after that. Even with my house's big windows on the lake, I had to keep the lights on all day, and there were enough reports of ice on the roads in early morning that I was very glad I didn't have to commute to work anymore. The air was starting to smell like winter, even though winter in this area was typically more about rain than snow, and people were starting to talk about holiday plans.

I did remember to text Laxmi's parents to try to arrange a time for her to visit, but apparently middle-schoolers have very busy calendars in December – tests and projects due before winter break, holiday parties, concerts – so we put her visit off til early January, after New Years but before the end of her holiday break.

Andrew, our self-appointed town liaison to the George group, posted:

> **Andrew:** Don't forget about the town tree-lighting this Friday evening, December 3, at the covered bridge! Rory and Eva, whom some of you have met, will be there playing fiddle and leading the singing. We'll be lighting a tree and having carol-singing.

> **Andrew, again:** Yes, this is pretty much just about Christmas, because that's what the town council has approved every year, but we will be sneaking in a more diverse list of carols.

I didn't know if anyone else in our group was

going, but I decided to walk over to the covered bridge where the tree was set up. It was definitely winter now, cold and damp with a few wet snowflakes falling, so I pulled out my lined pants and a heavy sweater and coat, since I didn't know how long I'd be standing around there. I added a Yule-themed hat and mittens I'd knitted myself. There were few streetlights in our small town, and the nights were very dark this time of year, but enough others were out heading the same way that I felt safe. A lot of houses were already decorated for the holidays, which added enough light to make the path visible. The town had set up a school bus shuttle from the high school parking lot to the bridge, but I decided to walk the whole way – it was under a mile.

The covered bridge, an exceptionally large one, had once spanned a small creek that flowed near the far side of the current lake. When they built the dam that created a lake where once apple orchards had stood, the covered bridge was retained as a landmark. The memory of the trees that once stood here was also preserved in the name of Orchard Lake. A new, much longer, bridge for cars crossed the lake, starting right next to the old bridge. A parking lot had been added, with benches by the lake where people fished in the warmer months. The covered bridge itself held signs with historical information; right now it also boasted a large tree at one end whose lights were dark at the moment.

The wind was biting as I crossed the lake, but once I got into the bridge's shelter it was a lot warmer, with the wind and snow buffered and enough of a crowd forming to add some warmth. Both ends of the bridge were open, of course, and there was a gap between walls and roof, so there was enough ventilation to make me feel relatively safe, though this was the biggest crowd I'd been in for more than a year.

Just inside the bridge's entrance, Andrew stood with some others – I recognized Deb, whom I hadn't seen since our initial George meetup – at a table offering cookies and hot drinks.

Andrew said, "Macrina! Thanks for coming! Would you like some hot chocolate or hot apple cider? They're free, though the cookies are for sale to benefit after-school music programs."

I accepted a small cup of hot chocolate and bought some snickerdoodles from Deb, who greeted me in a way that said she recognized me but wasn't quite sure from where, then sauntered toward the other end of the bridge. An older woman was marshaling kids onto some stands in front of the tree. A sign in front informed us they were the Percival School District Junior Choir.

I hadn't been in the bridge before, though I'd driven by it many times, so I wandered around looking at the historical signs until the crowd all started heading toward the tree. Since I was too short to see over people, I headed toward the edge of the crowd and was able to find a way around to stand near the front, where I could see.

Mayor Nell stepped up onto a small platform and turned her microphone on. "Hello, Percival!" she called. The crowd clapped politely. She went on, "Welcome to the annual tree-lighting! We are delighted to resume our tradition again, since we had to call it off last year. First, the Percival School Junior Choir will sing some Christmas songs for us, then our friends Rory and Eva will lead the rest of us in song – look for the high school elves who will be passing around song sheets with all the words on them. And now, for the tree – whether you celebrate Christmas, Yule, Chanukah or Diwali, we can all agree that some light to cut through the darkness is very welcome this time of year!"

The tree lights went on, showing that the tree was even bigger than I'd realized, helping to block the opening at that end of the bridge and making the space cozier. It was covered in multicolor lights; someone from the town had spent a lot of time making sure there weren't any dark spots on the tree.

A girl stepped down from the choir riser with a microphone in her hand and I realized it was Laxmi, the future magic user I'd met at Thanksgiving. She began to sing Away in the Manger in a clear, pure soprano, with the rest of the choir joining in after the first verse; I recognized Oliver also among the singers. The young choir were very good, and I was especially impressed at their quality, coming out of such a small school system. They followed that up with Andrew's 'more diverse' carols, including Ocho Kandelikas and Matunda Ya Kwanzaa with the kids tapping small drums, then Nell stepped back up on the platform.

"Weren't they great?" This time the applause was loud and enthusiastic. She went on, "Don't forget to get yourself a hot drink, for free! And buy some cookies; the proceeds go to after school programs including the choir you just heard! Now, if our elves will hand out the music sheets, we'd like you all to join us in song."

This time they kept it to familiar secular Christmas songs, starting with Jingle Bells. I admired the way Nell and the choir teacher had combined their goals of diversity and practicality for this occasion, with a wider repertoire for the rehearsed choir pieces and simple pop songs like Frosty the Snowman to lure more adults into song.

Afterward, the crowd dispersed. I waved at Rory and Eva, but the crowd was still too thick to talk to them. On the way out, I passed a fire truck, apparently there in case of accidents, and waved at Rob, standing with his coworkers. Cayden was by his side and seemed to know the rest of their group well. The walk home was cold and dark again, and though I hadn't put up any holiday decorations (nor decided whether I was going to), I was pleased that I'd remembered to leave some outdoor lights on for my return.

***

As I went up the front walk, the house felt oddly inhabited, as if someone was there waiting for me. Someone was, of course; as soon as I stepped through the door and felt warmth settle over me, the cats rushed up, complaining because I had dared to leave them. It felt like more than that, though; a feeling of welcome settled over me with the warmth, as if the house itself was glad to see me back. The long yellow wall and lamplight made the whole place glow, and though I'd intended to go right to bed, I added some wood to the fireplace, used the same fire spell I'd demonstrated to the kids at Thanksgiving to kindle a blaze, and made myself some more hot chocolate, with a good slug of coffee liqueur added.

I grabbed my book and sat on the sofa close to the fireplace, but before I started to read, I tried to tune into the house. Had it really welcomed me in a magic sense, or was it just the lights, warmth, and warm colors that had created the welcoming effect? I couldn't be completely sure, but I felt more at home here now than I had anywhere for years. The cats seemed to feel it too; they curled up beside me, though not before Merlin stared into my eyes and said, emphatically, "Myeowp!" as if he were trying to tell me something.

The next day I encountered a new problem. When I opened my work emails, there were notes from a couple of my steady customers. They weren't complaining, exactly, but they were wondering why I'd upgraded my spells without notifying customers or updating my documentation. Ever since making the changes to make the house more my own place, I'd been super careful to monitor my product's power levels, since an overpowered spell could result in disaster.

My own spells were flexible, able to be used to adapt many other kinds of spells, so the effects of overpowering my products could vary widely – anything from turning someone's hair a lighter blond than expected to causing large explosions. Based on Sulis's information, I'd worried that having the house more in tune with me could boost my power levels, and I'd been testing the power of every spell before sending it on to a customer. What I hadn't done, though, is to make any changes to my functional testing. Why would I? My spells did what they did and their functionality wasn't likely to change.

Except now it had, apparently, though fortunately

(so far!) only in good ways. My customers reported that the spells seemed to be more flexible; a software equivalent might be to say that they were becoming "plug and play", with no code needed to link one routine to another. Customers had added my spells into their own, but before they could make the necessary adaptations to link my spells to theirs, the spells had somehow self-adapted, making the link by themselves.

This was utterly baffling.

On the one hand, simply increasing power levels wouldn't do that. And on the other, it couldn't simply be due to the changes I'd made to the house – could it? After all, I hadn't done anything unusual. I'd brought pets home, painted walls, rearranged furniture, added some automated cleaning – nothing that even NMCs didn't commonly do to their own houses.

This could be a problem. For now, I resolved to send out older stock whenever possible, products I'd created before whatever was happening had happened, and to thoroughly test anything new. I could also do some diagnostics on Solstice: if Samhain was a good time to imbue ingredients and spell-stores with power, Solstice, as the shortest day, was the worst time to do it. So I'd try a few rituals, and if they worked at all I would know that the house's ambient power levels had increased.

Meanwhile, I tested copies of the products I'd sent out lately every which way I could think of, wrote up some documentation to explain the odd new capabilities, and sent that to my recent customers with an apology and a note of thanks to those who had alerted me, explaining it away for now as a simple case of sending out the wrong version of instructions.

***

Merlin and Morgana had now been with me for around a month, and seemed to be settled in happily. I'd worried about whether they'd be content as indoor-only pets, but for now, at least, that didn't seem to be a problem.

It was cold and wet outdoors, and the kittens seemed happy to have no part in it. They were affectionate, curling up on or near me in the evenings while I was reading, and so intent on being close by while I was working that I'd had to shut them out a few times – fortunately there was a door at the bottom of the attic stairway! A stray cat hair from a tail waving in the wrong place could ruin some of my more chemically-based spells, though of course there was no such risk with my verse spells. The only problem with those was when Morgana insisted on sitting on the edge of the desk between me and my keyboard. Or when Merlin decided he wanted to chase my mouse.

They insisted on sleeping on my bed, of course. At first, they'd wanted to lie on either side of my neck, which made sleep impossible when they got cozy by kneading the tender skin of my neck with their tiny sharp claws. After I pointedly removed them to the foot of the bed approximately 5,375 times, they started getting the idea. When Gil had visited, they'd retreated to the foot of the bed on their own accord, and, thankfully, had continued to sleep there after he left. I sometimes had to thread my feet down between two stretched-out sleeping kittens – it's astonishing how long a small cat can become – but that didn't keep me awake.

Merlin, especially, could be very conversational sometimes, as with his comment after I came home from the tree-lighting, but if he was actually trying to tell me something it wasn't clear yet. Sometimes MC pets got a little unusual – they might be smarter than the average dog or cat, or develop more unique capabilities. I'd even met one woman whose pet lizard developed wings – fortunately they weren't actually large enough to fly with. I was keeping a sharp eye on the kittens to see if they'd do anything unusual; so far, they seemed to be bright but nothing out of the ordinary. They were young yet, though, with plenty of time to learn new tricks.

CHAPTER THIRTEEN: THE SHORTEST DAY

Over the next couple of weeks, I spent some time thinking about holiday presents. I sent cards to my steady customers every year – that was just good business – and to some old friends around the world. This year I decided to send cards to my local George friends as well. Those friendships were too new for me to send them gifts, but sending cards felt right. I'd been seeing them less often, as the weather got worse and going out of the house unnecessarily felt less inviting, and also as everybody was busy with year-end activities and holiday planning. I knew most people wouldn't send cards back, but I enjoyed choosing the perfect design each year, and while writing messages and addresses out could be tedious, I liked the idea of telling people I was thinking about them.

Of course, a truly organized person would have ordered cards and even started writing them out well before Thanksgiving. Fortunately for me, this was one of those times when magic could help – not my own magic, but one of the suppliers I'd worked with for years. I waited until we had a night where the rain actually stopped and clouds parted long enough to let me see sunset from my kitchen window facing the lake. Then I gathered up the cats, brought them to the kitchen, set them on the window sill, and gave them a small magical 'push' to ask them to stay in place for a few minutes. I hadn't tried that before, and Morgana looked almost hilariously startled. I snapped as many photos as I could before the cats jumped down and the light faded, then checked them out on the screen. I had a couple good candidates – and even better, I'd been quick enough to catch Morgana's look of startlement in two of them. I chose the one that showed her expression most clearly and sent it with a quick email to my supplier:

> **Macrina:** Hi, it's me being late with my holiday planning as usual. Could you please make me sixty cards with this image on it? You can use the same cardstock as the ones I bought last year from you – those were great! Please add the words "It stopped raining!" below that startled cat on the front, and then inside, "Happy holidays, and may you have some light even on the darkest days. From Macrina Magid (with Merlin and Morgana)". Oh, and would it be possible to show just a hint of a lit Yule tree, as if it was reflecting in the window?

My supplier, Lauren, was a wizard at processing and printing images – and I mean that literally. Half an hour later, she sent back an image that was exactly what I asked for – and a suggestion.

> **Lauren:** You celebrate Solstice and Yule rather than Christmas, right? And you'll be sending this mostly to customers and other magic people? What if, instead, on the front it said, "Don't worry, the sun will come back" instead?

I liked the new wording, approved the change, and asked her to send me the cards via next-day shipping. While I was waiting for them, I made a list of recipients: all my usual customers, new customers I wanted to encourage, longtime suppliers like Lauren herself, the locals I'd spent time with over the past year, and a few old friends scattered around the world. And of course Gil; I'd be seeing him over Yule, but he always liked seeing what card I'd chosen this year.

I already had all my supplier and customer addresses in a database, so it was easy enough to print out address labels. What I didn't have were addresses for my local friends. I had to ask for those even with people I'd visited, as I'd realized that out here, many people picked up their mail at the post office instead of having it left in rural mailboxes. The conversation was completely predictable:

> **Macrina:** Can I get everyone's mailing addresses, for cards? You can PM or text them to me – probably not smart to put data on this site.
>
> **Cayden:** Um, sure – but I warn you, I'm not good at sending cards back.
>
> **Rob:** Same here.
>
> **Menzy:** Ditto.
>
> **Macrina:** That's fine. I like sending them out, and there's no expectation of a return.
>
> **Genna:** I've got mine almost ready to go out.

Much as I like Genna, organized people can be a little smug sometimes! I decided that I wouldn't push: if people sent me their addresses they'd get cards, and if not, they wouldn't. I wouldn't ask again. Anyway, I did get messages with mailing addresses in them from the people I most wanted to send cards to: Genna, Brigid, Sulis, Menzy, Rob, Cayden, Andrew.

The cards arrived next day. I just signed the ones for business contacts but tried to write a small note in all of the cards going out to friends. My wrists ached from all the unaccustomed handwriting, but in three days I'd gotten them all done, in time to start planning my Solstice rituals.

Of course, I also needed a present for Gil, in addition to my own presence. (Ha!) He liked techie toys, so I bought us a pair of WiFi-enabled devices. These were basically small thin screens, each with a stylus attached, with magnetic backs enabling them to be mounted on a refrigerator door. The idea was that we could write each other short notes back and forth that we'd see when we were apart, sort of like the whiteboards we'd all had on our doors in my college dorms. I did realize that we could just send texts, but I liked the idea of having something up on the fridge that he'd see as he walked into his kitchen each day. I might look up some good quotes, just to have something more interesting than "I miss you" to write to him each day. They were actually a very clever combination of magic and technology, using ambient magic for the minimal power they needed while connecting to WiFi for communication between the two. (There were pricier versions that relied solely on magic, so that they could be used even in areas with no internet, but since these were for our homes and we both had good WiFi, that wasn't needed.)

***

While I did usually observe Solstice, the shortest day in the year, in some way, many years it was just with a glass of wine or some good whiskey and an evening sitting by a fire as I thought over the past year. In a nod to my Jewish heritage, I also lit menorah candles every night of Chanukah; while I wasn't at all observant, kindling candles at the darkest time of year was important to me as a way to push back at the darkness. Though this year Chanukah had started a few days after Thanksgiving and ended well before Solstice, it was the symbol that counted.

This Solstice, though, I'd be doing a ritual I'd never done as an adult. While most rituals didn't work well on the shortest, darkest day of the year, there was one category of spells that were mostly done then. The cold weather and short days made this the right season for nesting, for snuggling into your home like an animal in its burrow. This was when MagiComms did spells to bond to, protect and strengthen our household; while I knew people with families and settled homes who did them every year as a matter of course, I never had because I lived alone and every place I'd lived in felt temporary – either a rental or a place I intended to move on from in a relatively short time. But this house felt like home: I owned it and I planned to stay unless and until there was some reason to move.

It felt right to do this in my living room, in front of

the fireplace, rather than in my lab, so I didn't want anything with chemicals or messy ingredients. I scanned the websites of my favorite suppliers and found one that was sold in crystal spell-store form; it had to be invoked with a piece of music that could be selected by the user to suit their particular situation – and I knew exactly what I wanted to use.

In the days right before Solstice, I gathered my ingredients and set the stage – not for the spell itself, which needed nothing but the crystal and song, but to set the mood I wanted. Like everyone else, in the early days of the pandemic I'd gotten into baking sourdough bread. I'd found a no-knead recipe in the New York Times that took 3 days to make, but only a few minutes of actual work between long rising times. I timed that, feeding the starter two nights before Solstice, so I'd have bread emerging from the oven just a little before my ritual. Solstice morning, I started a pot roast in a slow-cooker and set that to low, so it would cook for hours, and the smells of cooking bread and meat would permeate the house.

***

While the roast was cooking, I started preparing the other test I'd wanted to run today, to get some measurement of the increased power I'd been seeing in the house. I wrote out a few verses of Lewis Carroll's Jabberwocky, which I liked using for test spells that weren't meant to do anything much. I was going to imbue the written verses with power to act as a spell-store, load up a simple spell, and execute it. Normally, it would be difficult or even impossible to imbue power on this date. If I was able to do that, loading up the spell shouldn't be too hard, though I'd decide how big a spell to use based on the amount of power I'd been able to load. Then when executing it, I'd need to gauge how much energy that required from me, as well as how well the spell worked overall. I'd expect a spell to be more difficult to execute on Winter Solstice than it would have been on Samhain, let alone in summer.

I took the verses up to my lab to work on there – if something went wrong, I'd rather mess up the lab than the living room. The power flowed into the verses astonishingly easily – this was what I'd expected it to feel like on Samhain, when instead I'd felt more like I was lifting weights. I'd have expected Solstice to be much more draining, if I could imbue power at all today. At the end, I'd used only a bare fraction of my own power for this, and it felt like the energy around me was cradling and bracing me, the way a kayak holds you off the water and lets you brace your legs to get maximum power through your body and arms to the paddle. I even had a sense that there was more power I could have accessed, but that didn't seem like a good idea – I didn't want to strain myself or let out energy without being able to control the flow.

I'd planned to load up a spell to store and play back music – which must have been a much more impressive spell way back before gramophones were invented, let alone MP3 players. Nowadays, it was mostly used in to train young magic users — in fact, this might be a good one to teach Laxmi — or to do power checks, like the one I was using now. Depending on the amount of power imbued into this spell-store, I should have been able to store anything from a grainy recording of a single voice singing 'Happy Birthday' to a full-length, digital quality symphony in surround sound. I decided to shoot for somewhere in the middle – I wanted something with a lush enough sound that I'd really be able to assess sound quality, and with enough segments that I could load it up bit by bit. So I pulled up my phone and dialed up Metallica's S&M album, on which they played their greatest hits with backing from the San Francisco symphony orchestra. I left that playing into the spell and went off to check on my cooking, coming back periodically to see whether the spell-store had run out of space yet.

To my surprise, it kept going until the entire album was loaded up – I might even have been able to squeeze in another song or two. When I played it back, the sound was as lush and full as the original digital file was able to produce. There was clearly something about this house that was bolstering my work – I only wished I knew what or why!

***

Solstice evening, I set a table and comfortable chair in front of the fireplace, poured myself a glass of good wine, set out bread, sweet cream butter, and my pot roast and its attendant vegetables. I put another plate with a small bit of pot roast on a mat on the floor, so the cats could eat with me just this once. Taking the spell-store crystal from my pocket, I held it in my palm and breathed on it, selected the living room speakers from my phone and pulled up the song I wanted: Our House, an old classic by Crosby, Stills, and Nash.

As I listened to the words, I realized I had goofed in a few ways – for instance, I didn't have a vase and flowers to place in it, to match the song's exact words. Oh well, the spell didn't have to be that literal in every detail. But as it went on, describing the perfect home and those in it, I realized I'd made a bigger miscalculation.

I had the house and the cats, but it was very much a song about building a home with another person. Gil wasn't here, and didn't live here anyway, and I reminded myself that I was very happy with him and had no desire to dump him and find the indeterminate 'you' of the song. I wondered if the spell would even work.

But as the song concluded, I felt the magic build and then release, an increase of pressure within me that crested and broke with that satisfying "whoomp" in the air that means it's discharged properly. A feeling of peace and safety came over me; the cats finished their dinner and then came over and snuggled by my feet, purring as they groomed the gravy off of each other's whiskers. It felt somehow as if Gil were with me, and I wasn't surprised when the phone rang. I muted the music and answered it.

"Happy Solstice, Macrina-Meli! I didn't call too

soon and interrupt your ritual, did I?"

"No, you have perfect timing for once. I had just finished and was thinking of you."

"Me, too – I mean, thinking of you. I just had a picture come into my mind of you and the cats snuggling in front of the fire and wanted to talk to you."

Hm. I mean, not that I had any doubt of the spell's working – I was a professional magic user, after all – but this one wasn't made to have an effect at a distance. I reminded myself to investigate that more later, and focused on talking to Gil for now.

"Too bad you're not here – I made pot roast!"

He groaned. "And me stuck here with leftover pizza. Glad I get to see you soon; do you think I can tempt you into making another roast while you're here?"

"Mmmmmmmmmaybe. If I can get you to take me out for some good Tex-Mex another night."

"It's a deal. I can't wait to see you, and Jimmy and Deepak are looking forward to your visit too. You'll see them all when we go to Christmas dinner at Jimmy's – you won't believe how big the kids have gotten! Though in a way I'm sorry that I'm not coming to visit you this time – I want to see how the cats have settled in, and how your house looks since you've painted in those colors we picked together."

"You'll get to see them next time you visit – maybe February? I think the cats will be full-grown by then, though they'll still be acting like kittens. And I'm looking forward to Christmas dinner – you know how much I like those guys, and their families."

I put the phone on speaker, so I could keep talking to him and still finish my dinner before it got cold. We didn't talk of anything of consequence, but with his voice in the room, I could close my eyes and imagine the two of us there, with the cats, and the house – it definitely felt like something had changed and settled, in a good way. After finishing dinner and ending our call, I put the plates in the dishwasher, moved the table to its usual place, settled in my reading chair with another glass of wine, and carefully widened my senses, trying to trace the impact of the spell more analytically. If the house could have purred along with the cats, it would have; it felt safe and solid, as if I'd encased all of us in a fleece-lined box – but it wasn't quite complete. It felt like I'd built a puzzle, one of those three dimensional ones, with one piece missing, then I'd encased it in a box so that it was stable even without the lost piece. My choice of song had given me the wrong puzzle, one I didn't have all the pieces for, but the spell had worked well enough despite that. It bound me, the cats, and the house together in a way that would keep us safe and would hold together. I made a note to remind me to re-evaluate next Solstice, but in the meantime, I'd take it.

CHAPTER FOURTEEN: OVER THE HOLIDAYS

Sulis had volunteered to watch the cats; she said it was easy for her to just "pop in from the lake". I shuddered at the idea of being *in* the lake this time of year, but I guess for a naiad it was home. She came over the morning after Solstice, to pick up a house key, meet the cats, and for me to show her what to do. Since Sulis hadn't been inside my house since Solstice, I was very curious to whether she noticed any changes to the house, now I'd implemented so much of her advice.

As soon as she walked in, both cats came streaking into the room and went straight to her, rubbing their heads against her legs. Apparently her love for cats was reciprocated. I still couldn't figure out what the connection was between naiads and cats, but maybe it was just Sulis herself rather than a general naiad thing.

She said, "Well, aren't you a fine pair!" and got down on the floor to pet them. "Yes, you're such beautiful kitties!" She stood up with Morgana in her arms in her usual "I'm the baby and you **will** carry me everywhere" pose, looked around, and said, "Wow, what a change in this place!"

I smiled, very happy that the changes were real enough to register on her so quickly. "What do you see? And I didn't do anything unusual, just pets and a little redecoration, except that I did do a home-binding spell at Solstice."

"The new colors and the cats are hard to miss, of course, but it's also that the house feels like it's waking up. Not like a person, of course – it isn't about to start talking to you or anything like that, or at least I don't think that's possible – but it's all centered on you now. Well done."

"Thank you – your advice really was the start of it, you know."

"But how often do people take advice?" she asked, wryly. "Well, maybe when their livelihood is at stake. And just, how does it feel now? Are you noticing any differences in your work? Any differences you notice in living here day to day?"

"Definitely changes at work – in fact, I have to test carefully to make sure my spells aren't overpowered or running amuck and trying to add features. But it's a good problem to have…as long as I'm careful. As for how it feels and if that's changed, hard to tell. If anything, it just feels cozier. Warm. Very welcome this time of year!"

"Oh, good. I'm so glad my advice worked out. It will be interesting to see what happens when you leave, but I'll play with the kitties so they don't get too lonely without you. Now show me what I need to do for this diva and her brother?"

I handed Sulis a spare house key and showed her their favorite toys (still the stuffed owl their fosterer had given me, along with a small fuzzy ball they loved to chase and tumble over), their food and the litter box. I showed off the clever spell that kept the litter granules and dust contained so they didn't end up all over my lab, and explained how to use the equally clever gadget that let me clean the litter daily but kept the results in a sealed bag so there was no smell. (Before this was invented, I might have used a spell for that too, but this was easier and cheaper, though it did occur to me that there might have been solid reasons for the historical link between MC people and cats.)

The cats were used to getting their wet food as a treat first thing in the morning, and dry food later, but they'd just have to adjust. They'd probably complain loudly, being slaves to routine like most cats, but Sulis wouldn't be there to get woken up by it. I thought they ought to be grateful to have a cat-sitter they liked so much, but of course cats don't really do gratitude!

Sulis promised to send me daily reports and photos

of Merlin and Morgana so I'd know how they were doing. I was feeling a little overprotective – this was the first time I'd left them overnight since bringing them home. I was confident they wouldn't admit it even if they did miss me.

***

I was nervous about taking my first flights since the start of the pandemic, especially during the busy holiday season, but after all it was my turn – Gil had visited me at Thanksgiving. At least I had smaller, less busy airports on either end, though there was a stop in San Francisco one way, and Denver the other. I had decided to wear my mask the whole time, and noticed that most others were doing so in the Eugene airport, not so many on the Texas end.

I was happy to see Gil again for only the second time after our long involuntary separation, and I enjoyed the chance to reconnect with his friends, whom I'd met many times over the years. I gathered that their kids hadn't been enjoying going to school online, but luckily, Deepak's wife had teaching experience and didn't have an outside job. She'd taken a few years off to stay home with her kids, and now her youngest was just emerging from toddlerhood, so they were able to transition the children of both families to homeschooling with her.

I stayed in Texas just over a week, enjoying time alone with Gil as well as a raucous Christmas dinner with his friends' families. Though I celebrated Solstice and Yule rather than Christmas, a tree with ornaments, a big log fire, faith that the sun would return, presents, and peace-on-earth-good-will-to-mankind all struck me as Good Things, no matter what tradition they stemmed from.

Also, it was nice to see some sun again. It had been a while!

We even had a chance to go dancing (at an outdoor venue) with some more of Gil's coworkers – not that either of us were any good at the two-step or line-dancing! I'd decided to return home before New Year's, though; Sulis had refused to take any pay for cat-sitting and I didn't want to take advantage of her. She'd sent photos frequently, and it was evident that both kittens were enjoying her visits, so I wasn't worried about them. I was a little homesick, though; I missed my own house fiercely. Gil had a sleek, comfortable modern apartment, with a pool and gym, in a trendy neighborhood, but it didn't feel like home to me in the same way.

I said as much, nestling my head onto his shoulder in bed one night. "I love being with you, you know that. But I miss home, and Merlin and Morgana."

In a sleepy voice, he said "Me too," but roused more when I said, "You what?" registering the confusion in my tone.

"I miss them too, in a way. I liked having your cats around – I haven't had any pets in my adult life. First I was working long hours and partying a lot, and then I was working even longer hours, and by the time I finally realized work-life balance was a thing and I should get some of it, I'd gotten out of the habit and didn't even really think about getting myself a pet. When I was at your house, working with you and the cats around, it just felt so much more homelike. Though I'm not so sure I was as productive, what with being solicited for head-scratchings every thirty minutes!"

"They let you go that long?"

***

There was an unexpected issue when I got home, though. I'd texted Sulis when my plane landed so that she'd know I'd arrived safely, but I wasn't expecting her to be there when I got home. She walked up from the lake as I got to my front door, though, and held up a hand to stop me from unlocking it. "Hang on, before you go in, there's a small problem I wanted to warn you about."

I was instantly worried. "A problem? Are the kittens OK?"

She took a step back and waved both hands in the

universal don't-worry sign. "No, no, they're fine – sorry, I should've led with that."

"What then? Don't tell me I had a break-in!"

"No, nothing like that. It's just – I think the house was lonely."

"The what was what?"

"The house. I think it was missing you. Did you say you did a binding spell at Solstice? What kind of spell?"

"Nothing unusual, just the sort of thing lots of MagiComms do every year, to make their homes safe, comfortable and welcoming for their families."

"Well, you must have put a lot of juice in it. You might want to just poke your head in the door and tell it you're home, before you step inside."

Well, that didn't sound odd at all. Still, she'd been right with her original advice to wake the house up by changing things around to be more "me", and this couldn't hurt anything, right? So I carefully unlocked the door, opened it partway, stuck my head in, and said, "Hi, honey, I'm home!" Then I pulled my head back in a hurry as a cloud of dust came hurtling toward me. But when I eased the door all the way open and walked in, it looked…exactly the same as when I'd left it.

Sulis poked her head past the door, very tentatively, walked in, and said, "Huh."

Now I was completely baffled. "What was all that about?"

She said, "Like I said, it missed you. Good thing I took some pictures – I was going to send them to you, but I decided not to. It would only have messed up your holiday and it's not like any real harm was being done." She pulled out her phone (I had no idea what happened to it when she went into the lake – but most phones were waterproof these days anyway, weren't they?), pulled up a photo and handed it to me. "Go ahead and scroll through the next several."

I did, and saw photos of the various rooms in my house, full of dust. All of the areas where the cats liked to hang out were as clean in the photos as I'd left them, but in places like my lab, there was a clear path from the stairs to the litterboxes, with a thick layer of dust everywhere else. "Maybe we'd better take a tour of the place."

We did, walking through both bedrooms, both bathrooms, and the attic office, lab and storeroom. The whole place was exactly as I'd left it. "I guess all the dust came out in that puff when I opened the door. That is completely and entirely bizarre. You think the house was…what, sulking because I left it alone with just the cats?"

"That's my best guess, anyway. I still don't understand it either. I know I said you should make it more alive by making it your own, but it sounds like you didn't do anything that should have had that kind of effect!"

"Nope. Anyway, I'm so sorry you had to deal with all of that!"

"Oh, no, no problem at all. After all, I only had to go where the cats went, and those areas stayed perfectly clean. I guess it still appreciated their company."

"Good thing I turned off the robot vacuums before I left! I usually leave them programmed to run a couple times a week, but they sometimes get stuck in strange places, so I turned them off. I can only imagine the mess that would have made!"

I gave her the dark chocolate-covered pecan pralines I'd bought for her at an artisan shop in Austin, and thanked her again.

"I told you, I love cats. It was no trouble at all. Anyway, keep bringing me chocolates and I might start *asking* you to go on vacation and let me cat-sit!"

She left, and I took my bag to my bedroom, deciding to unpack it later. As I came back out to the kitchen to get something to drink, I realized that not everything was exactly as I'd left it, after all. On the kitchen table was a small package with a note from Sulis saying, "Brigid dropped this off for you, so I brought it inside." When I opened the package, there was a welded snowflake, not too heavy, with a base that formed a tripod so that it could stand alone or be lashed to a Yule tree to serve as a topper. It had a card that said, "Happy Yule, and thanks for the listening ear! From Brigid". It was a beautiful thing, and she'd clearly made it herself, making it doubly precious. I hadn't set up a tree this year since I was traveling and wouldn't be around to water it, but this was definitely going on top of one next year. Meanwhile, I set it in the kitchen window where I'd see it every day.

***

Busy as I'd been with all my preparations for Solstice and then traveling, I'd made no plans for New Years' Eve and was anticipating a quiet glass of champagne at home with the kittens. I'd even bought some new cat treats so they could celebrate the holiday too, but when I checked the latest George messages that evening, it looked like my plans were changing.

> **Menzy:** Anyone else have no NYE plans? Want to have a small party? We could do it at my place. I have champagne and popcorn!

> **Macrina:** I don't have plans and that sounds like fun. I could bring my bottle of champagne too, and could make some brownies (from a mix)

> **Genna:** Duncan and I were just going to have a quiet night at home, but we could come for a bit, though I'm not sure if we'll stay up til midnight. We're not great party animals!

It looked like we might have a full house: Brigid and Sulis were going out to dinner but didn't have plans later in the evening and even Rob and Cayden said they might stop by.

I made *verrry* sure to tell my house I was leaving, and that I would be back after midnight.

I hadn't been to Menzy's little house before. Not surprisingly, it was on the edge of the forest, just barely within town boundaries, and was full of plants. Dryads aren't much bothered by weather and cold, any more than trees are, but in consideration of everyone else's frailties, she'd rigged some tarps over and around her back patio to ward off rain and wind. She and Genna had apparently done some planning after we'd all agreed on the party and Genna had lugged along an electric heater that Menzy plugged in and set up in the middle of the patio, allowing the party to flow from the living room to the sheltered outside area. As was becoming usual with this group, everyone had brought both food and wine, and we had far too much of each, so the small party grew louder quickly.

***

Duncan started telling us about Hogmanay traditions in the areas where he studied in Scotland, and since Rob and Cayden were both tall, dark-haired men, we somehow decided a midnight torchlight procession was required. It wasn't raining for once, and the town was plenty small enough to walk to all of our homes. We did at least retain the sense to avoid using real torches. As we got closer to midnight, we concluded our preparations: Brigid found a candle app and chivied everyone into loading it on their phones, Genna grabbed a bag of pretzels so we could eat bread and salt in each house, and Menzy ruthlessly emptied out an 8-pack of bottled water and poured a shot of whiskey into each one so that we could take a sip of whiskey likewise in each house. Sulis, who had spent some time in Scotland, relentlessly reminded Rob and Cayden to enter each house right foot first, and we put them at the head of the parade.

It may not have been our finest hour. There was definitely some stumbling as we paraded around town with our phone "candles" held high, shushing each other so we didn't wake anyone who might have decided to sleep through the year's transition. Rob and Cayden took turns being the "first footer" to step into each house in turn, and we had to stop them more than once to keep them from stepping in with left foot instead of right.

Genna and Duncan had managed to stay awake until midnight, but once we got to their house they elected to stay there and pick their car up from Menzy's place the next day.

The rest of us were still in hilarious moods as we approached my house, the last stop for the evening. I had remembered to leave my porch light on to light my way home, but I was bemused to see all the lights on as we walked up the path. Everything else seemed normal and quiet, but I carefully took a look inside without stepping over the threshold, just in case. Then I had to grab Cayden once again, as he was about to step into the house with his left foot. He stepped back and I asked everyone, "Can you please all step in right foot first? My house seems to be, um, in a sensitive state right now and I don't want to take any chances!" Luckily, Sulis and I had told them about the Great Dust Incident earlier in the party, so this was less confusing than it might have been.

We walked in step, right feet first, and before we took our obligatory bite of pretzels and sip of whiskey, Rob said, "Maybe we should toast the house? Do you have a name for it?"

I said, "No, not yet, though it clearly needs one. I'm taking suggestions!"

Rob replied, "No ideas, but – a toast to Mac's house!"

Everyone echoed, "A toast! Happy New Year!" and drank. The cats came up, nosing at our ankles to smell where we'd been (possibly because of the dogs in some of the houses we'd visited) and I quickly grabbed the small tubes of paste cat treats from my counter so they could have a "toast" too.

Once again, I was careful to tell the house I was leaving and would be back soon, and just in case, I whispered "Happy New Year, house!" back over my shoulder as we headed out and back to Menzy's. The party lasted for another hour – or at least, that's how much longer I stayed, waiting for the whiskey to wear off so I could drive the three blocks home. (Of course, I could have walked, but the whole reason I'd driven there in the first place is that walking home alone at 2AM can be a little scary, even in a tiny town like ours. Also, cold – not that I'd noticed the cold during our impromptu parade, where I'd been insulated by alcohol and camaraderie.) This time as I approached my door, only the porch light and the entryway light were on, and I couldn't really remember if I'd left both on myself. Did the house have some way to know when more people were coming? And how? I really hadn't done anything unusual to wake it up – if paint, pets and a "homeplace" spell had this kind of effect, then self-aware houses would be common among MC people, and I'd have known about them.

At least so far, the house's actions had been innocuous. Some dust in areas no one went in, some welcoming lights on – nothing to harm me, the cats or any visitors. I hoped it would stay that way.

CHAPTER FIFTEEN: THE MAGICIAN'S APPRENTICE

I did very little the next day other than watching bits of online coverage of the Rose Parade and Mummers' Parade, and occasionally fondly remembering the days when staying up til 2AM was completely normal and didn't at all impede my activity level the next day. That is the real reason for televised New Years' parades, you know: to give you something to do the day after that doesn't involve moving out of your chair. Late in the day I managed to do a little bit of neatening in my office and lab, since Laxmi would be coming to visit me on January 3rd.

The day before her visit, I set up a simple spell I could walk her through, a variant of the same color-changing ones I'd used on the walls. I'd use a single-use version that was stored in a crystal. The spell could be turned on or off or be adapted slightly once it was invoked, but it would only last a limited time and couldn't be recast or transferred to anyone else. That way, Laxmi could take the emptied crystal home as a remembrance, but couldn't get herself into trouble with it. I chose a pretty blue sparkly one that I thought she'd like.

I did a little bit of research on some MC-only web pages, too: there was a bit of information about some houses that were as responsive and self-aware as mine, or even more so, but some fairly intensive spells and a lot of ongoing magic work while living in the house had gone into those.

At least I found some reassurance: I'd had some vague worries in the back of my mind about horror scenarios where the house turned on me, like the computer

HAL in the movie 2001, but apparently that was vanishingly unlikely. As with dogs, once the house liked you, you just had to treat it well – but as with cats, and as I'd seen myself, it could sulk if you went away or didn't pay it enough attention!

I was unexpectedly nervous on the day Laxmi was due to visit – I hadn't really ever taught children, only adults. But Laxmi had been easy to talk to at the Thanksgiving dinner where we'd met, and she'd certainly seemed eager to talk to me. Maybe I'd only have to field half a million questions – I could certainly do that!

The doorbell rang right on time. I was still tweaking a few things in the lab, trying to make it look exciting, welcoming – anything that might attract an 11-year-old. I ran downstairs. Laxmi and her dad, a tall man with braided hair and a pleasant face whose name I vaguely remembered as Leo, stood uncertainly on the mat until I said, "Glad to see you, welcome to my house!"

With that they stepped inside. Laxmi looked around and smiled, almost a satisfied expression, as she said "Hello, house!"

I looked a question at her father, who shrugged and said, "I don't know why, you'll have to ask her. But houses are kind of her thing; she says they each have a different feeling. We think it might be because one of my great-grandfathers was a duende, a household spirit, though I don't feel what she does."

Laxmi shrugged and said, "They do all feel different. This one is happy to have company, and just happy overall. It likes you."

"Good to know. So you want to be a magic user? I mean, as a job someday? It sounds like you already do some magic – your feeling for houses is definitely not something NMCS have. Sorry – by NMCs, I mean, people who aren't in the MagiComm."

She said, confidently, "Oh, I know all about the MagiComm. We're in it, even though we don't really do much magic stuff at all, only tiny stuff. Dad says even with boughten spells, he and Mom don't have enough magic to make the big ones work."

"That may be true, but it doesn't mean you won't be able to do big spells, if you decide you really want to. It's like singing or art: it helps to have a talent but being able to do it really well is all about study and practicing. And how much energy you want to put into it."

I introduced the cats, who had wandered out to check out these new people. Laxmi and Leo gave them the proper attention (Merlin and Morgana always made sure of that!) then she asked, "You said I can ask questions, right?" as I led them upstairs to the lab.

"Sure. Ask anything you like."

Leo shook his head and said, "You might be sorry you said that! She always wants to ask *all* the questions."

I smiled at her. "That's fine. Go ahead."

"Since you're a magic user, how come you don't have magic spells all over the house? Dad says this house used to be really magic!"

He looked a little embarrassed. "I worked here for the old man, when I was a kid."

I asked, "You worked with Rob?"

"Oh, you know him? Yeah, old Ray hired both of us, but he mostly had Rob do the outside stuff. Well, I did too – he didn't play favorites on handing out the hard jobs – but because I was MC he had me do more of the inside tasks. Rob did some stuff like changing smoke detector batteries, and we both helped organize the garage, but he had me help with a few of his bigger spells. Mostly just handing him stuff or lending energy."

Now I was really confused. "But this house doesn't have a garage, just a covered parking spot. You saw my car out there, when you came in."

He looked baffled too. "Oh, of course. Maybe he just had stuff stored out there? Or I'm misremembering and it was his workshop up here we organized? It was a long time ago. The house seemed bigger, too, but maybe that's just because I was smaller."

Laxmi pulled my sleeve and asked again, "So how come you don't have more magic working? Like, Dad said the old man always used to have the door open itself when he rang the bell. I thought since you're a magic user, you'd have all kinds of stuff like that."

I answered, "Maybe because I'm not old enough to mind getting up to answer the doorbell. There's always a cost for magic – if it's a spell you can do yourself you have to put time and energy into implementing it and if not, you have to pay someone else for it. Also, everyone has their talents; maybe manipulating doors was easy for him, while I do stuff more like spell accelerators and amplifiers. I sell those for other people to use on their own spells. Besides, I work with magic all day – it's my job. Sometimes it's a nice change to get up off my butt and do things the mundane way."

She said, with utter confidence, "If I'm ever a magic user, I'm gonna do everything with magic! Like, I'll point my finger and the dishes will wash themselves."

I tried not to laugh. "Maybe you will. Just remember, sometimes it's easier to grab a dishrag and do it yourself. But we can do a little magic now if you want to."

Her eyes got really big. "Of course I want to! Can you grant me a wish?"

***

That time I did laugh. "Sorry, that's not how it works. Tell you what, let's have a lesson about how magic works and then we'll do an experiment. And you can ask any question you want. OK?"

"OK!"

"So, lesson first. We don't grant wishes because they're always more complicated than they sound. Let's say you wish for a million dollars. First, where do we get it? Do we take it from someone else? That's clearly a bad thing to do – after all, they didn't wish to lose a million dollars! Do we just make it out of nothing? That's another problem. Banks can tell when money is counterfeit – that means fake –"

She said indignantly, "I know what counterfeit

118

means!"

"OK, I'll just assume you know all the big words, and if I use one you don't know, you can ask. Anyway, all money has serial numbers on it and if we made more, it wouldn't have the right numbers. And how would I give you the money? A million dollars would be ten *thousand* hundred dollar bills – where would you store them? But that's about the biggest bill you can use to actually buy something without people wondering where you got it and why you're not just using a credit card. Of course I could give you a prepaid credit card with a million dollars on it, but then banks can track everything you spend. See? It all gets too complicated."

She still looked interested, so I warmed to my lecture. "OK, so let's say you decide to stay away from money wishes. I have a couple of friends who are in love – " I looked at Leo. "Have you met Rob's Cayden?"

He smiled. "Yeah, I don't run into Rob too much these days, but I saw them out shopping – they're cute together."

"Right, so let's say I wish Rob and Cayden a long, healthy, happy life together. But if I want that to be a real wish, and not just something I write on a card, it's actually seven wishes, not one. Remember what I said about all spells taking energy? I want Rob to be happy, to be healthy, and to live a long time – that's three separate wishes. I want the same for Cayden, so we're up to six wishes. And I want them to stay together, seven. If I specify that I want them to find happiness in each other, that's eight – no, nine, because I have to wish it for each of them. And those are big wishes, not like doing the dishes, so they take lots of energy. And over time, those wishes would start taking some energy from them to stay in place, not just the energy I put into them originally, and that might keep them from being as healthy as they would otherwise. So it's just not practical."

She looked doubtful, but said, "I see. But we can still do magic for some stuff, right?"

"Right! Just let me borrow your dad for a moment

to check some stuff, and we can start. But first, what's your favorite color?"

"Purple! Or, like, violet – purple with a lot of pink in it."

"All right, we'll just be a sec."

I took him to the other side of my office, and explained what I wanted to do and that the effects would be strictly temporary and could be controlled. Once I got his OK, I crossed back to Laxmi in the lab.

"All right, the spell we're going to do will be stored in this blue crystal, but the results can be any color you want. First, I want you to fix the exact color you want in your mind, and keep thinking about that. Next, we have to say or sing a few lines of a song or poem that tell the spell what to focus on. I have the song ready, but I think you probably don't know it yet." I cued up the music on my phone and played her a few lines from the title song of the 1970's musical Hair. "I know you're a singer, because I heard you at the tree-lighting. Can you sing just those two lines?"

"I think so…." she began.

"OK, now can you sing those two lines while keeping the color you picked in your mind's eye? Maybe you can imagine the song words typed out in violet, or on a violet background."

"I can do that," she said, with determination.

"Great! Here, take this crystal, hold it in your hand, remember your color, and sing!"

She did, and her father gasped. She looked around. "What? What happened? I don't see anything different." Then her hair, in two braids longer than her father's, swung out as she turned her head, and she caught a glimpse of the ends. "Oh!"

I walked her over to a mirror, and she beamed at her now bright violet hair. Then her face fell. "But I have to go back to school tomorrow, and our dress code says we have to have natural colored hair." She hooked her fingers into quotation marks around the word "natural". "Do I have to stay home from school? I wouldn't mind, but I haven't seen my friends since before break."

I reassured her, quickly. "Nope, I made sure I grabbed a spell that could be controlled. All you have to do is to pull out a strand of hair and hold it, sing the same two lines, but this time think about your natural hair color. Then you can put it back to violet, or even another color, after school – just pull out another piece of hair and sing those lines, focusing on the color you want it to be."

"But do I need to pull out another strand of hair every time? I'll go bald!"

I laughed again – I couldn't help it. "It's fine. We all lose hundreds of pieces of hair every day."

"Except me," her dad put in ruefully, running his hand over the braids that, I noticed, started an inch further back from his forehead than they probably had in his youth. "I lose more than that!"

"Anyway," I went on, "You can just run your fingers through your hair and use one of the strands that come out naturally. Or if you see a strand stuck to your shirt, you can use that. Just make sure it is your own hair. It won't work with anyone else's – and it won't turn their hair different colors either, before you start thinking up pranks."

"I wouldn't do that! But thanks, I love it!"

"Oh, and one more thing – this is only a temporary spell. It's meant to last two weeks. Toward the end of that the effect will start fading, then it won't work. It might last a little longer," I qualified, remembering what had happened when I'd used a similar spell on my house walls, "but it's guaranteed for two weeks."

"Can you show me how you set this spell up?" she asked.

"Sort of – I can tell you how it works and maybe make a simple version, like to change the color of a piece of paper one time, but I can't make one this professional. I buy spells like these, since it's not my area of expertise."

"Then what do your spells do?"

I'd been dreading that question. I usually explained my work to adults using a software analogy, but I didn't think I could explain APIs to an 11-year-old (to be fair, many adults didn't understand them either, but for those people I just used vague words like "hooking spells together" or "accelerator".) But I'd underestimated Laxmi again. It turned out she was an accomplished coder and had participated in a summer camp last year where they learned to create apps and games. She just nodded as I explained, and it was clear she got it.

Her dad beamed. "She's got a surprisingly subtle understanding of software. She's good on music theory too. I have a pretty amazing kid."

I agreed. "You do!"

Laxmi asked, "Can I come again? I could help you, like Dad did for old Ray when he was young."

Leo said, "Not nearly as young as you! I was 17 or 18 when I worked for him."

But I said, "I don't think I need that much help. But," I held up a hand as her face began to fall, "maybe you could come and help me once a month or so, if your parents agree."

Now her face was alight. "Can I, Dad?"

He hedged a little. "We'll need to check with your mother – you know we make decisions as a family. But I think so."

Laxmi was confident. "Mom will like the idea. You know she's excited about anything she thinks will teach us responsibility. And it's only a few blocks; you don't even have to bring me here."

He said, firmly, "Yes. But let's get her sign-off before we arrange anything." He looked over to me. "Thank you, Macrina. This has been a big thrill for her, and if you really meant it about meeting monthly, we'll be in touch after I talk to my wife."

"I did mean it," I said with equal firmness. "Laxmi is a delight, and I'll enjoy working with her. But I need to keep it to monthly to make sure we're working on really useful stuff that will help me with my work and teach her, not just made-up lessons for the sake of lessons. And of course you or your wife can come with her and hang out; I know parents have to be careful."

He was clearly grateful. "Thanks, we do, of course. We try to teach them to be independent and use good judgement, but you know how it is."

"I can only imagine. Not something I've had to worry about – my kittens aren't even allowed outside. Though I'm sure they will be wanting to go out, as soon as the weather gets better."

"Meerp!" concurred Merlin.

CHAPTER SIXTEEN: THE WELCOMING COMMITTEE

Nothing notable happened over the rest of the month, except our usual weekly outing to the bar. Until lately, Genna hadn't joined our weekly Antlers nights except for that first one, but now she came out most weeks; Duncan had left for his semester in Aberdeen, and I think she was lonely. Also, there was one glorious week at the end of January when the weather pretended it was May; it was so sunny and warm that I got out in the kayak several days that week. I was very cautious, though; much as I loved being out in my boat, I was no expert and had never learned to roll my kayak and pop back upright. The water was still icy even if the air was warm, and there weren't many other boats out at this time of year, so I made sure to stay close to the banks at all times, and I always wore a lifejacket.

Gil came to visit for a week in early February. Texas was nice and warm, while in Oregon the hyacinths were just poking out leaves that would probably get snowed on, so I volunteered to fly down to see him, but he insisted on coming to me; he said that he wanted to see Merlin and Morgana before they completely emerged from kittenhood. They'd reached their full size now, but were still playful.

They were rambunctious in the week leading up to his arrival, though they may have been simply reflecting my excited mood. The whole house felt a little on edge, though again that may just have been me. Still, I'm *sure* I hadn't yet taken out the clean sheets on the day before his arrival. When I got back from grocery shopping, they were sitting in the middle of the bed, as if it were saying Change Me!

I did hope the house was not going to begin criticizing my housekeeping skills. I'd moved out of my mother's house long ago, and didn't need that kind of nagging! On the other hand, if it was going to actively help, as with blowing out dust or taking the sheets out so I didn't forget to make the bed, I could get on board with that. Since Laxmi's visit, I'd started saying "Good night" and "Good morning" to the house, in addition to telling it when I would be back any time I left. Just in case.

Gil had gotten a better sense of how things worked around here on his first visit, and knew how rarely I actually left the house, so he didn't bother renting a car this time. One of the things I'd had a hard time getting used to in rural living was the lack of car-hire services or public transportation – but I was so looking forward to seeing him again that I was happy to go pick him up at the airport.

This was the first time I'd picked someone up in an airport since the pandemic. (There were so many "first time since the pandemic" occasions these days! After over a year of seclusion, returning to the world was a strange and fraught process.) However, there was one minor consequence I hadn't anticipated. I was wondering if I'd have trouble recognizing him from a distance, in a mask, but that was no issue – we recognize people by their walk and by the way they move, more than we realize. As he got close, though, I realized one other problem and doubled up laughing.

So his first word when he got to me was "What?"

I chortled. "I was planning to grab you and give you a big kiss, but," I stopped to gesture between his mask and mine, "I guess that's not going to work."

His eyes laughed, above the mask. "It gives a completely new and different meaning to the phrase 'bumping uglies', doesn't it? Let's get out of here; I didn't check a bag. Since we'll mostly just be at your house, I didn't need a lot of clothes, just a couple nice shirts for teleconferences."

On the way to my car, I told him, "It's good that you
brought a nice shirt, though – I have a surprise for you.
One of the best steakhouses in Eugene has opened back up
– they just did take-out for a while. They've got heated
outdoor seating, so I made a reservation."

"As long as it's covered, great." A thought hit him.
"You should have warned me, though – my shirts will be
OK, but all I have to wear with them is jeans."

"This is Eugene, silly. Jeans will be fine."

By then we'd reached the car. I opened the trunk for
him to put his bags away, but before I could close it, he
grabbed me, gently lifted my mask off over my head, and
kissed me thoroughly. Very thoroughly. My knees felt a bit
wobbly.

"Do you want to just use the trunk?" I asked, only
partly joking. "We could move the bags."

"Don't tempt me," he rumbled. "But, Macrina-Meli?
I'm OK with it if you drive fast."

When we got home, the porch light was on. I know I
hadn't left it on, because it was the middle of the afternoon
and for once it wasn't cloudy and raining. I pointed it out
to Gil, "I did not turn that light on – I think the house is
welcoming you." I had told him about all the house's
recent weird behaviors (the weirdest part of all was even
talking about how a house 'behaved') and after all, he'd
been in on the start of the plans to wake it up, back in
November, so I didn't have to explain any more than that.
He stepped onto the porch, bowed gracefully – I didn't
even know he could do that – and said, "Thank you,
House. I am happy to be here."

Then he stepped back off the porch, to where I stood
on the walkway, and muttered out of the side of his
mouth, "You don't think the house, uh, monitors us while
we're in there, do you? I don't think I want to be watched!"

I snorted. "I have no idea. But even if it does, it's not
like it talks to anyone else about what it sees, right? Think
of it like another cat. You were joking about them sitting
on the bed and watching you, last time."

He rolled his eyes. I handed him a spare key and said, "You can keep this – I forgot to give it to you last time."

He opened the door, and both cats were right there. He quickly moved to block their exit with his bag, called "Macrina! Hurry up so they don't run out!" and walked in. They had been getting bolder lately, and I'd let them out on the back deck in a harness a few times during that one week of nice weather we'd had, but they hadn't been trying hard to make a break for it and get outside. Yet. From the looks of them, it might not be long.

But no, this time they weren't trying to make a break for it. They sat side by side with their tails curled around them at the far edge of the entryway until we both were inside, then simultaneously walked up to Gil, stropping against his shins until he put the bags down and squatted down to skritch them both behind the ears, one under each hand. They purred in harmony, and he grinned at me over his shoulder.

"Between the house, the cats, and you, this is a great welcome! No wonder I wanted to come up here instead of you coming to Texas."

Then he stood up and faced me. "Remind me when we go to that steakhouse, there's something I wanted to talk to you about, and that will be a good place for it. No," and he held up a hand, then waved it side to side in a 'don't worry' gesture. "It's not that kind of 'we have to talk'. I hope you know my heart better than that."

He wouldn't talk about it further then, and I had better things to do with him than talk, anyway.

I made bacon and eggs for him the next morning, having decided this was a good tradition for the first day of his visits here – I wanted him to have *many* reasons to keep coming back!

We didn't really have many plans for this week: the steakhouse dinner tomorrow night, the weekly outing to Antlers on Wednesday, and maybe a visit to a couple of local wineries on Friday afternoon, if we could both knock off early, or else on Saturday. Otherwise, we'd just work,

hang out, and enjoy being together, until he had to fly out
next Sunday.

***

He did have an idea, though. "You know, I don't
have much foul weather gear. Austin is so much warmer,
and not as wet. And boots are heavy to bring back and
forth. You didn't have any plans for today, did you? We
said we'd wing it. What if we go shopping downtown and
buy me a few things, like a raincoat, boots, and a sweater
or fleece? Would you mind if I kept them here?"

Sounded like a good idea to me. I hadn't been to the
REI outdoor-gear store here and was curious how it
compared to the ones in Portland, and if that didn't work,
there was also a different store, Cabela's, on the north side
of town.

Visiting REI was an odd experience. They were still
controlling the number of people allowed in the store at
one time – and enforcing the wearing of masks, which I
was glad to see – so after finding a parking spot in the
small lot across the street, we had to stand in line for five
minutes before we could enter the store. It was a bit
smaller than the Portland ones, but Gil had no trouble
finding a jacket and a lightweight pair of hiking boots he
liked. I had enough spare backpacks and water bottles that
he could borrow, if we decided to go hiking once things
warmed up a bit, so he didn't need to buy any of those.

We considered buying him a bike, but decided that
could wait for another time – after all, I'd only taken that
one trail ride so far. If it turned out to be something I
wanted to do more often, and if he wanted to go with me,
we could consider a bike for him then. He also found a
lightweight fleece jacket he liked, that could be worn under
the rain jacket to make it warm enough for winter – this
way he wouldn't need to bring a coat on the plane.

Even though we'd gotten most of what we needed,
we decided to head over to Cabela's too. Like REI, this was
a chain of stores that sold gear for outdoor activities, but

the vibe was very different. The gear here was aimed more at hunting and fishing, with none of the climbing or cycling gear we'd seen at REI. There was no control of how many people could be in the store, and only about half of the customers were wearing masks, despite the mandate still in place. It was interesting to walk around and check out the wide range of cooking gear – for grilling or making sausages or drying meats – as well as stuff for car camping, where REI seemed to be oriented more toward backpacking.

Cabela's had a lot of clothing at reasonable prices, and Gil decided to pick up a couple of flannel shirts while we were here. I teased him that, in the flannel shirts and hiking boots, he only needed a beard to fit right in, in Oregon, so he threatened to buy an axe for the complete lumberjack look!

CHAPTER SEVENTEEN: DINNER AND DECISIONS

The next evening, we dressed up for the Rodeo Steakhouse dinner. Of course, 'dressed up' in this context meant a polo shirt and jeans for him and something a little fancier than the leggings and fleece pullovers I usually wore around the house, for me. Back in the days when I used to actually see people on a daily basis, I'd bought a few lightweight wool trapeze dresses from a Portland company. In one of those, with tights, nice boots and a cardigan added for warmth, I was just as comfortable as in my lounging clothes, with the added benefit of no tight waist to make me uncomfortable if I ate too much.

I wouldn't be able to drink much wine with dinner, though – this was where I missed being able to Uber home! But Gil was my guest so I should suck it up (or rather, not suck it up) and do the driving like a good host.

Just then, he looked over at me and said, "Tell you what. I'll drive home tonight and on Friday when we go to the vineyards, if you'll do the navigating, since you know I don't know this area well yet, and choose the wine. You know I hate figuring that out."

I did know that, but the offer still seemed too good to be true. I squinted one eye and looked at him sideways. "You're trying to butter me up for something, aren't you?"

He laughed. "Maybe. Just go slow on the wine, because I do have something we need to discuss." I gave him another questioning look, but he just smiled and moved to the passenger side of the car. "You can drive there, so I get at least an idea of the route."

I hadn't been to this restaurant before, either. It was

nice, set on the north bank of the river, and it was clear that there would be great views of the water when it wasn't February and drizzly. We walked through the inside area, which was warm and welcoming, to get to our seat. I hoped we'd be able to come back one day when it felt safer to be indoors unmasked – hopefully, it wouldn't be too much longer now.

They'd done a great job setting up the outside seating, in the area that was usually only open in summer. It was roofed, with electric heaters attached to roof beams, and framed walls hung with tarps on the outside to keep us dry, and patterned carpets on the inside to make it feel cozy. They were probably cheap indoor-outdoor rugs in daylight, but tonight they looked like exotic tapestries, glowing in the lights from the candles on each table and the dimmed lighting overhead. The booths were set in little niches all over the place, giving us the illusion of privacy. As I'd heard, they'd returned to serving their full menu and the steaks all came from local farms. The service wasn't at the level you'd find in the most luxurious restaurants in bigger cities, but it was fairly good and attentive, and it wasn't hard to catch the server's eye when we needed something.

We placed our orders and asked the sommelier to recommend a bottle of wine that was more or less reasonably priced, telling him we'd prefer something local. He recommended a Syrah that was bottled locally, though the grapes were grown south of here, telling us that the wine had "starting notes of warm spice and cola with a hint of Tahitian vanilla, which transition to refined but supple tannins". With some effort, we managed to keep straight faces until he'd left.

Once the wine came, I tasted it, and nodded to our server to tell him the wine wasn't corked – because at least I could tell that much, though I wasn't sure I'd know a supple tannin if it bit me.

***

When our server had poured the wines and left, I said, "OK, you wanted to talk? I think this must be the most romantic outing we've had in years, so you'd better not be breaking up with me!"

He laughed. "What, after we've spent all these years breaking each other in? It would be way too much work to start over with someone new. But, Macrina-Meli," he was more sober now, "We really have broken each other in over all these years, haven't we? We're not the people we used to be; the rough edges have worn down. The thing is –"

He paused, as the server arrived with the wine and a basket of bread – sourdough bread and home-made herbed butter, yum. The server poured our wine and left, and Gil took a piece of bread, broke off a bit and buttered it as he continued, "The thing is, my company has decided that we can go fully remote. We had a lucky accident of timing; you know I've always said that one thing I really like about this company is that our management listens to data?"

"It turns out my boss and our quality engineer started a project two years ago to measure productivity – they've created some metric based on the number of lines of code created, the number of defects found and the complexity of each module. With that they were able to show that we actually became more productive working from home – there was a dip at first as everyone adapted to quarantine, but then it got better and better, especially when most people's kids were able to go back to school. So after the big presentation a few weeks ago, they talked about it and polled employees to see what people want, and it turns out people wanted to keep working from wherever they want to be."

Our appetizers arrived – a beet salad for him, and mushrooms cooked in the style of escargot for me. (No snails were involved in the preparation of my appetizers; the mushrooms were essentially just a delivery mechanism for garlic butter and I did them full justice, attempting to keep the garlic butter from dripping onto my lap.)

But Gil was still talking, so I wrenched my attention away from my mushrooms. "So, Meli, I was wondering – if I can work from anywhere, what if I moved up here?"

I thought about it. I'd love to have him nearby, but we'd tried living together way back when, and it had almost broken us up. And there were other issues…

He continued, "I know, it's not going to be simple. But I do really think we've mellowed. Our jobs have also forced us to get better at communication over the years – we can promise ourselves this time to bring up problems before they fester. Also, now we can afford to have more space, and that should help – remember that little apartment we were in, where we couldn't get away from each other?"

We smiled at each other at the old memory. It was funny now, but it had been horrible – a one-bedroom flat, with a tiny kitchen and only one sofa and one uncomfortable chair. It had been only about a quarter the size of where either of us lived now.

I asked, "Were you thinking of buying a house in Percival?" Were separate houses close together a good compromise?

Completely serious, he said, "I'd really like trying to live with you. It took that year and a half of complete separation for me to see how much I just like having you around, going to bed together every night and waking up together – even on weekdays when all we do is make coffee before we rush off to our desks. I think it would be worth it, even if it wouldn't be simple."

It wouldn't. My house wasn't large, and while the spare room was fine for him to use as an office during short visits, it didn't feel like a long-term solution.

He apparently agreed, because he went on, "I think I'd need a separate office, which would still let us have a guestroom. Your office and lab upstairs give you some space, but I'd be in your hair whenever we weren't working, and we wouldn't have any room for company to stay with us. But I'm not asking you to move; you really can't right now, can you? I don't understand what's going on with your house, but it seems to be connecting with your magic and leaving it feels like a bad idea."

He took a breath. Then our steaks arrived, and the potato gratin we were sharing, and we spent a few minutes tasting them and talking about how good they were. Finally, when we'd slowed down a bit, Gil said, "So all I'm asking you right now is to think about it. My lease in Austin isn't up for another six months anyway, so we have plenty of time. Maybe we could think about remodeling, or I could rent office space somewhere. Or maybe there's another brilliant solution I haven't come up with yet."

His warm brown eyes were intense now, and I thought they looked a bit nervous, as he finished, "But, if we can figure out how to make it work…would you want to?"

I carefully put down my fork and knife, because accidentally stabbing your boyfriend with a steak knife in the middle of a romantic question is not good for the relationship. Then I tugged his fork out of his hand, set it on his plate, and put my hand over his.

"I'd love to." We sat there grinning at each other for a few minutes before we returned to our food.

His relief was palpable. "Whew. I don't think the rest of this visit would have been any fun if you'd said no! Should we order champagne with dessert, to celebrate? Even if we're not really changing anything, right now."

I shook my head. "I have some at home – let's have it back there. After all, you still have to drive us back there!"

***

We did have dessert before leaving – I spotted tiramisu on the menu and couldn't resist. On the way back home, I said, "Can we please not mention the possibility of moving away while we're in my house? I think it's OK to talk about you possibly moving in, but I don't know how this house would react to the idea of me moving out. I don't think I want to find out, unless we really need to."

"Fair enough. Do you think the house really understands what's said inside it?"

"Maybe? Honestly, I have no idea. I'm being cautious."

Of course I didn't really have "Champagne" – I had a couple of bottles of sparkling wine, one made in Oregon and one in neighboring Washington state. But the difference wouldn't matter to anyone but a wine pedant. These were bubbly and festive, and that was what counted. We opened the Washington bottle, got out my champagne flutes and filled them, then sat there nestled against each other on the couch in front of the fire, talking about local things we could do if we had the time to do them. The problem with long-distance visiting was always that we wasted so much time on travel that it cut into the time we had together to go anywhere.

CHAPTER EIGHTEEN: YUP, STILL WINTER

We managed to finish work on Friday by noon, giving us time to do some wine tasting. I'd wanted to give Gil a taste of Oregon winemaking, but I also wanted to visit some wineries I hadn't been to before. I'd asked all my local friends for suggestions on which ones to visit, but there was so much disagreement that I ended up ignoring all of their messages. Instead, I charted a tasting route based mostly on which places were close together and whether there were nice views from the tasting rooms at each place. We ended up visiting two wineries and a sake brewery. At this time of year, the wineries didn't get as many visitors as they did in better weather, so we took a chance and didn't make any reservations.

On the way to the first one, Gil said, "Don't forget to look for supple tannins!" so of course I answered, "And warm notes of wet leather and elderberry spice!"

We were still laughing as we reached the tasting room at the Moonacre Estates winery and told the people behind the counter that we would like to try their tasting flights. It was a beautiful room with tall glass walls and views across the vineyards, but fortunately their staff didn't seem too stuffy. The man serving us introduced himself as Leon and asked if we had done much wine tasting and if we'd like some pointers on what to look for.

When we agreed, he said, "First you want to look at the color. You can swirl the wine if you like – if you see "legs" where the wine drips down the inside of the glass, that tells you it's got a higher percentage of alcohol – which isn't necessarily good or bad. Then you want to hold the glass up to your nose and sniff the wine, to see what you can smell. Last, take a small sip and hold it in your mouth. You can swish it around your mouth if you like. Try to see what notes you can taste, like different fruits or spices or even minerals, leather or tobacco. There is no right or wrong, just what you like."

Gil said, "Can you please tell me, what on earth is a 'supple tannin'?"

Leon laughed. "Honestly, I have no idea. I think people usually say that about a wine that has no harsh or discordant flavors. It feels sort of smooth and rounded in your mouth and the flavors seem to flow well from beginning to end."

We liked both Leon and his wines (though Gil kept telling me he tasted "lingering notes of lion's mane mushroom and effervescent hints of chocolate-covered lime jellybeans", when he wasn't telling me the wine "mostly tasted of grapes"). I bought several bottles of different types of wine to take home, and even took a leaflet for their wine club, so I could think about whether I'd like to join and get sent a couple of bottles every three months (or go back to the winery and pick them up, which, as Gil pointed out, sounded like an *absolutely terrible* situation).

The second place, Coq de Noir, was much snootier, but their wines were really, really tasty. They were also really, really pricy. I bought just one bottle there, on the off chance we might have something to celebrate soon, if we could just figure out practicalities of living together.

The third place we visited was Saijo Sake Brewery, and the main thing we learned there was that neither of us were big fans of sake – though it was objectively interesting to learn how they polished grains of rice to make progressively better grades of sake, and Gil did seem to enjoy deliberating whether he was tasting notes of melon or of lychee.

I missed Gil just as much after he left on Sunday as I had after his previous visit, but at least now I had wine to drown my sorrows, plus a lot of decisions to make. At least one of my decisions was low-stakes; there was really no way to go wrong with a wine club, and even if it did I could just quit. If Gil and I found a way to make living together practical, on the other hand, I'd have another human around every single day. We'd have to talk through all of our life decisions, plan meals together, schedule around each other…and if things did go wrong, it would hurt even more than last time because we had so much more history now.

I decided to think about Gil later. Wine decisions were much easier to make, though maybe I needed to research more local vineyards before deciding. By "research" of course, I meant more wine-tasting. Maybe enough wine would help with the bigger decisions too? No, probably not.

***

It had gotten cold again after he left, and there was even some snow in the forecast, all of which made me miss having another warm body in my bed even more.

My phone dinged, and a text appeared to distract me from my thoughts:

> **Sulis:** Would you be willing to let me hold a Frost Fair on your dock?

What was a Frost Fair? It sounded like a carnival, and I didn't think my dock had room for one of those.

> **Macrina:** A what?

> **Sulis:** A Frost Fair. Basically, a party on the ice.

> **Macrina:** What ice?

> **Sulis:** That's the part where it's useful to have a naiad on hand.

She went on to explain that, during the coming cold spell, she'd be able to channel enough heat from the lake surface into the surrounding cold water to freeze the lake solid for some distance surrounding my dock. She'd set up a booth on the ice to serve drinks and food, and would have a fire pit on my dock, where people could warm up.

Macrina: Like an ice-skating party?

Sulis: No, that's probably not a good idea. If people bring skates, they'll tend to get too far away from the dock, where the ice may not be as thick – I don't want anyone falling in! But they can slide a bit, just with their regular shoes. I can bring some Kool-Aid powder, and we'll sprinkle it on the ice to make a safety line, so they'll know where the safe area stops.

Macrina: How many people are we talking?

Sulis: Just the George group and a few of my closest coworkers – the ones who know what I am. If they could use your bathroom, that and the dock would be all you'd need to provide. I can take care of the food and everything else.

I did owe her a favor for watching the cats when I went to Texas. More importantly, this sounded like fun, so I agreed and we set the date for the next Saturday. (Sulis also lived by the water, as you might expect, but her house backed onto a creek rather than the lake itself, so she didn't have a dock.)

Of course, when she invited the group to her party, Genna's first thought was historical:

Genna: A Frost Fair? Like the ones they had on the Thames during the Little Ice Age in the 16th century?

Sulis: Um, sort of. Only with just us, and just one booth serving food and drink. I'm not inviting the whole town.

Genna: Pity.

Genna: Just kidding. It sounds like fun! What can I bring?

Of course, Sulis told he she didn't have to bring

anything, and of course Genna said she wanted to – we all knew how things worked with this group by now! So Sulis told her anything that worked with the Frost theme would be very welcome.

Naturally, I wanted to bring something to the party too – the use of my dock and bathroom wouldn't be any effort at all – so I looked up recipes and decided that Spicy Fireball Shots would be appropriate. All I'd need to get hold of would be cinnamon-flavored whiskey, white rum, a tiny dash of cayenne pepper, and those tiny shot-sized red plastic cups. Easy.

I still missed Gil fiercely (and was starting to think that yeah, it might be worth making the adjustments required to live with someone else) but having something to look forward to made me feel a lot better.

True to her word, Sulis had everything in hand. She came over and froze the water around the dock the evening before. I watched her, but there wasn't much to see; she arrived in the water, slithered out onto the dock, stood up with her head bowed for a moment, and voila, there was ice for a good twenty feet around the dock. She filled several large containers with water and left them on land to freeze overnight.

She and Menzy showed up again the next morning and assembled a food stand out of the ice blocks she'd frozen overnight. Sulis told me, "I saw a video on YouTube of someone who built a bar out of ice behind their house and kept it up all winter, but that was in Minnesota. It's not something we can do here, except when we get one of these cold snaps, where it stays well below freezing." Sulis didn't bother with a cooler for the cold food and drinks, just set them directly on the bar, but she'd brought boxes full of hay to keep her hot food insulated. Her showpiece drinks looked like the kind of thing they sold at ice bars, served in shot glasses made out of ice. (Now I understood why she'd reminded us to bring not only hats but gloves!)

I felt like my little red cups had been outclassed, but she thanked me for them, saying that they'd work for anyone who didn't want their drinks quite that cold, or for when we ran out of the ice "glasses" – she'd had a limited number of molds for them.

It ended up being a lot of fun, having an outdoor party in winter; we'd all spent so much time indoors over the last few months that it felt great to be outside, and the previous week had been so quiet for me that I was enjoying having everyone on my ground. The cold sharpened everyone's appetites, and though I thought we'd have way too much food with the stuff everyone brought, almost all of it got eaten. Sulis's icy drinks and my fire shots were popular at first but after a while, hot drinks sounded more appealing, and we ended up repurposing my ingredients to go with the hot chocolate Sulis had supplied. We invented Fire Chocolate: hot chocolate combined with the cinnamon whiskey, rum, and cayenne I'd provided. Tasty, as well as warming.

The party only lasted a couple hours; by then, we were all chilled enough despite the fire pit's warmth to be ready to go home and take a nice hot bath or shower, but it was so much fun I had a feeling we might be doing this again next winter.

CHAPTER NINETEEN: RETURN OF THE APPRENTICE

Laxmi was right: her mother had enthusiastically agreed to the idea of her visiting me monthly, with one stipulation that she called me to discuss. "Please don't make it nothing but fun," her mother Deepthi said firmly. "I want her to learn. Teach her and feel free to make her work – you called it an 'apprenticeship', so treat her like an apprentice and let her help you. She can help you prepare ingredients or even clear your lab, as some compensation for teaching her. Leo and I are agreed that our children can be anything they want and we will support them, but we don't want them to choose a career because they think it will be all fun and games. If she really loves the field, and I think she might, she'll like it all the better to be doing real work and not a child's game version of it."

I bore that in mind, but for our second lesson I wanted to talk, mostly, to find out how much she knew already and to discuss the different types of magic and see what directions she might want to go. I also wanted to assess her ability to read and follow directions. So I came up with a short list of simple spells we could do, depending on how the conversation went.

We arranged a meeting time on a Sunday afternoon, and she showed up promptly, again with her dad in tow. After they took off all their warm layers, coats and hats and mittens, and hung them up on my coat tree, this time I took them over to the kitchen table. Laxmi seemed a little disappointed.

"What's wrong?" I asked.

"Aren't we going to be in the lab today?

I smiled. "Some magic users do more magic in a kitchen than a lab. Some do all their work on a computer and don't use a lab at all. Also, we're going to start out today by talking about different kinds of magic, and the kitchen table is a comfortable place for all of us to sit. My lab only has one chair!"

"There are different kinds of magic?" she asked.

"Yes, but before we do that, I want to learn more about you. Tell me about yourself. What things do you like to do? Do you like working with other people or by yourself? How do you like to learn, by seeing things, or hearing things or doing things?"

She started off with what I recognized as the standard speech every child is used to giving adults: "I'm Laxmi and I'm eleven. I like reading and music and programming computers and hanging out with my friends," but then she faltered, trying to remember what else I'd wanted to know.

Oops, bad teacher. Stick to one question at a time. I prompted her, "Do you like to do projects together with other people, or to work by yourself?"

"Um...I'm not sure. At school we sometimes do projects in groups, but we're all working on our own thing, just sitting together. I like talking to other people, anyway."

"OK. That's not something you need to know right now, anyway, but maybe we can experiment sometime. Do you know how you learn best? I mean, do you remember things best by reading them or being told, or by doing something for yourself?"

"Definitely doing things. Dad, remember when I had that one math teacher, who expected us to understand everything just from her telling us, without giving us easy questions to practice on before the hard ones? That was awful!" She shuddered. "But I like to have directions where I can read them when I need them, instead of being told and having to remember."

"Good to know! I want to help you figure out what kinds of magic you want to do, so it's good if we understand who you are first."

***

"So what kinds of magic are there?" she asked.

"You already know at least some of them. For starters, some people do magic spells, like me, and some people are magic. You've met Menzy – she was at that Friendsgiving dinner where I first met you. Menzy is a dryad, and our other friend Sulis is a naiad, so they are magic. They can do some magic too, but it's related to who they are – all of Menzy's magic is related to trees, and all of Sulis's is related to water. As an example, I once saw Sulis make part of the lake freeze. That might take too much power for me to do as a spell – or if I did manage it, I couldn't keep it frozen for long. But it's a lot easier for her because it fits her nature. She couldn't do that spell to change hair color that we did last time, though."

"Could they learn to do magic spells too, so they could be magic and do all kinds of magic?"

"Well, maybe. You do have to have some talent and inborn magical power as well as learning to do spells, or all humans could do them. I don't know that there's any rule that a dryad or naiad couldn't have that talent, and they definitely have the power, but they usually just don't do human-style spells. I'm not sure if it just feels wrong to them, or if they feel like there's no point studying spells when the other kind of magic comes so easily. I've never asked."

Her dad was paying attention, and spoke up then. "And if you do meet Menzy or Sulis and you want to ask that question, make sure you ask politely, young lady, you hear me?"

"Da-aad, of course I'm polite!" She turned back to me. "But you said there are more different kinds of magic?"

"Yes, of course. There are more different magic species, and you probably know some of those too. But also, among human magic users, there are different things people can specialize in. I already told you that I do background magic, things to make other spells work better. Some magic users are kitchen witches; all their spells are about making food more delicious, or quicker to prepare, or more nutritious, or different tasting. Some are healers, and they make spells to make sick or hurt people better. Some people do magic to make art, or to build things."

"How do they choose?"

"It's like choosing any job: you pick something that you are interested in, that you're good at, and hopefully that other people need and will pay you for."

Her dad interjected, "Remember that last part, it's important. I want you to be able to pay for your food and rent when you grow up! That's why you can't just decide that your job is playing video games, or why your mom is a doctor and can't be just a painter even though you know she loves painting."

"But people want her paintings! They buy them sometimes."

"Yeah, but not enough, or they don't pay enough, to earn a whole living from. So it's her hobby, and she does it in her free time, and then it's just a nice bonus when someone buys one."

Way to snag a teachable moment, Dad! I smiled at him, and went on, "There are also different ways people do magic. I mostly store spells in crystals or in words, and invoke them from there. Some people do spells in music, or make chemical potions or whatever. Last time you were here, we combined some of those, where a spell was stored in a crystal but you sang to invoke it."

"Cool. Are there other kinds? And will we be able to do some today?"

"Yes, lots. You said you liked to do things, and with written instructions, so I was thinking we could try some kitchen magic today."

She looked at me curiously. "But can you do that? You said your specialty is background stuff."

"I can do at least basic things. It's like... OK, your

mom is a doctor. She's an obstetrician, right? But when she went to college, she didn't only study how babies grow; she probably had some basic classes in math, chemistry, physics, and maybe even languages and then some more classes in the basics of medicine before she could study her specialty. So, when I went to college, I learned the basics of all kinds of magic – plus math and science and languages – and then I studied my own specialty in more depth, my own field. Also, I do background sorts of magic because that's what my business is, but I do a variety of things within that. Just like some doctors do general medicine while others like your mom specialize."

She tucked that way to think about later and changed the subject back to immediate matters. "What are we gonna do today?"

"I was thinking we could bake cookies."

"I can make cookies! I do it a lot, all on my own. Mom and Dad let me, they only say they need to be there when I'm using the oven. But I do it all myself. But what's magic about cookies?"

"Partly it's training, to let you practice following instructions – a recipe, in this case – without me telling you what to do at every step. But of course I'll be here to answer all your questions along the way. Also, we can use magic to change some flavors. I was thinking you can make blondies – have you ever had blondies?"

"No, what're blondies?"

"Not really cookies, they're like brownies, only without chocolate."

"Wha-a-at? Why would you even want brownies without chocolate?"

I snorted. "Don't worry, we'll put chocolate chips in. But they have a nice butter-scotch caramel flavor even without those. The thing is, I don't have chocolate chips. I only have peanut butter chips. And cocoa, but I don't think cocoa would be good in blondies. At least, they wouldn't taste like blondies if I put cocoa in."

"So what do we do? Do we just go to the store?"

"Well, we could. But sometimes you need

something and the store is closed. So we're going to use magic to turn the peanut butter chips into chocolate chips. Also, I only have light brown sugar, and the recipe calls for dark brown sugar. So we'll transform that too. Here, take this."

"This" was a surprise I'd gotten her: an apron with a picture of Mickey Mouse in his Sorcerer's Apprentice role. "You can leave that here, in the lab, so it's ready for you no matter what we work on."

"Cool, thanks, Macrina!"

Her dad said, "Just be glad she doesn't make you call her 'Master', or maybe 'Mistress', like they used to make real apprentices do!"

"Ewwww!"

I laughed. "Plain Macrina is fine."

***

I pulled out the recipe she'd follow, but explained the ingredient conversion first. "We're going to do these conversions two different ways, and we're going to work a little differently than I usually do. Normally, I create the spell and store it in a spell-store – I usually use either a crystal or some lines of poetry that can be printed out or brought up on my tablet. That lets me sell the spell so someone else can invoke it, and that's how I make my living. In this case, though, we want to do the spells ourselves one time, right now, right here, so we don't have to store them at all. We just set up the spell and run it right away. Does that all make sense?"

She thought about it – I was really pleased that she did that instead of just answering automatically without thinking. Young as she was, Laxmi was serious about her learning, and it made her fun to teach. "Yes, I think so," she finally answered. "What was that about doing the conversions two different ways? Is that just to teach me, or is there a real reason for it?"

"Oh, there's a real reason. With the peanut butter chips, what we want to do is to take the peanut butter flavor *out* of the chips, and put chocolate flavor *into* them, borrowing the chocolate from the powdered cocoa I have."

"If it's borrowing, will we put it back afterward?"

"Nope, just a figure of speech. The cocoa will be a flavorless powder after that and it will be useless, so I'll just throw it away."

"That seems like a waste!"

"It is – though on the other hand I'm sure there are waste products when they manufacture chocolate chips, too. But you're right. Sometimes it just makes sense to do things the mundane way, like buying the right ingredients in the first place. But there are some tasks you just can't do without magic. Or, maybe you can't do them at that particular time – like, say you promised to bring chocolate chip cookies to school the next day and you forgot until it was too late to go to the store."

Leo answered that one. "Oh, that never happens at our house! We're always organized," he said, keeping a completely straight face until Laxmi dissolved into telltale giggles.

"OK, so how do we do all that to convert the chips?"

"First we start with the amount of chips the recipe calls for – how much is that?"

She looked over at the recipe I'd handed her. "Half a cup."

"OK, then measure that out," I said, handing her the measuring scoop and a bowl to put the chips in.

"First, we take the peanut butter flavor out of the chips – that's the easy part."

"How?"

"We could run water and magic over them at the same time, but then they'd be all wet and they might dissolve. So we sort of…run the idea of water over them to dissolve the flavor away."

"The idea of water???"

"Yep. Run the tap water, put the bowl of chips next to the sink, think about dissolving the flavor out, and push your magic into it."

I put my hands on her shoulders and lent her some extra magic to make it easier for her to feel the flow – that's always the hard part when you're starting out. "Feel that?"

"I do! It's like a current running through me!"

"Push that toward the chips and think about the flavor running out of them, like washing it away."

The chips abruptly turned white.

"You did it!" I cheered. "Go ahead and taste one."

She did. "It mostly just tastes like sugar and wax now."

"Right. So next we add the chocolate."

"How do we know how much cocoa to use?" she asked next.

I digressed a little, and asked her "Have you ever wondered why not just anybody can make magic spells?"

"Um, yes…" she answered, clearly wondering where I was going with this.

"It's because that part is an art, not a science. I need the amount of cocoa that has the right amount of chocolate flavor for half a cup of chocolate chips. Chocolate chips and cocoa are both made by grinding up cocoa beans into paste, but then they take all the liquid or pasty parts out of the cocoa to make a dry powder." (I'd looked all this up beforehand, since I'd known I'd have to explain it to Laxmi.) "They both get some more processing and choc-chips get sugar added, but that's the basics. But the amount of flavor in cocoa depends on how ripe the beans were when they were harvested, where they were grown, and a lot of other things. They come from a plant, which means they can vary a lot. So I estimate, and that takes practice. I can go a little overboard, but if I go too far the chips will come out bitter tasting – unsweetened chocolate doesn't taste too good. And I might even get some flavor from the alkali or other chemicals they use to make cocoa, which would taste even worse."

"Is it all just experience, or can you also use your magic to figure out how much?"

"A little of both. I estimate, and if I have nearly the correct amount it just *feels* right, but that takes experience too, to train your magic that way."

"So how much do we need, and do we need any other ingredients?"

"Measure out about 3/4 of a cup, dump it over the peanut butter chips, and then I'll check. This is a transformation spell, so we are going to use three things: you're going to draw us pictures of a caterpillar and a butterfly, I'm going to play a song called 'Changes' on my phone and we'll grab a cup each of water and ice to symbolize changing state."

She'd already measured out the cocoa while I was talking, so I handed her two pieces of paper and a box of crayons. "Draw a caterpillar on one and a butterfly on the other."

Leo said, "Changes by David Bowie?"

"Yes – Phil Ochs did a song with that title too, but the Bowie one is easier to sing." I started playing it while she was drawing.

Laxmi was such a talented kid in so many ways, it seemed only fair that she was an absolutely *terrible* artist. I could see she knew that – she looked a little embarrassed, handing me her drawings, but I said, "Great! The symbols are what matter, in magic. Listen to the song for a minute – you just need to be able to sing the ch-ch-ch-changes lines from the chorus."

She said, "I know this! Dad likes David Bowie." The kid did know her music.

The rest went pretty smoothly. I lent her some extra magic again to make it easier to feel, and had her put the caterpillar drawing in the sink and pour the water over it, then wrap the butterfly one around the ice, hold both drawings, sing and focus on directing the magic to infuse the chocolate flavor into the chips. It was a lot of things to do at once, and nothing happened for a minute. Then she took a deep breath, held it…and the chips turned brown.

She swayed a little. "You OK?" I asked.

"Yeah. It just felt like when you run really fast and then you have to catch your breath," she said.

"You did great. The next conversion won't take

quite so much energy from you, and then from there out it's just normal baking. But it is good practice in following written directions on your own."

***

Laxmi asked, "So why are we doing this differently than the chips?"

"Good memory!" I commended her. "It's because of how brown sugar is made. Do you know the difference between dark brown sugar and light brown sugar?"

"Um, one is darker than the other?"

"Brilliant deduction, Holmes. But why?"

"I d'know."

"Basically, brown sugar has molasses in it – if it has more molasses it's dark brown and if it has less molasses, it's light brown. So the flavor is already there, and we just need more of it – in fact, most cook books tell you that you can substitute light brown sugar for dark brown by just adding some molasses. But this is tricky, because we don't know how this sugar here is made – sometimes they just filter less of the molasses out when they're making the sugar, but sometimes they start with refined white sugar and add molasses back in." (I'd looked that up, too.) "I don't want to monkey around with trying to figure out which kind we have, so we're going to take some of our light brown sugar, extract the molasses, and then pour it over a cup of some more light brown sugar."

"That sounds really complicated! Couldn't we just use the light stuff as is?" I could tell Leo was biting his tongue to keep from agreeing with his daughter – there actually were plenty of blondie recipes that did just use light brown sugar.

"Sure we could. They'd come out just fine – but they wouldn't have all the caramel flavor that they will this way. *And,*" I held a finger up, "You wouldn't get to try another spell. Also, don't worry, honestly, the spell itself isn't as complicated as the explanation of why we're doing it."

This time I used ice as the only other ingredient, just a few small chips. I had her measure out a half-cup of the sugar, and told her, "You are going to take these ice chips and hold them in your hand. They'll melt and you can let the drops of water fall on to the sugar – that little bit of water won't hurt anything. Say, 'What you were, you now must be,' and think *hard* about the sugar dissolving to molasses. I'll lend you a bit of magic again to make it easier to feel the flow of it. Ready?"

She did exactly as I instructed, the droplets of water fell on the sugar, and the sugar turned into a thick brown liquid. I sniffed it, just in case. (Once you've seen a few spells go wrong, you learn to double check; after all, there are lots of different thick brown liquids and I had no desire to take a bite of blondie only to find that her mind had somehow wandered onto the topic of fertilizer! But no, this was definitely molasses. Phew.)

"Good job! You look tired now, though – you sure you want to go ahead with making the blondies?"

She took a breath and valiantly squared her shoulders. "I get to eat them, right?"

"You can take the whole panful home to your mom," I told her. Then I let my shoulders and the corners of my mouth droop. "Unless you want to be extra kind and leave just a couple for your poor starving teacher..."

She laughed. "OK, you can keep a few. Where's the recipe? This is the easy part, right?"

***

She finished making the blondies and they were delicious. As they were leaving, Leo gave Laxmi a stern look and, reading it correctly, she said, "Thanks for the blondies and the lesson, Macrina!"

Leo added, "And thanks for tiring our girl out – I bet she sleeps well tonight!"

Before they left, Laxmi turned to me and said, "Can I ask one more question?"

"Of course – that's why you're here."

"Isn't it possible to do big things with magic?"

"Like what?"

"Like, I d'know, like flying or turning invisible or reading someone's mind?"

"Well, not quite mind reading – we've never figured out a way to do that with human magic – but talking with no sound, yes, and flying, and bending light rays to make something more or less functionally invisible. But they all take a lot of energy, and it takes a whole lot of practice to be able to build up that much energy. You're just starting, that's why you're so tired from these small spells today. Even for people who can do them, they can be exhausting so they don't do it often, only when there's a need. And often it's easier to just, say, buy a plane ticket."

"So I might be able to do them someday, if I work really hard?"

"I think you might – you have a lot of potential."

***

Telling Gil about our lesson later that night, I said, "I was so proud of her – she kept going even when she was tired. I remember when I was first learning to use magic, and when you're not used to directing it, it takes a lot out of you!"

He said, "But you loaned her added magic?"

"Yes, it's a lot easier to feel the flow when it's already flowing into you, and when there's more of it. But she still had to do all the directing and that takes focus. A lot of kids her age can't hold that concentration."

"So do you think she'll be a magic user?"

"No idea. It all depends on what she wants. But I definitely do think she can do it if she decides she wants to!"

CHAPTER TWENTY: SPRING IS SPRINGING

My hyacinths had indeed gotten snowed on during that cold spell, but by the middle of March they were budding anyway. The weather started to open up, with occasional warmer days and even some sun now and then, though never for a whole day at a time. The kittens were about ten months old now, definitely adolescent, and were lobbying hard to be allowed outside – I had to get through the doorway quickly any time I entered or left the house so they couldn't run out, because I didn't quite trust them to find their way home.

Morgana wasn't much of a problem; as soon as she got outside she always wanted to roll on the cement of the pathway, and it was easy enough to pick her up and drop her back inside. Merlin, though, was a runner, and he was fast and sneaky. He liked to hide under bushes where I couldn't reach him. Worse, he didn't seem to know his way home; once or twice I'd caught him in front of a next-door neighbor's door, yowling to be let in. (Maybe he just wanted to be adopted by a new mom?)

I decided that they needed to learn the neighborhood, so I dug out the harnesses I'd bought with the rest of the cat's gear. As far as Morgana was concerned, they were a total flop: when I put a harness on her, "flop" was exactly what happened. She hit the ground, went limp, and gave her best impression of a cat who had been saddled with all the weight for the world, like Atlas. Funny, because as soon as I took the harness off, she hopped back up and went about her business as if nothing had ever happened.

Merlin didn't seem to mind the harness so much. He went on exploring, though it wasn't much like walking a dog. He had to investigate every single plant, nibble the leaves and think about how they compared to every other leaf he'd ever tasted, apparently. Still, we got a bit farther from the house every time I tried harnessing him, and I resolved to keep going for cat-led walks, even if we didn't get any farther than ten feet from the door while he sniffed every plant in range. (Funny, because when he got out on his own, he had a tendency to run through the neighborhood.) I tried to vary which door we used to come back in, in hopes he'd eventually learn all the doors into the house. I considered adding a cat door, but decided to wait – no point in having one until I was sure he knew which house was his.

So far, the cats had reacted to the house a few times, such as when they welcomed Gil on his last visit, but they hadn't given any other indications of being anything other than normal, nonmagical pets. On the other hand, humans at the same equivalent age didn't have fully-developed brains either so I wasn't giving up hope yet.

They had developed a few nemeses, though. One day, I'd brought my laptop down to the kitchen table after completing most of my workday. I was answering a few more emails, completely absorbed in my work, when a loud scream erupted right next to me. I jumped about five feet in the air. Once I landed back in my chair, my heart still racing, I looked over and saw Morgana sitting at the sliding door onto the back deck, nearly nose-to nose with a large fluffy cat.

I hadn't known she could be that loud, and I'm not sure she did either, but she apparently wasn't fond of what she considered intruders on her territory.

I finished the email and sent it off, then slipped outside, closing the door to keep Morgana sealed indoors. A rotund and stripy mass of orange fluff with a white chest and the jowls of a tomcat sidled up to me, ostentatiously ignoring Morgana's protests and purring loudly. He angled his head under my hand, so I scratched his chin, hoping Morgana would forgive me later. After a few minutes I started getting cold, so I regretfully stopped petting him and stood up. He walked over to the door as if he wanted to come in, but I said "No!" and gently pushed him away so I could get inside without him trailing me.

Once I was in, Morgana fixed me with those green eyes and said, loudly, "Miiiiinne!" I scootched down and petted her, saying , "Yes, this is your house. Yours and Merlin's." She seemed calmer, head-butted my hand once and stated, authoritatively, "Meerp!" before stalking off.

So I guess I'd been told off! If Morgana didn't like strange cats, she was even more resentful of other animals sauntering by *her* door, and that wasn't the last time I found myself levitating in startlement at a sudden scream, when unexpected guests visited the deck. At various times I saw possum, raccoons, nutria, and even skunks wander by. (The latter made me even more determined to keep the cats indoors until they developed a lot more sense!)

As spring wore on, ducks and geese came back and settled in the meadow between my house and dock. I'd seen geese threaten humans before, so I wondered how these would react when I started taking my kayak out again, but they seemed happy enough to get out of my way if I got anywhere near, even after little yellow balls of fluff hatched out and began following the adults around.

I managed to find time to go out mountain biking again a couple of times, once with Rob and once on my own, as I grew more confident. I really needed to buy a bike rack for my car, but at least there was an easy trail just outside town to practice on.

I spent a bit of time coming up with a short syllabus for Laxmi's training – mostly just a list of things I wanted to teach her, building on simple concepts. She had little interest in the sort of background magic spells I did, which wasn't unexpected for her age, but given her talent for music I made a note to myself to do a little research on spells that used music instead of poems or crystals for their spell-stores.

***

Spring also meant that it was finally time for Genna to go visit her husband Duncan in Scotland. Duncan's university's spring break lasted for three weeks, apparently, unlike the shorter breaks US universities took in spring. Genna planned to visit him for four weeks, starting in the last half of March: one week before his break to explore the local area around Aberdeen, then three weeks while he was off, to travel around Scotland together.

She'd booked her usual dog-sitter to walk the dogs, water the plants and check the mail; Menzy had promised to drop her off at the airport, so everything was ready for her to go. Even though she'd traveled alone before, she was busy as her departure approached, getting her house into spotless shape. Fortunately, it would just be time to plant her garden with annuals when she got home, so there wasn't much to do outside before she left, other than prune back her blueberries, and she'd done that in January.

Genna had certainly traveled alone before, but that had been a few years ago, back before the pandemic, and she seemed unexpectedly nervous. With more complaints about how much she needed to do than her actual preparations warranted, though, she was off. Duncan would meet her when she arrived, and we all knew she'd be glad to see him again.

Genna's discussion of her gardening plans had started me thinking about some gardening of my own; it was far from my favorite thing to do and I wasn't good at growing things, but any spell ingredients I could grow, I wouldn't have to buy. There were some ingredients, like clover, dandelions and poppies, that I wouldn't even need to plant; I knew there would be plenty of those behind my house. Or in the park nearby. If only blackberry had magical uses, I'd have been set, but unfortunately it was a magically neutral plant – except that it was hard to explain how fast it grew and multiplied, unless it used magic. I invested in a machete to deal with the blackberry bushes that kept coming back around the edges of the lake.

There were several half-barrels clustered beside the northeast corner of the house. It looked like maybe

Grandpa Ray had used them as planters, but now the willow in front of the house hid them from the street view, so I hauled some of those out back and set them along the side of my deck. I'd arranged to have some soil delivered, and hoped to plant mint, vervain, and rosemary in them, which should all be easy enough even for me to grow. I'd also pick up some flower baskets I could hang along the deck railing on the other side.

Behind where the barrels had stood, there was an odd gate, or grate, or something, made of some kind of black metal and wood and set into the foundation. As far I could tell, it didn't open out, so maybe it was just some sort of ornament. It seemed to be attached firmly to the foundation and clearly wasn't doing any harm, so I left it there.

***

I'd stored the kayak under a tarp on the other, more sheltered, side of my house for the winter. Now I took it out, hosed it off, and took it down to the dock. I tied it down so it wouldn't blow off the dock when spring storms came through, and started going out in it whenever we had a nice day.

I still liked doing some spellwork from the kayak, whenever I had spells to create that didn't require any tools and that could be stored in a spell-store that could get wet – either in a crystal, or in written verses that I carefully sealed in a plastic bag. Or virtual spells that could go on my phone, which I always took out in the boat for safety anyway, safe in a waterproof case that would float if it ever did fall in the lake. I stuck with spells that only required my voice to create, since my hands were busy padding.

I added kayaking to Laxmi's training syllabus too; I felt strongly attuned to water, so for me spells worked well any time I had the lake under me. This summer, I'd teach Laxmi to paddle and that way, she could try it and see whether that worked for her. And if she wasn't more effective on the water, at least she'd know how to kayak! Water-proofing kids is always a good idea for safety's sake anyhow. Hmm, speaking of safety, she'd need a lifejacket. I thought I had an old one that might cinch down small enough for her. If not, I'd ask her dad if they had kid-sized ones, or I'd buy one or maybe a couple of widely adjustable ones, just to have in case of future visitors.

I was also feeling spells go more and more smoothly in the house; I'd adjusted by now to the higher energy levels, and my spells' power levels were predictable enough now that I felt comfortable easing back to my previous, less rigorous, testing protocols.

***

Of course Gil and I had continued to talk about the idea of him moving in here. We both knew that it couldn't be as easy as just moving him in with me; much as I loved my house, it was just too small for the two of us. We'd both been living on our own for years, and we were set in our ways. The absolute last thing either of us wanted was to relive the arguments that had made us decide to live apart in the first place. I thought that we'd each need spaces of our own that we could escape to – not necessarily when we were fighting, but any time we wanted quiet, or to be alone, or just to spread our stuff out where it wouldn't be in anyone's way.

We talked it over and decided there were three alternatives: either we could add on to my house, Gil could buy his own house nearby or we could buy a bigger house together. Over several phone calls and texts, we talked out each of the options to figure out their pros and cons.

I told him, "I like the idea of adding on to my house in theory, but then I'd have contractors in every day for *months*. I'd probably have to rent a workspace somewhere to get away from the noise, and where would I find a setup like I had now, with my lab and office together? Plus my house would be open to the elements for all that time, so it wouldn't be all that comfortable to live in even when they weren't working."

He responded, "It would take a while even before we even got to all of that – there would be lots of planning, and we'd have to find a trustworthy contractor."

"And from what I've heard, any remodeling that opens up the house might cost almost as much as a whole new house."

"Hm. So it would be simplest just to buy a new house big enough for both of us."

I frowned, though of course he couldn't see me. "The big problem with that is that I don't want to move! I love where I live. I love living right on the water – both for having the view from inside the house and on the deck, and for being able to keep my kayak on my own dock. And I love the house itself. It fits me so perfectly, especially after rearranging things and painting those walls." What I didn't say was that more and more I was beginning to feel that it liked me in return, somehow.

Gil asked, "What if we just get another lakefront house? We can decorate it however we want, together."

"The problem is, I don't think we can."

I knew already that there were no lakefront houses for sale in this town, and the other lakes nearby didn't have houses on them at all. It was clear this house wouldn't fit the two of us so well; more space really was needed – even just one more room would help, and maybe some storage space. But I didn't want to leave here!

Honestly, if Gil had scoffed at my feelings about leaving this house, the whole issue would have been moot, because we wouldn't be moving in together at all. But he took them seriously, and I loved him for it – in fact, it was one of the reasons I had hope that maybe we really had mellowed and could live happily together now. Anyway, he loved my house too. He was happy about moving in with my cats, too; he'd mentioned getting a dog as well, but I was OK with that, as long as he could get Merlin and Morgana on board with the idea!

Buying a separate house for Gil would solve all the problems of the other options, but then we wouldn't be living together. We'd get to see each other a lot more than we did now, and we'd have all the space we needed, but I didn't think he'd be entirely happy with that idea. He'd said he wanted us to sleep together every night and wake up together every morning. Still, there was nothing to prevent us doing that, at either house. And if we ever felt like we'd had a bit too much togetherness, we could always choose not to sleep together on any given night. I thought this was probably the best of our three possibilities.

I'd be visiting him soon, so we agreed to wait and talk through our options and opinions, and what kind of space we each needed, when we were face to face.

CHAPTER TWENTY-ONE: FURTHER DEVELOPMENTS ON ALL FRONTS

Now that I'd been living with these fuzzballs for several months, I'd realized how much I'd forgotten about living with cats. For example, there is the part where you will never again get an unbroken night's sleep, between the bedtime in-your-face snuggling (which I don't mind, as long as it doesn't involve claws in any bare skin); the midnight yowl when someone realizes they're lonely and wants company; and the three AM zoomies.

Last time I'd had cats, though, I hadn't worked at home. So I had a whole new list of affectionate feline behaviors to learn, like the way they try to help with keyboard ergonomics by keeping your wrists warm and supple...by laying *on* your hands while you're trying to type. They also 'helped' with my lab work, though I have no idea how they always seemed to shed right by the heating register, where the fine hairs would be caught by the breeze from the vent and wafted into any potion I might be mixing. There is probably a reason why "Bring Your Cat to Work Day" is not a thing in chemistry labs.

There had been a while when Morgana liked to sit on the back of my desk chair and would sometimes purr so loudly that my customers or suppliers could hear her during our online meetings – since I lived alone, I rarely used headphones. When I had the camera on, she'd even poke her head up to say hi, and to try to figure out what all those faces on the screen were doing. They seemed to like her; two or three times, a shipment from one of my suppliers arrived packaged with an added cat toy "for your assistant".

The cats also liked to play with my tablet. A few times, I'd been injudicious enough to load up and let them play on it with a cat game, designed to entice cats to tap the tablet screen with their paws, to draw on the screen or chase an animated fish. The lesson they'd taken from that was that tablets were fun, and any time I was working on mine it was fair game for them to join in.

Despite minor annoyances, I loved being owned by a pair of cantankerous cats. Odd creaks from the house in the middle of the night or dark shadows in the edges of my peripheral vision no longer worried me, because I just assumed it was the cats and not a roof shingle blowing off or an intruder sneaking in. When I went out, they trotted to the door with me and welcomed me back in, and I'm completely sure it was because they missed me and not at all to see if they could sneak outside. Definitely, completely sure.

I'd swear the house liked the cats too; there always seemed to be a warm spot on the floor conveniently near where I was sitting or working, and any time I happened to shut an interior door, it seemed that it hadn't quite latched properly if a cat happened to want to push it open (which is one reason I couldn't just keep them out of my lab and office, in addition to the inevitable yowling). Mostly this just meant they were able to push a door open, but a few times I saw one working claws into the gap where a door opened toward them and pulling it open enough to slip through. Fortunately the house seemed to agree with me that the cats should stay inside, because this never happened with the external doors – or maybe I was just more careful to close them firmly.

The cats' determination to get in anywhere they wanted, and the house's evident inclination to let them, did have some unfortunate results. More than once I tracked down the source of some distant yowling, to find that one of them had pushed their way into a room or closet, leaned on the door, and gotten themselves stuck inside. (I wasn't sure why the house wouldn't let me shut the cats in a room, but was perfectly happy to let them do it to themselves. Maybe the house had a sense of humor?)

As it got warmer, I kept trying to take Merlin for walks. Morgana never did take to wearing a harness, but Merlin didn't seem to mind it – he not only didn't run away when I took it out, he'd purr the whole time I buckled him into it.

I'd seen a post online somewhere from a woman who took her cat out kayaking, but I decided to hold off on buying a kitty life jacket, because Merlin wanted absolutely nothing to do with the lake. I carried him to the dock a couple of times, but he'd struggle to get away as we got close to the gangway, then once I stepped onto it, he'd hold on like Velcro and try to burrow into my shoulder, using claws for traction – ouch. So I was on my own for water sports.

Still, he was growing more comfortable on the leash, and I hoped he would at least learn to recognize our front and back doors, in case he did get out again.

***

One day while I was working in the office and the cats were batting a ball around in a sunbeam nearby, an order came in from my favorite customer and former landlord, Meg, with a note attached.

> **Meg:** Hey, I've got a two-week business trip to Portland coming up at the end of April, so I'll have a free weekend in the middle. Any chance I could come down and visit on Saturday the 30th, see what you've done with the house and meet your feline coworkers? I can take you out to dinner or bring food over, if you tell me where to get it, then I can stay in Eugene and head back Sunday, maybe hike up the Butte before driving back or hit a winery near Salem along the way.

I'd known Meg for so long that she was more of a friend than just a work contact, so I promptly replied,

> **Macrina:** I don't have any plans for this weekend,

and I'd love to catch up with you – but don't be silly about a hotel in Eugene, of course you should stay here with me, in your grandfather's old house!

Macrina: Oh, almost forgot – you aren't allergic to cats, are you?

Meg: Nope, and I'll enjoy meeting yours – I saw their photos on your holiday cards.

That would give me some motivation to get the house ready for guests. Food would be easy; we could eat in town or get pizza, and I could get a spread of bagels and flavored cream cheese for breakfast. I had plenty of coffee, both regular and decaf, and several different teas, so we'd be set. I also had some wine still left from my purchases on the tasting trip with Gil, but we'd see how the supply was as her visit grew closer – I could always buy more if needed. (I really should get around to joining one of those wine clubs, but I wanted to visit a few more wineries first.)

I also wanted to do some more decorating before Meg's visit. The house felt much more welcoming with the new colors I'd added in autumn, and I'd gotten all my old treasures out and displayed them around the house. I'd recently found a few items tucked in the back of a kitchen cupboard that must have belonged to Grandpa Ray: a pair of surprisingly heavy brass candlesticks and a goblet that seemed to match them. Funny, because I'd been through all the cabinets in this house, I thought, but I hadn't seen those until now. I polished them as best I could and set them on display over the fireplace so I'd remember to ask Meg if she wanted them.

***

So the inside was in good shape, only needing some last-minute cleaning and tidying, but I wanted to do more outside. Meg's visit was well-timed – I'd needed a spur to get some things planted, and this was the right time of year for it. Local plant sales were popping up everywhere: at the commercial nurseries, of course, but also at the schools, the town's grange, the local arboretum...I visited a few and managed to pick up starts of some of the herbs I wanted and even some hot pepper slips (the latter were intended for eating, not for magic spells) as well as a few bags of soil. I spent the next afternoon getting them all planted in several of the half barrels I'd found beside the house and moved to the back deck. While I was at the plant sales, I also picked up three hanging baskets with vervain and nasturtium for spells, and petunias that I hoped would attract hummingbirds.

I wanted some art outside too, so I visited the Saturday Market, which had now reopened at full scale after being closed for the pandemic, and picked up a wind chime and a wind spinner, plus a gazing ball on a pedestal that I wanted to place along my path to the water, where it would be a focal point to reflect the lake and sky. I considered a swing seat, but decided not to get that this year.

I remembered I had an old hammock somewhere, though, and was able to find a couple of trees between my house and the water that were just the right distance apart. This wasn't something that I'd necessarily use with company, but I could see myself spending a lot of happy summer hours reading there.

The deck hadn't been washed for a while, and I didn't want to buy a pressure washer. But the same neighborhood app where we'd formed the George group was full of people advertising all kinds of home services, so I found a local high school kid who would bring their own pressure washer (well, probably their parents' pressure washer) and clean my deck and dock for a reasonable fee.

The house was starting to look very much my own, and I looked forward to seeing what Meg would think of it.

***

Once that was all done, I left for another visit to Gil
– just a short one this time, under a week. Spring was a
busy time of year, as clients bought spells to accelerate
their plants' growth, so I couldn't be away from my lab for
too long. Sulis volunteered to watch my cats again, saying
how much she'd enjoyed them. She wouldn't need to
water any of my outdoor plants, since it was still raining
most days, and the indoor ones wouldn't need to be
watered until my return. After she'd watched the cats at
Christmas, I'd asked her to hang onto my house key so
there was always someone who had a spare key just in
case.

I did take one additional precaution, though, before
I left. Really, that whole incident with the dust had been a
little embarrassing, as if one of the pets she was watching
had behaved badly. She had the key and knew where
everything was now, so there was no other reason for her
to come over before I left – but I asked her to stop by just in
case.

She rang the bell, and both cats raced to the door.
How did they know it was someone they liked? I didn't
have to worry about them running out this time – they
both stayed right by Sulis's feet, sniffing at her as if they
were trying to learn where she'd been since her last visit.

"Hey, Sulis, thanks for coming over! Come on in.
Want something to drink?"

"No, I just stopped over on my way out to do some
errands. No problem. What did you want to show me?"

"Not show you, exactly, just – well, don't laugh. I
walked her over to the middle of the floor and said firmly,
"House! This is Sulis. You know her. I will be leaving
tomorrow and I'll be gone five days, then I will come
back." I held up five fingers, though I doubted the house
had any way of looking at me, then went on. "Please be
nice to Sulis. She will take care of you, Morgana and
Merlin. " Sulis giggled.

"I told you not to laugh," I said, grumpily.

"I'm not laughing at you. That was probably a good

idea. But you have to admit the dust thing was funny."
"Oh, *fine*."

***

Gil picked me up at the airport and took me to his apartment. It was around 8 by the time we got there, but he had very cleverly pre-prepped all the ingredients for burritos, so that we only had to re-heat the meat and microwave the tortillas for a few seconds.

As we ate, he said, "I'll make you steaks tomorrow night."

"Are you trying to impress me with your usefulness around the house?"

"Is it working?"

"Actually...yes. These are delicious, and I already know how good your steaks are."

"Then yes, I am."

He paused to take a big bite, chewed and swallowed, then asked, "Do you want to start talking about what we want out of a house tonight?"

I said, "Do you realize this is our fourth time seeing each other since the year we spent apart?"

"Yes, but is that connected?"

"Sort of. I think four visits is enough to have established a new tradition."

"We have a new tradition?"

"Yes," I said firmly, "We have a 'first night of the visit' tradition now. Our tradition is that we spend the first night of every visit...not talking."

"Oh. I'm good with that. One more question, though.

"What's that?"

"Is moaning allowed?"

"It's encouraged."

***

The next day was a Friday so we both worked all day, but that night over *fantastic* steaks and a big salad, we did talk about what we wanted and needed in a house.

Gil asked, "Do you need any more space than you have now?"

"Hmmm. I don't think so. More storage is always nice, but on the other hand it might just convince me to keep more stuff I don't need."

"And what rooms are you OK with me sharing?"

"You mean in my current house, or in a theoretical bigger one?"

"Let's talk about your current house for now – I think it will be easier to visualize."

"I think I can manage to tolerate you in my bedroom."

"Glad to hear it. Am I allowed in your kitchen too, or do I have to have my meals out back?"

"Depends," I cracked. "Are you going to keep cooking for me like this?"

"At least when it's my turn to cook. We're going to need to have a lot of discussion about who does what, I think – better to talk it out than to find a year later that one of us has been quietly pissed off for months. Anyway, so I get to share the kitchen. I feel like we're making progress here."

I gave him the most exaggerated, sulky-teenager eyeball my middle-aged eyeballs could muster. "I guess, if I have to, I can share the living room and dining room too." I dropped the snarky tone and quit joking. "I really don't think either of us could work together if we shared an office, and you know I need my lab space. But those two rooms are the whole attic floor, aside from a small storage area. If I want to do crafts or have a quiet place to read or whatever, there's plenty of room for me up there. I'm fine with sharing the whole rest of the house, but I don't think that storage area is nearly enough for an office for you, plus it's open to the lab."

"I agree," he said. "But we should still keep a spare bedroom, in case we want or need to have company – and that room is really a little small if I want space for hobbies or anything *but* work. Plus, you don't have a garage at all, do you?"

"No, just a little covered area where I keep my kayak, and a tiny shed for lawn tools and soil and stuff."

"If I'm going to bring my convertible to Oregon, I'd really like to keep it in a garage," he said, wistfully.

"You do know it rains for three quarters of the year and then it's smoky for another month, right? You won't be able to put the top down much."

"I know. See how much I love you? I'm giving up the wind in my hair, just for you."

"You did say you were getting a bald spot," I said, heartlessly. "I'm just protecting you from skin cancer!"

"Anyway, so that's my wishlist. A home office big enough to have a comfortable reading chair or hobby area, and a garage." He was hit by a thought then. "What about building a detached office? Like maybe a separate garage with a loft area over it? Then if we don't need offices later on, we could think about making it into a rental."

"Maybe. That would be a lot better than cutting into my house!"

We talked about it some more throughout the rest of my visit, and agreed that we'd each do some research: I'd find out what would be entailed in expanding my house or building a separate structure, and he'd look at real estate listings in the area to see if there was anything available that would work for one or both of us at all. If he found something, I could always go look at it and report back.

We wrote each other notes, too, after I got back home, using the message boards I'd given him for Christmas to keep a running wishlist of what we'd each like to have in a house. I talked about wanting good light and plenty of bookshelf space, while he commented that he'd love to have three bathrooms (one apiece and one that was always pristine for guests) and to *finally* have a big enough pantry in the kitchen. It was a lot of fun to generate ideas for our dream house, though we knew we wouldn't be likely to get everything we wanted.

CHAPTER TWENTY-TWO: IT TAKES A VILLAGE

I'd been following along with Genna's travels in Scotland via her Facebook posts; she'd been posting fabulous photos of nearby standing stones Duncan's colleagues told her about, as well as cobbled streets and stone buildings in Old Aberdeen. She seemed to be having a great time and was looking forward to doing some longer driving trips once Duncan's break started.

On the day after I got back home, we were all shocked to see a message on the George forum from Duncan, posting on Genna's behalf:

> **Genna:** Duncan here. Genna asked me to tell you that she's broken her leg. It's a bad one: she'll be wearing a cast and not allowed to put any weight on that foot for up to a couple of months. We're not sure yet what will happen next, but she's got great medical care.
>
> **Macrina:** Oh, no! Please tell her we will keep her in our thoughts, and pass on our wishes for speedy healing.
>
> **Brigid:** ^What she said.
>
> **Andrew:** Nell and I will be praying for quick healing, and minimal pain.

Everyone else chimed in with their concern for Genna, and Duncan was great about keeping us updated as the situation evolved. She had a spiral fracture of her tibia and was kept in the hospital for a week, for surgery and recuperation. There was a lot of confusion about who was paying for it – I never got that whole story, but eventually the various insurance companies involved settled it among themselves, with a strong push from the university, so Duncan and Genna weren't going to be out of pocket for much.

The problem was where she'd convalesce; she'd be in a cast for weeks. They'd put a metal rod in her leg and she wouldn't be allowed to put any weight on it until the bone grew around the rod. She'd be using first a walker, then crutches, for eight weeks or more. She could take medical leave from her own job, but if she stayed with Duncan in Aberdeen, she'd be not only housebound, but possibly stuck living on one floor for weeks – the quarters they'd given him were on the second and third floor of a picturesque old building. So she'd need to either sleep on a cot in the living room or else sit in the bedroom all day, until she could handle stairs. (She told us later that getting her into the flat in the first place required calling in several of Duncan's stronger students and was not a lot of fun.) If they came home to their own house, it was all on one floor, but then he'd have to give up the visiting professorship.

Once Genna herself was back online, out of the hospital, and able to use a walker, she lobbied hard for going home, claiming that she'd be fine on her own if Duncan just stayed for the first week since her house had only one floor and no stairs inside or out. Picturing the difficulty of even making a pot of tea while needing both hands on her walker, I winced. There was discussion of nursing homes, or of trying to find alternate housing in Aberdeen that might be more walker friendly.

***

It was Menzy who came up with a solution:

Menzy: What if Duncan stayed until the end of his break, then we set up a rota to help out? We can help with cleaning, cooking, and whatever else she needs. She's got a fenced yard, luckily; if she can manage to let the dogs in and out of the house a few times a day, her dog walkers can come to exercise them. If enough of us pitch in, it wouldn't be too much work for any one person.

Macrina: someone would need to keep track of who's doing what, so she doesn't get her house cleaned two days in a row and then not for another two weeks!

Brigid: OK, so what is needed? And most importantly, while she's using the walker, can she get to the bathroom on her own?

Genna: Bathroom: Yes, thank God. And it would probably only be dinners; I could manage cereal or yogurt for breakfast, and simple stuff for lunch. But it would be a ton of work, and I couldn't ask it of you all – this will go on for a couple of months. I really appreciate the offer, though!

Menzy: I think we can do it. And look, we live in a small town in an earthquake zone. We have to take care of each other! This is good practice. I don't mind being the one to set up and maintain the rota.

Rob: I can help out with any first aid needs – changing bandages or whatever.

Cayden: What about getting the house set up? Grab rails, that kind of thing. I'm a pretty good carpenter.

Sulis: Menzy and I could handle weekly cleaning together – you'd be amazed what the two of us can do with an old-fashioned twig broom and some water!

Brigid: What else? She'd need dinners brought over, and probably at least one person to check in daily to do stuff like loading and unloading the dishwasher, if she can't bend over. And just for company. And she can have groceries delivered, but someone would need to bring in the bags and put stuff away.

Rob: Once she's able to take showers, someone should probably be there while she does, in case she falls.

Macrina: I like cooking things like chili or stew – I could make a bunch of frozen meals she'd just need to reheat. Also, I work from home and I work for myself – I can be the contact person if anything comes up where she needs help but not emergency services.

Brigid: And maybe some nights, a few of us could just make dinner over at Genna's and eat together. It would be fun – hey, we could all hang out at her place instead of Antlers on Wednesdays!

Menzy: I'll bring the wine!

Genna: You guys are the absolute best.

***

Everyone wanted to help Genna. I hadn't even realized Deb, the older blonde lady from our first meeting, was still in the online group, but she chimed in now – maybe someone told her to log in. She explained the situation to others at her church, and they promised to make some casseroles and cakes to help fill Genna's freezer for the first few weeks. A few of Genna's neighbors and coworkers volunteered to help as well. Andrew and Nell lived only a block away, and their kids Oliver and Charli offered to come over and play with the dogs after school as well as fetching anything Genna needed when they visited.

Duncan would fly home with her and stay three weeks – in view of the situation, his colleagues would take over some of his classes to give him an extra week off.

I realized, once again, that I needed to quit making assumptions about people; somehow I would not have expected a dryad to be a great organizer, but Menzy did a phenomenal job setting up the rota and making sure someone was covering every slot.

While Duncan was there, we'd mostly come over for company, but once he had to leave, we'd swing into full action.

Menzy and Sulis insisted on signing up to do the cleaning once a week. I made stews and chili and sealed them into one-serving packets, and also volunteered to take Genna's Labs to the dog park three times a week, so she wouldn't need to pay dog walkers every day; Oliver and Charli would help tire them out, but they were still a bit small to take two high-energy dogs for longer walks. I'd been meaning to do more walking myself, anyway. Genna could let them out into the yard in the morning and evening, but the Labs needed more exercise so they wouldn't be too rambunctious around her.

In addition to the kids' daily visits to play with the dogs, at least one adult was signed up to visit every day after Duncan left, and we'd have "dinner parties" a couple times a week taking turns to cook in Genna's kitchen, as well as the Wednesday night gatherings at Genna's instead of Antlers.

We'd ease into those dinners; Genna wasn't sure when she'd be off painkillers and pointed out that at present, she was barely managing to stay awake through dinner.

***

Menzy coordinated Genna's homecoming, too. While she was still in Aberdeen, Cayden and I got into Genna's house (Duncan had instructed the dog walkers to

let us in, since they had keys) and installed grab bars in
both bathrooms. Or rather Cayden did; I was grunt labor
to pass parts to him and provide extra hands when
needed. Nell and Andrew had a small RV, and even had a
ramp to get into it, left over from when Nell's late mother
had traveled with them. They and Rob would pick Genna
and Duncan up from the airport, so Genna wouldn't have
to cram herself and her walker into a car. Then they'd drop
Genna off with me for a couple of hours because the main
floor of my house was all on a level and there were no
stairs at the entry, while Cayden and Duncan rearranged
furniture in her house to make sure she had wide
pathways with no obstructions.

I'd never thought too much about accessibility, but
this all made me look at my own house in a new light. As I
said, the main living area had no stairs, and also had no
narrow hallways in case I ever needed to use a walker or
wheelchair. My doors already had lever-style handles
instead of doorknobs. The house was at least fifty years
old, but Meg had had it checked by an electrician. All the
wiring was up to present-day code, and the electrical
systems had apparently been redone at some point because
all my switches were the modern rocker style instead of
older ones that could be harder to use with arthritis or
hand injuries. Even the showers had handles that were
easy to use, not the kind that needed a firm grip and lots of
finger strength, and I wondered if maybe Grandpa Ray
himself had had a touch of arthritis, and had remodeled
accordingly to make things easier for himself.

If a time ever came when I couldn't handle stairs, I
wouldn't be able to climb up to my lab and office, but at
least I could use all of the living space. This was definitely
a house I could easily imagine living the rest of my life in.
For now, I pushed aside thoughts about whether I'd be
living here on my own, or with Gil, and focused on getting
ready for Genna's visit. Not much was needed, since she
wouldn't be staying long; I just moved the coffee table
aside to make it easier to get to the sofa, and put a lap
blanket and pillow ready in case she was tired after her

long flight.

In fact, she was not only tired but groggy; they must have given her some stronger pain relievers for the flight. So I didn't try to make conversation, just let Duncan help her visit my bathroom, then gave her a bottle of water, asked if she wanted anything to eat (she didn't) and settled down with my own book while she napped on the sofa. The house was very quiet; even the cats seemed to know not to jump on Genna or wake her up, and just curled up next to me for their own naps until Duncan and Cayden came back to fetch Genna and take her home.

She was much livelier the next day, though, once they'd gotten her into her own house and she'd had a good night's sleep. Of course everyone wanted to check in, so we coordinated and spread our visits over the next few days.

Menzy and Sulis were the first to visit, because they wanted to try something. Genna had told us, way back at our first meeting, that she had naiads and dryads in her family tree, so they wanted to try their healing on her and see whether it would help.

"The problem with broken bones," as Menzy said later, "is that they're not like wounds. You can't just look at them and see if they look any better."

When Rob had heard about the healing plan, he'd warned Genna to stay off the leg even if the healing did seem to work. "Better wait til the doctor checks it," he'd said. "No point healing your leg and then re-breaking it because it wasn't better enough to put weight on."

So Genna had to wait until the next appointment with her doctor to know whether the healing had worked, but Menzy and Sulis both felt they'd had some effect, and Genna herself said she thought it was hurting less. Genna told us about it the next day when Brigid and I both visited, as well as telling us the whole story about how she'd broken her leg.

"Stepped off a curb wrong in the city and got tangled with a bicycle," she said with disgust. "I didn't even manage to trip on a cobblestone or the uneven stairs of a ruined castle, much less while doing anything in the least exciting. I think I'm going to tell people I met the Highlander and he challenged me to a sword duel, and I fell while parrying his lunge. Or at the very least, that I fell while climbing a mountain on Skye or stepping over a peat burn on Islay, not while I was crossing a street with the light at a marked pedestrian crossing!"

Brigid stayed with her to chat some more, while Duncan and I went out in the backyard with the dogs. I'd met them before at Genna's house, at her Friendsgiving dinner and since then, but Duncan wanted to make sure they were comfortable enough with me to behave well on walks, so I called them to me, put their collars and leashes on, and we walked around the block. They clearly knew something odd was happening and seemed more subdued than usual, but there was just one problem.

Duncan said, "I think they know Genna is unhappy or ill and they want to console her – they keep wanting to come up on the sofa with her! At least they haven't tried to sit on her lap, like they did when they were younger and hadn't realized they weren't puppy-sized anymore, but even if they just sit next to her they can jostle her. So we're not letting them up on the sofa at all until her leg starts to knit."

Since Genna was able to invoke small spells, I'd brought along a present – a spell I'd bought from an old college friend who specialized in medical spells and equipment, stored in a small metal spring for symbolism, to help boost her up into the walker. I knew that later on she'd be better off using her own muscles to get up with crutches and then a cane, but for now, while her leg needed to stay as still as possible, this would help her get up more easily.

A few days later, Rob and Duncan helped Genna climb into the car for a checkup with her own doctor. She was thrilled when the doctor checked her X-rays and confirmed that the healing from Menzy and Sulis had indeed sped up her recovery. According to Genna and Duncan, the doctor, who had had naiad patients before, had said that she looked like she'd been healing for more than a month instead of under three weeks, and that she, the doctor, only wished this could be done for all of her patients. With luck, she thought that Genna might be able to switch from the walker to crutches a few weeks sooner than expected.

CHAPTER TWENTY-THREE: HOME MATTERS

When I wasn't at work or walking Genna's dogs, I did the research I'd promised Gil I'd do. Getting construction permits, whether for an expansion or a separate building, looked complicated. If I found a good general contractor, they'd take care of a lot of that for me, but looking for one reminded me of what friends had told me about being pregnant or needing surgery: once people found out you were in that situation, they all wanted to tell you their horror stories. I heard about GCs who ghosted their clients, workers who only turned up when they felt like it, contractors who did shoddy work and had to be sued in long-drawn-out court cases. I was confident they couldn't all be that bad or no one would ever remodel their house, but finding a good one was beginning to look like a crapshoot.

I spoke to Nell and Andrew, who had built a tiny home for Nell's mother behind their house several years before. They reassured me that it wasn't always the kind of nightmare I'd been hearing about, but also warned me that the cost of building materials had been rising dramatically.

Worse, I looked at the city's rules, and it appeared that I would need to get a special variance to be able to get a permit to build at all. My house was within city limits, and much of the land between me and the lake couldn't be built on at all due to Federal rules. The house parcel was governed by city rules that demanded easements between a house and the borders of its land, and my house, small as it was, was already close to the limits. It was beginning to look like I'd either have to add a story to the house and raise the roof, which would be very expensive, or build the garage in front of the house, blocking it from the street. If I did that, it would block the light from my front windows in the morning, and I wasn't sure if it would look odd. Also, it would have to be small, barely big enough for one car and a matching space above.

I told Gil all the bad news on our nightly phone call, and he comforted me. "They do variances to those building codes all the time – we'd just need to talk to a contractor and find out how rigid your City Council's Building Committee is. And I know it would be expensive, but after all, the other option is buying an entire house. If we can afford that, and you know we can, we can afford to remodel yours."

I spared a thought to whether the house might have an opinion on being cut up and changed, but that wasn't a question I wanted to talk about inside its walls... just in case it threw another dust-storm hissy fit. Or had its feelings hurt (if it had feelings). I wasn't sure which would be worse.

***

I didn't tell Gil why, but I didn't discuss the other options in our housing dilemma on the phone at all. I hoped he didn't notice that I kept that chat to text and email only. Don't ask me why; he'd been nothing but supportive about magical matters, even those he didn't understand, as long as I'd known him. I just felt silly worrying about hurting a house's feelings.

Gil sent me the listings of four houses for sale and asked me to take a look at them. There were two in each category – two for him to live in, and two that he thought might work for the two of us together. I really didn't want to sign up with a real estate agent at this stage – for one thing, if we decided not to buy I was sure they'd be checking back with me forever, saying "I just wondered if you're ready to buy now? No?" and then a few months later, "How about now?" – but luckily all four had open houses over the next couple of weeks.

The first house was only a block away from mine. I

could tell by looking at it what Gil had in mind; superficially it looked a lot like mine, with two bedrooms and a cottage-y style. It might have been built around the same time. But this one hadn't had the same loving care Grandpa Ray gave to my house. The kitchen hadn't been updated and there was a vague smell of mildew in the bathrooms. The attic was smaller than mine and unfinished, just room to store a few boxes. A few of the lights were in ill-chosen places, and it became apparent that the photos of this house had been taken on a very sunny day by a very clever photographer to make it look bright and cozy.

Gil was out with his friends that night so I didn't talk to him, but in our call the next night, I told him, "I'm afraid that house might take almost as much work as building an addition on to mine, just to make it into something you'd want to live in."

"What about the second house? You saw one of the big ones today, right?"

"Complete opposite. This one was a palace."

"Oh? That's good, right?"

"Well...It's a mile down a dirt road, and it's on fifty acres. There's a smaller second house, but the main one is 3000 square feet, and it's beautiful and in perfect shape."

"That sounds like a lot of house for what they're asking. What's wrong with it?"

"Nothing, if you want a preppers' compound. Or a commune. It's off the grid, runs entirely on solar and diesel generator. There's a well, which they assure me has reliable flow year-round, and about an acre of garden. There's a pantry with shelves and shelves of home-canned food."

"Oh."

"Yes, oh. The house is wonderful. It's us, Gil. We are the problem. I don't think we are up to living in that house!"

"No, I see what you mean. We're not exactly 'live off the land' types, are we?"

***

The next two open houses were a few days later, but no better.

I told Gil "The big house has all the room we need, and is brand new…"

"I can hear a 'but' coming. Go ahead, Meli, get it off your chest."

"But…it's pretty much charm-free. Builder spec, builder quality, everything as generic as it can be. It doesn't feel like a home."

"You don't think it will be better once we have our own furniture in it?"

I was doubtful. "Maybe, but I think it would be difficult. Also, it has plenty of space, but it's not a great layout. The downstairs rooms are all open to each other, so you couldn't have a separate office there, and the bedrooms upstairs are small. I don't think I could easily have a lab in any of those rooms, either."

"What about the other small house?"

"Sorry to be such a downer, but I didn't like that one either. It felt like it was built out of cardboard – it looked good in photos, but the house felt like it would blow down in a high wind."

"So you don't think any of them would work for us at all?

"Well, you might be right that we could add some charm to the second big house, but even so, we'd still need to do some remodeling there, to combine some of the bedrooms and plumb in a lab."

"And if we have to do remodeling anyway, we might as well do it to the house you already love – *if* we can get an exemption from the easement rules."

"Maybe I should just start researching contractors, and meanwhile we can wait to see if anything better comes onto the market."

He said, softly, "I'm sorry."

I was surprised. "For what?"

"I just wanted to be able to live with you and have

you in my arms every night. I didn't mean to make your life more complicated!"

I laughed so hard I couldn't talk for a moment. "You didn't want to make my life more complicated? You? When have you ever done anything else?"

"No fair. I can't pout at you over the phone."

"Never mind. You're worth the hassle, anyway." I paused. "I think I really do want to live with you, Gil. I'm just scared, because it went so badly years and years ago. I want us to have the perfect house this time, because I want this to work out."

"I know. And don't worry, I trust us. I don't know what we'll end up doing, but I know we'll find a way to make it work."

CHAPTER TWENTY-FOUR: THE VILLAGE PITCHES IN

We'd all been dropping over Genna's house now and then for the past couple of weeks, to keep her company and give Duncan any help he needed, but he'd been taking care of her without needing too much help. Now he had to go back to Scotland, but at least Genna was back to her usual self, organizing everything around her. She took the rota back over from Menzy, with much gratitude, so that at least she could feel she was running her own schedule. Rob firmly cautioned her not to try anything her doctors wouldn't allow, reminding her that she wouldn't want to set her recovery back.

"Don't go by feel. If you overdo it, you might not feel the pain until it's already too late. And be extra careful any time you're moving around, especially with the dogs in the house!"

But she was able to order her own groceries and grab food for breakfast and lunch, as long as it was stored high enough in the fridge, freezer or pantry that she didn't have to bend over much. She couldn't load and unload the dishwasher without help, but she could wash dishes by hand, leaning on the counter edge. I was really enjoying walking her dogs a few times a week – it was a bit warmer by now, so I'd just put on my rubber boots and rain jacket and be perfectly comfortable walking them, whatever the weather, and it got me out of the house on rainy days.

After the walk, when the dogs were calmer, we'd sit and chat while I knit on a lightweight summer pullover project and Genna crocheted toys. She'd given a few to Oliver and Charli but they were getting too old to want anything more than a little mascot to hang on a backpack, so she was building up a stash to be donated for a community project that gave out toys to local kids at Christmas. She told me it did help to feel that at least she could do something useful while she was stuck on the sofa. She also reported that she was making great inroads through her 'to-be-read' pile of books, which had been growing for years. On sunny days, though, Genna still was mourning the loss of the garden she never got to plant this year. She probably wouldn't be short on fresh produce, anyway; I was sure she'd be receiving more produce than she could handle once her friends' and neighbors' gardens were ready to yield fruits, herbs and vegetables.

We'd started having the 'dinner parties' Brigid had suggested, and those were fun! We kept them to two or three people, so that we could make a pot of something and still have leftovers to leave with Genna, and we took turns being the one to bring ingredients and cook the meal or the one to do cleanup (Genna could wash dishes now if she had to, but there was no reason she had to when we were there, especially since putting things away was still tricky for her). One day, Sulis and I were over there for dinner, for which I was trying out a new recipe I'd found that was basically a caprese salad: fresh mozzarella cheese, heirloom tomatoes and basil, with white beans added to make it a filling main course. (Some people don't like trying new recipes when cooking for other people, but I like living dangerously. Or at least, having my friends live dangerously!)

While I was mixing the salad, Genna said, "I just can't believe you all are doing all of this for me. I can't tell you how much I appreciate it, the company as well as the practical help."

Sulis told her, "We're having fun. You know it takes me and Menzy about twenty minutes total to clean your bathrooms and kitchen, once I get some water swirling around and she gets that broom going. It's made from fir twigs, so as a fir dryad she can control it – it's like watching that Disney clip with Mickey Mouse as the wizard's apprentice! And Macrina here loaned one of her robo-vacs, since we couldn't do that part with water and a broom."

Genna replied, "And it's so much fun, having the kids visit every day to play with the dogs. They've showed up every single day, and even brought friends over a couple of times. I don't think I've spent enough time with kids for years now, and I've enjoyed having them around. The dogs really love it. "

"So do the kids," I called over. "Andrew told me that they'd been asking for a dog, and he and Nell weren't sure they'd be responsible enough to take care of one. Your dogs are giving them practice as well as evidence their parents can't argue with. They love taking care of yours."

Genna said, "Maybe, if Andrew and Nell do let them get their own dog once I'm better, it can have play dates with mine!"

The salad was ready by then – it didn't take long to make and if it tasted good, it was definitely going on my recipe list. Genna was still being careful about alcohol, since her body was healing and she still took the occasional pain pill, but Sulis uncorked the bottle of wine she'd brought and poured glasses for the two of us, as well as a tiny bit for Genna so she could feel like she was getting back to normal.

While we were eating, (with the dogs giving us big eyes, just in case someone might possibly be kind enough to share some food with them) Genna said, "I can't thank everybody enough for all this. Especially Menzy – she was the one who had the original idea, and she's done so much work pulling everyone together and organizing a schedule – I'd like to do something special for her, but I don't know what. Any ideas? I could have flowers sent, maybe."

Sulis' face was a picture. Clearly trying hard to be tactful, she asked, "Do you mean a bouquet made from cut flowers? That might not be the best thing."

"Really? I thought flowers since she's a gardener..."

"Yes, but she's a dryad too. Cut flowers would be dead, or at least dying. I think dying flowers would be distressful for her."

Now it was Genna whose expression was indescribable. "Oops. I guess I hadn't quite thought that through. Thanks, I'm glad I asked!"

I suggested, "You could go with a living plant, but she's got plenty of those. What about flowers in another form, like a book with photos of the world's great gardens, or one with native plants?"

Genna seemed relieved. "That does sound like a safer idea! Thanks."

***

The next time I was on the schedule to have dinner at Genna's, Brigid was the one doing the cooking. She brought a pizza stone over, and some dough she'd made the day before, and had us each make our own small pizzas, with an assortment of toppings to choose from.

While they were cooking in the oven, she told us how she'd learned to weld from some distant cousins who lived just south of Portland, and how they'd taught her to make pizza on a cast iron pizza "stone". "They've been in that area a long time, and there used to be some iron mines," she told us. They've got a history of all kinds of metalwork with that iron."

Genna told us about her physiotherapy, and that the bone was healing well and faster than expected, thanks to the healing from Menzy and Sulis. "I thought my dryad ancestry was so far back it wouldn't have much effect on my genome," she said, "but I guess you never know what traits will crop up down the line. Anyway, I'm just glad I'm dryad enough for healing magic to work on me, even if it is still slower than it would be on a full-blooded dryad!"

I recounted my recent visit to Gil, and summarized our discussions on housing. They sympathized, but didn't know of any more suitable houses in the area or GCs looking for new projects. Then Brigid mentioned that she'd started going to her parents' house for Sunday night dinner every few weeks. "I hadn't talked to them all that

much the last few years," she said, "because they'd been so
pushy about getting me married off, and then when I did
marry, they didn't like my partner. But I think her death
shocked them, and now they're really trying to behave
better. They even stopped my brothers from teasing me too
badly. I'm still not going there for dinner every single
week, like they'd want, though!" I took it from her careful
wording that she wasn't discussing her Sasquatch heritage
with most people, and felt privileged that she'd told me.

I also told them all about how Laxmi's training was
going, and how her parents had asked me to give her a
true view of my discipline, not only the fun parts. Genna,
professor that she was, instantly suggested an independent
study.

She said, "You said she was asking questions about
the difference between people who do spells and people
who are magic. What if you ask her to do a trial: learn a
spell or two herself, then teach it to someone who is magic
and see if they can do it? I'll volunteer myself to work with
her if you can't find anyone better, but I bet Menzy or Sulis
would be happy to do it."

"But it's not a new question," Brigid objected.
"Macrina just said that *she* doesn't know. I'm sure some
human scientists must have done studies on it, and of
course the other species would know even if they don't
talk about it widely!"

"Sure, but she's only eleven," rejoined Genna.
"That's a bit young to be required to add to the sum of
human knowledge. And if she does think to Google and
find the answer before doing her experiment, you can
commend her for doing her research. It's still good practice
for her to run the experiment on her own. And who
knows, working one on one, she might notice more details
about how things work than a larger study would find."

"I'll think about it," I said. "I still need to teach her
the basics, and I'm not sure she wants homework from this
apprenticeship."

Genna said, with complete confidence, "A chance to
do magic on her own? And to teach an adult? Trust me,

she'll love the idea."

***

Once Genna felt up to it and didn't need pain meds any longer, we implemented Brigid's other suggestion: Wednesday night drinks at Genna's house, which we rechristened Antlers Too. The first night we were there, everyone brought wine or beer, which ended up leaving Genna with several unopened bottles, which she put aside for the next week. The next day, though, Brigid posted on George:

> **Brigid:** How do you all feel about mixed drinks?

> **Cayden:** ?? I don't think I have feelings about them. I mean, some taste good and some don't, but I don't get emotional about it.

> **Menzy:** I do! I get very happy when someone buys me a mixed drink. Especially if he's cute!

> **Brigid:** Ha ha. What I was thinking was, I took a bartending class years ago and even worked as a bartender while I was learning to weld, but I never get to practice any more. What if we picked a signature cocktail each Wednesday for Antlers Too?

> **Macrina:** And just took turns bringing ingredients? We could do that.

> **Menzy:** Or just tell Genna to add what we need to her regular shopping order each week, and we could all pitch in to cover it. That would be less work.

> **Genna:** You've all done so much for me, I'd be glad to cover the tab.

> **Brigid:** I don't think that would be right. Good liquor can get expensive, and on a night when

everyone shows up, that could be… *pauses to count on fingers* up to ten people.

Genna: Maybe I could cover half?

Brigid: We might already have some things, too. Like, I've got bitters on hand, and I never actually use them. Genna, you usually put in your shopping order on Mondays, right? I could pick drinks and post a recipe every Sunday, so people can check if they've got any ingredients.

Menzy: I'm in!

Macrina: Just one thing, Brigid – if you expect Genna to be able to order and get the ingredients delivered, you'd better keep it simple. Last time I was looking up drinks – when I brought those Fire Shots to Sulis's Frost Fair party – I found recipes with all kinds of things I wouldn't know where to buy. Yuzu syrup (what's yuzu?), and prickly pear flowers, and I don't know what all.

Brigid: Yuzu's a citrus fruit and you can buy the syrup online fairly easily, but I take your meaning. No, I was definitely thinking we can start simple. I've got some orange-infused whiskey that I've had for a while and wasn't sure what to do with it. In fact, I was looking up recipes for it when I got the idea of doing cocktails at Genna's. I haven't had an Old Fashioned for a while, and all you need for that are Angostura bitters and sugar.

Genna: I've got both simple syrup and sugar on hand, so it sounds like no shopping is needed this week!

And it was a blast, that Wednesday night. Even though more and more bars and restaurants had been opening up at full seating levels, it still felt odd to be unmasked around crowds of strangers, so we'd kept sitting outside on our visits to Antlers'. Here where it was just us, it felt safe to be indoors by now, and it was nice to be able to hear ourselves talk.

The second time we gathered, Brigid decreed that the cocktail of the evening was a Tequila Sunset. Simple but lethal. Rob and Cayden were both working late, and Andrew and Nell were spending the evening with their kids, so it was just the single or temporarily-single women – me, Sulis, Menzy, Brigid and of course Genna.

Genna told us gleefully that her doctor thought she'd be able to walk with a weight-bearing cast in just three more weeks, thanks to the healing from Menzy and Sulis.

As we got through the Tequila Sunsets, we found the one drawback of an out-of-practice bartender – Brigid tended to mix them strong. Secrets were shared. I didn't really want to know about the role of sap in dryad procreation (TMI!), or where Sulis had gotten her latest tattoo put, for instance, and I hadn't really been intending to go that deeply into the whole question of whether Gil and I should move in together or keep separate houses. (Oops.) Though I did appreciate Brigid's stories of how hard it was for her as a teenager to date human guys when her Sasquatch brothers and cousins kept butting in on her dates and scaring off her human boyfriends. (I'm still not sure if everyone there had known Brigid was a Sasquatch before, but they did now!) And the story of how Genna and Duncan had met in college reminded me vividly of my college days:

She told us, "My friend Brianna wanted to go to a college party because this guy Pete whom she liked was supposed to be there – and he was, with his roommate, Duncan. They wanted to go make out in the guy's room, so he wanted to get rid of Duncan for the evening, and she didn't want to desert me at the party, so they kind of pushed us to dance together.

Then after the dance, we kind of looked at each other and realized they weren't coming back, so we went for a walk, but when he walked me home, my roommate had a 'Please do not come in' sign on the door – apparently *her* boyfriend was visiting from his school an hour away, and she knew I was likely to be out late. So we went back to his room, but Pete and Brianna were still there, and Pete had a sock on the door – that was the signal he and Duncan used. Just as we got there, Pete's old girlfriend came around the corner. Duncan told me his roommate had broken up with her, but tried to be so tactful about it, because he didn't like people being mad at him and she had a temper, that Duncan said he had a strong suspicion she hadn't quite realized what he was saying. She tended to be oblivious to anything she didn't want to hear anyway.

So she walked up, saw the sock, saw Duncan outside the room, realized what had to be happening, and started pounding on the door. We turned right around, went up on the roof of the building, and ended up talking all night. Brianna ended up going back to the party because she knew other people there, telling Pete he could call her back when he dumped his old girlfriend for real, but by the time he did, she had a new boyfriend. And as for Duncan and me – well, here we are, thirty years later."

Brigid said, quietly, "You two are very lucky," and things got very quiet for a moment.

Poignant memories aside, we had enough fun on those nights that we decided that we might need to keep our Antlers Too nights going, maybe just on a monthly basis, even after Genna was on her feet.

Helping Genna felt like just the right thing to do, but it had also felt like an investment in a connected future for all of us. When I'd moved to the area, living alone, even with nightly calls with Gil and lots of calls and meetings for work, I'd had the occasional thought that if something terrible happened…well, I'd bet that every woman has had the conversation with herself about what she'd do if she were assaulted or raped…I wouldn't have even known who to talk to that was nearby enough to help, and it was a very lonely feeling. Now, for the first time in years, I felt like I had a community nearby whom I could call if I needed help, whether that involved the need to borrow a cup of sugar or take me to Urgent Care. And I could do the same for them. It was a very good feeling.

CHAPTER TWENTY-FIVE: MEG'S VISIT

I was still visiting Genna a few times a week when the time came around for Meg's visit. Her meetings ended before lunch on Friday, so she called to ask if it would be all right if she drove down and arrived early on Friday afternoon. I'd planned to visit Genna and walk the dogs that day, so I checked with both Genna and Meg to make sure they were OK if I just brought Meg along to Genna's house.

When Meg texted me that she was here, I walked to the front door…to find the door already opening as I got there. Okay, then. I hoped this was because the house remembered her, or recognized her relationship to her grandparents, and not something it was going to start doing with every visitor!

She saw me just entering the entryway and looked a little confused. "Sorry, I didn't just push the door open, I swear! It just opened as I got here."

"I know. Apparently, the house likes you." I showed her to the spare room to drop her stuff off, then gave her a quick house tour of the downstairs before we went anywhere else. Both cats were sleeping on her bed, presumably their idea of how to welcome a guest.

"I love the colors! It has a whole different look than when Grandpa Ray lived here. Definitely a lot more up to date." She eyed the walls with a practiced eye. "Did you use my company's paints for this?"

"Well, obviously. Got to support my customers. Besides, if I'd used nonmagical paint, I'd have had to do three coats to get the color that even, instead of one."

She stood in the middle of the living room and tilted her head as if she were listening to the house. "It feels welcoming, but I miss the cookies."

"The cookies?"

"Yep, every time I walked into my grandparents' house, it smelled like someone had been baking cookies. To be fair, my grandmother probably *was* baking cookies if she knew my parents and I were coming to visit. After she died, though, I don't think Grandpa ever baked anything, but it still smelled like cookies every time I walked in."

"It's probably just as well," I said dryly. "I don't bake cookies or cake often either, and it would be false advertising!"

She grew thoughtful. "What would you want your house to smell like, if you could choose anything?"

I'd never thought about it, and said so. "I don't know. I don't have a signature scent. I don't even wear perfumes, because they always smell fake to me, and I'd rather just smell clean. I don't think there's any one smell I'd ever want in my house. And I don't use candles anymore, because now they all just smell like burning things to me, and after living through years of fire seasons in Oregon, where the whole outdoors can smell smoky for weeks at a time, that just puts me on edge. I guess..." and now it was my turn to be thoughtful. "I just like the smell of the forest out here, pine and cedar and growing things and clean fresh air. And I wouldn't mind some variation with the seasons – to smell hyacinths in early spring, and then the damp smell of growing things and unfurling leaves. And smells of baking and cooking around holiday time, or really, any time I have something good like sourdough bread or a pot roast going..."

Meg laughed. "Very poetical for someone who's never thought about it!"

"Yeah, well. I guess there was more in the back of my mind than I realized. Anyway, before we go to Genna's, do you want anything to eat or drink?"

"Nope, I'm good. I ate junk food all the way down here – that's the guilty pleasure of road trips! Hey, when we get back, would you mind showing me the upstairs? After buying from you all these years, I'd enjoy seeing where the magic comes from, literally, in your lab." Her voice went softer. "And I'd dearly love to see our old playroom, from when I was really little – I think it was up there too. For some reason, I never used it when I was older, so I'm not quite sure. I think Grandpa took me there when he wanted to do some work in his workshop and keep an eye on us at the same time. I used to build enormous cities there with my blocks – well, they seemed enormous to me when I was tiny!"

I wasn't sure which room she meant, but assumed it was either my office or the storage niche off my lab. "Of course. Oh, and don't let me forget to show you – I found some old things that must have belonged to your grandparents, that you might want to have."

"Great! It's going to be so much fun to stay here again – thank you for inviting me!"

***

Genna had so much company these days that she'd taken to leaving her door unlocked in the afternoons, so that she didn't have to get up and balance on her crutches to get to the door every time someone came by. She was counting the days until she could switch over to a weight-bearing cast and walk on her own, or with just a cane. So I knocked just to give her some warning, and we walked right in.

I'd already told them a little about each other, but I introduced everyone just to be polite. "Genna, this is Meg, my friend, longtime customer, and former landlord. Meg, Genna is the one who started that whole George group I was telling you about. We're giving her some help right now, while she's healing from a bad break."

Genna said, "Welcome, Meg, nice to meet you. I don't know what I would have done without Macrina and the rest of the George group – they've been lifesavers."

I put my hand to my mouth and spoke behind it to Meg, but in a perfectly audible volume. "Pssshhh. We enjoyed it, and I think it's really cemented the group together. We're talking about continuing cooking dinner together even after Genna is better, maybe once a month or so."

Genna changed the subject. "Meg, Macrina mentioned that you sold her that house, because you'd inherited it from your grandparents. I've only lived in this area for about a year, but I used to come down here all the time for my research, and I think I might have known your grandfather. Was he Ray Hobb?"

Meg was delighted. "Yes, he was! How did you meet him?"

"My research is on the traditional relationships between dryads and naiads in this area, back before it was heavily settled. Someone I was talking to told me that your grandfather had been living here longer than anyone else he knew, and might have some good stories of the old days. So I wrote him a letter and he invited me to go see him."

I was intrigued. "Genna, you've never mentioned this."

"I wasn't a hundred percent sure – your house looks very different than it did twenty years ago, and some of the other houses on your street weren't there yet. But I met Ray's wife a couple of times before she died, and Meg looks a lot like her."

Meg was curious now. "Was he able to help you with your research?"

"Oh, yes, he was a huge help. He must have been very old when you were born; he said he'd lived here over a hundred years, and he had stories going back well before that."

Now I was curious, and also startled. "Over a hundred years??"

Genna smiled. "He told me he was a brùnaidh. Didn't you tell her, Meg?" (She said it like "BROON-ay" – I had to ask Meg about the spelling later.)

I said, "What's a brùnaidh?" I knew most of the common magic groups, but hadn't heard this one.

Meg said, "Most people say brownie, but Grandpa

Ray never liked that term. He said it sounded too much like little girls with merit badges. Grandma Rose was human and was forty years younger than Grandpa, even though he outlived her. My Dad is human too, so I'm only a quarter, and definitely didn't inherit any notable brùnaidh traits. You should see my house – well, you shouldn't, it's usually a mess!"

Meg elected to stay and talk to Genna about her grandfather while I put the dogs' collars and leashes on, then went off to get them exercised and give me some time to think over the fact that I owned a house that had belonged to a brownie – sorry, Grandpa Ray, "brúnaidh". Brúnaidh were house spirits; had he left some magic behind? Was there something I needed to do to maintain it? All I knew about them were the old stories of houses where they'd moved in and would clean the whole place every night as long as they were never thanked or given any clothing, but I didn't know how much truth was in the old tales. And wasn't there something about leaving a bowl of milk for them?

But that was all when the brúnaidh were alive and active in the house, which was certainly not the case here. And all the stories I'd heard were about brúnaidh living in humans' houses, not about what they might do in a home of their own. The stories might not be completely accurate, anyway; brúnaidh and similar spirits like hobs and gruagach were often described as "little people", but clearly Grandpa Ray had been human-sized, big enough to marry a human woman. His granddaughter was taller than I was – though that wasn't saying much!

When I got back, Brigid was arriving, bringing pizza to share with Genna – and that smelled like a good idea for dinner. We said goodbye to them and headed home.

***

Back at my house, we took our jackets off, and I said, "Before we go upstairs, I found something else that I want to show you." I pulled the brass candlesticks and goblet off the mantel and held them out to her. "Did these belong to your grandparents?"

She took them from me and looked them over. "Maybe, but I don't recognize them. These look old."

"Do you want them?"

"They're pretty, but I don't have any memories or attachment to them, since I don't remember my grandparents ever using them. You're welcome to them, or you can donate or sell them if you don't want them." She grinned. "If they turn out to be antiques worth thousands of dollars, you can give me half!"

I put them back on the mantel, and we headed upstairs for the rest of the tour. The cats followed us, clearly considering it part of their duty to help me show off the house. My office was just a desk, chair, and filing cabinet in the first room at the top of the stairs, but she was interested in my lab set-up. I showed her my stashes of crystals, herbs, stacks of verses and other stuff, and explained how I organized my ingredients and physical inventory, though a lot of the spells I created these days could be stored virtually. Still, I liked working with a variety of spell-stores so my customers could have the format they preferred.

"This was my grandfather's workroom too, you know. He liked trying different crafts – woodworking, leather working, paper making, anything he came across to make stuff for the house. That's why he installed the sink and gas oven up here, so he'd have heat and water and could even attach a Bunsen burner to the gas valve if he needed it."

"Did your grandmother like to do crafts too?"

"Not that kind. She did some embroidery and sewing – that front room that's your office now was her sewing room. But mostly I think baking was her art form. She'd make gingerbread at Christmas, and she and Grandpa would work together to guild and decorate the most amazing gingerbread houses and even castles. He loved anything that was about building or furnishing homes – I think it was his brúnaidh gifts coming out. And he loved working on gingerbread houses because he was working with Grandma Rose. Most of the things he made were for her, either something pretty for her or the house, or something to make her life easier. He loved her so much, even when she aged faster than he did. He was never completely happy again after she died, I think, though he still enjoyed it when we'd visit."

"Genna said you look like her."

"I do – there were some pictures of her when she was younger the old photos you sent me when you moved in here. But that wasn't why he enjoyed our visits, or not the only reason – he just loved kids. He was the best person to play with that I knew, and he mentored a lot of the local kids – I think he would have been glad if I'd had half a dozen siblings or cousins, but my mom and I were both only children."

"Yeah, a couple of guys around town who grew up here have told me they worked for your grandfather as teenagers. They have fond memories of him."

I saw her looking around the room and said, "If that front room was your grandmother's sewing room, then I don't know where your playroom would have been, unless it was that storage area over there. It's not really a separate room, just a small alcove, and I don't keep anything there except the litter boxes. "

She stepped over to look at the area, the cats crowding in front of her to make sure she didn't mess with their litterbox. (They came and watched me every night while I scooped the litter, too, with unmistakably disappointed expressions on their faces. I was sure they were thinking, "Hey, I made that! You can't just throw it away!")

"This seems like the right place, but I'd swear it was bigger, and more like a real room. But I was so little, my memory's probably not accurate. Is there anything behind these?" She pulled the old boards away from the wall. "Hey, what's this?"

"This" was made of black metal and wood. It looked like a small gate, but it was firmly attached to the wall. The funny thing was that I hadn't seen it before, even though I was sure I'd looked to see if there was anything behind the old boards when I'd moved in, or even when I'd put the litter boxes in there. It felt like something I'd seen before though…and then I had it. It was the same as that grating I'd seen attached to the foundation, over on the side of the house where I'd gotten the half barrels I was now using as planters. I had no idea why either one of them was there, though. They seemed like odd things to have for decoration, but I didn't know what else they might be. It was strange to have a matching set in two completely different locations.

The cats seemed interested too; they were peering and sniffing at the bottom of the object, and started scratching beneath it, as if they were trying to pull something out from beneath it.

CHAPTER TWENTY-SIX: A LETTER FROM GRANDPA

Merlin and Morgana definitely had found something – I saw a white corner beneath the gate, or whatever it was. They kept working at it, and eventually managed to pull an envelope out from under the gate, though I would have sworn there wasn't room for it in there. Then they both sat down as if satisfied with their work and looked at Meg for a moment, then settling down to wash their paws while clearly conveying "our work is done here".

My eyebrows rose. "Apparently it's for you." I picked up the envelope and turned it over, surprised to see "Meg" written on the back of the envelope. "Huh. It really is for you. I had no idea they could read." (This was sarcasm, if that needs to be said. Even MCs' cats can't read, not even if they'd decided to become familiars rather than just pets.) I handed it to her.

"Maybe it smells like me to them," she said shakily. "If it's from my grandfather, it makes sense that family would smell alike."

"Maybe. Do you want to be alone to read it?"

"Oh! Thank you, but it's fine. I think I'd rather have someone here while I read this, and I doubt there are any secrets in it – I'm sure Grandpa wasn't telling me where his ill-gotten gains are hidden. He was the most upright person I knew." She opened the letter, took out a handwritten letter on what looked like thick handmade paper, and began to read.

After a moment she said, "Macrina, I think you need to read this too. She tilted the letter so that we both could read – luckily, Grandpa Ray wrote a big, clear hand.

Dearest Meg,

Since you're reading this, I'm gone and you've inherited my house. I know you'll be missing me but I hope you're not sad about me – I had a long life and a very good one, especially the part of it that your grandmother graced. Remember me with happiness, not sorrow.

As for the house, it is entirely up to you whether you keep it and live in it or sell it – it's your life and I wouldn't presume to tell you how to live it. Whichever you choose, though, there are a few things you should know. Even if you do decide to sell, you'll need to come clean the place out, so I have magicked this letter to appear to you the first time you come up to my old workroom.

Before I get into details about the house, let me say this: I could not have had a better grand-daughter, or one I am more proud of, than you. I love you very much, and I hope that you fill your life with love, and make all your decisions with the good sense and fierce determination that have always been a part of you. You get those from your grandmother, and it's been a joy to see her live on in you.

You know that I am a brúnaidh. That means that you are too, by the way; though you may not have chosen to call out that side of yourself yet, the potential is always there regardless of your human grandmother and father. I never told you all about this house because I didn't want you ever to feel obligated to stay here unless you wanted to. But she is not an ordinary house. It's a brúnaidh thing; you've probably heard all of the old stories about brúnaidh either helping or pulling pranks in other people's houses, but when we are happy in our own house for a long enough time, the house may come to be aware of us. Don't expect her to talk to you – this isn't a fantasy novel about a magic house! More like a pet dog, who loves his humans and will help them if he can.

I was never sure how conscious you were of that – you used to talk to her when you were little, but I couldn't tell if that was just playing. We knew she liked you; you never so much as got a splinter when you were here, or burned your finger touching a hot pot, or tripped over a toy.

Right now, I have bound the house – her name is Nyssa, by the way – to your essence. The house herself and any pets under its roof will respond to other people, but never as strongly as it will to you. If you decide to live here, she will keep you safe and comfortable. I can't tell you what else she might do; the house responds to her owner, so she may be different with you than she is with me; a modern young woman might not want to live in the same ways as her decrepit old grandfather. I will leave you and Nyssa to build your relationship together.

If you do decide to sell, though, then you should break the bond with her – otherwise you will always want to come back here, and the house may not be able to bond with its new owner. How you do that will depend on whether you sell to someone who is familiar with the magic world, or not. If you sell it to someone who is not magical, you can just break the bond. If you don't do anything else, Nyssa will slumber – even asleep, her presence will always make this feel like a comfortable home to anyone who lives there as well as any guests they welcome, but that's all.

If possible, though, it would be better to sell her to someone who is magical, or at least familiar with the Community. This is partly for your sake, because it might be easier to sell her to someone who will appreciate that Nyssa is more than an ordinary house, and partly for hers, because I know she'll be happier if she can bond with whoever lives there. Nyssa is important to me; you might say she is my other child, because she was born out of the many loving years your grandmother and I spent living there. I guess that sort of makes her your aunt!

The spell to break the bond is simple. If you look in the back of the kitchen cupboards, you should find a very old pair of candlesticks and a chalice. My own grandfather brought them from Scotland, when he crossed this country and settled down with the local tribes and spirits living here. You know the old tales about telling the bees when there is a change in a household? Like Nyssa, they were tutelary spirits of a house, so this ritual is related. You will need beeswax candles and honey mead.

Brúnaidh spells are not like the formal ones human magic users do. All you will need to do is to light the candles, sip the mead from the chalice, focus your intent, and tell Nyssa what you want her to do. I know you're more used to human-style formal spells, though – if it would help you to have a verse to focus on, you can use that thing Kipling wrote – it's much younger than the ritual, but he got the spirit of it correct:

Marriage, birth or buryin',

News across the seas,

All you're sad or merry in,

You must tell the Bees.

If you want to bond Nyssa to a new owner, tell her that too. That person will need to be there with you when you light the candles. Have them sip the mead too, and ask Nyssa to let them live there, and tell her she is welcome to be part of their lives. Blow the candles out to close the ritual.

And that's it, about the house. Most importantly, Meg, always remember I love you. Wherever you decide to live, whatever your goals are for your own life, I hope you will find love, and that you and whoever you love will live as long and as happily together as your grandmother and I did.

Love,

Grandpa

***

Meg looked deeply shaken. I asked, "Are you all right?"

"Yes, I'm fine. It just brought back his voice – I miss him so much."

"Do you want some time to figure out what you're

going to do next? I mean, about the house?"

"No! I sold you the house. My life is on the East Coast. I want to do the ritual to bond the house – Nyssa – to you." She bit her lip. "I mean, if you still want to live here."

"Oh, yes –" and then I realized I wanted to tell her everything. "I think the house and I may already be at least partly bonded. I want to tell you about it, but would you rather wait until later? That letter was a lot to think about."

"Yes please."

"Anyway," I said more practically, "If we're going to do that ritual we need to go shopping first. I don't have any beeswax candles or mead in the house!"

We headed back downstairs and I got Meg a cup of tea, because tea makes everything better. I didn't usually keep many sweet things in the house, but I was grateful now that I'd bought some snickerdoodles while prepping for her visit – hopefully they would remind her of her grandmother's baking and be a comfort, even if mine were store-bought.

The cats followed me into the kitchen; while I was waiting for the water to boil, I asked them quietly, "Maybe you could go snuggle with Meg? She might appreciate it – she's a little sad right now." Just in case, I looked up and said, "Nyssa? Can you influence them?" I felt a little foolish talking to a house, and I wasn't even sure if it – she – would understand speech even after we were bonded, but it couldn't hurt. And it wasn't like the cats were going to tell anyone I was talking to a house! The cats ignored me, anyway, showing absolutely no signs that they had listened to me – because obviously that would have ruined their feline street cred.

While Meg was drinking her tea, I said, "Tell you what. It's only 3 o'clock. Let's wait until tomorrow morning to do the ritual, but I could go into town now to buy the candles and mead. Would you like to come with me, or do you want some time alone?"

"Thanks – if you don't mind, I'd like some time here alone." She managed a watery smile. "Maybe I'll talk to

Nyssa about my grandparents."

"OK, then. I'll be back in two hours or less. Is pizza OK for dinner? What toppings do you like?"

"Anything but pineapple. Or anchovies." She made a face.

"I'll just get the one with all the normal stuff then – they have one with pepperoni, sausage, onions, mushrooms, and olives. Is that OK?"

"Sounds good!"

As I headed out, I noticed that both cats were both curled up with Meg on the sofa.

CHAPTER TWENTY-SEVEN: BONDED TO A HOUSE

The beeswax candles were easy to find; there were a couple of fancy home-goods stores in Eugene's 5th Street Market area. There were wine stores too, and I picked up a bottle of a not-too-fancy red to have with our pizza, but the mead took a little thinking. Then I remembered seeing some bottles of mead at the Bier Stein, a Eugene institution with a fabulous beer selection, both to drink there and for sale to take home. Also, they had decent parking, always a plus.

There was a pizza place along the road home that I liked, so I called an order in to them from the Bier Stein parking lot, then went in to grab the mead. I wasn't a big fan of the stuff, but I bought two bottles in case Meg liked it and wanted more than a sip, as well as some beer I hadn't tried before just to have on hand – they had a much more interesting selection than my usual grocery store.

When I walked into the house, pizza, candles, and drinks in hand, Meg seemed more cheerful. She was reading one of my Calvin and Hobbes collections and laughing at it. I called to her, "Wine, beer or mead with the pizza?"

"Wine please! Let's save all the mead for the ritual tomorrow morning. On second thought, let's not do it too early in the morning. Not sure I can face mead for breakfast."

I grimaced. "I'm with you there. Think it's warm enough to eat outside?"

"Yes, please. I love the lake view here."

I set the table, and we ate our pizza. I wasn't sure

whether to ask about Grandpa Ray's letter or avoid the topic, but Meg introduced it herself.

"Did you say you thought you were already partly bonded to the house – to Nyssa?"

"I think so, though I didn't know her name until today. I'll have to look up what it means."

I told her about all the things that had happened with the house, even the ones I'd dismissed at the time, trying to remember them all in order. It had started with the problems in imbuing power into my spell-stores at Samhain. Then I'd done some painting and redecorating to make the house my own, and brought in plants and the cats. After I'd walked to the Christmas tree lighting in the covered bridge, it had turned on all the lights to welcome me home. I'd done the homeplace ritual at Solstice, and after that the house had seemed more awake – it had pulled the stunt with all the dust when I'd gone away at Christmas, turned on the porch light in the middle of the day and lined up the cats to welcome Gil on his next visit, and unlatched the doors for the cats – but only the internal doors, not the ones that would have let them escape outside.

I wasn't doubting Grandpa Ray's explanation; no one knew houses like a brúnaidh. The surprising part was that the house had been reacting so positively to me. Perhaps it was the Solstice ritual? But it had started before that, as soon as I began making the house my own.

Meg listened carefully to my recital, then said "That bit with the dust is really the only thing that couldn't be explained away. You could have turned on lights and forgotten about them, the cats could just have been curious about your first houseguest, and the old doors might just be a little warped so that the latches didn't click in. Though then again, Grandpa would never have built a door off true, or let one warp under his watch, and he's only been gone less than two years now, not long enough for things to go downhill."

"Plus, while I don't know anything about brownie houses, I've been a professional magic user for two decades now, and I know the feel of it. And there are too many coincidences – while any one thing could have been explained, all of them together are too unlikely."

"True. After all, we use spells from you at my company because you know what you're doing."

"Meg, can I ask a personal question?"

"How can I say no to that after this day? It's been all about my family and my heritage!"

"Then, what did your grandpa mean about you being a brúnaidh too? If you are one, why do you buy spells from people like me instead of working in that tradition?" I didn't exactly know how brúnaidh worked, but I was fairly sure they didn't buy commercially made paint, even the magic kind, online.

She looked a bit forlorn, and I was already sorry I'd asked. "My mom died when I was little."

"Oh, I'm so sorry."

"It's ok. I just have a few memories of her, mostly of how much fun she was. She and I spent a few summers with my grandparents. Afterward, though, my dad really worked hard to make sure I still had a relationship with them, but he never had time to bring me for more than a week or so. Then when I was old enough to go on my own, I wanted to go to camps, and then there were summer jobs and internships, and then I was working and had limited vacation time. So I always visited them whenever I could, but never for long enough for Grandpa to teach me, and I ended up following the human magic traditions instead."

She got up, closing off that topic. "Can I do the dishes?"

"What dishes? There are only two plates and two glasses to put in the dishwasher."

We went to bed not too long after that – it was early, but I thought she wanted some more time to process her grandfather's letter, and I was happy to read in bed for a while. I had my tablet with me, too, and wanted to do a bit of Googling. I wasn't able to find any stories or information about brúnaidh in their own houses, only in other people's, but I was able to look up the origin of the name Nyssa. It meant 'willow' – the house must have been named for the big willow tree out front, or maybe one of its ancestors, since willow trees don't live as long as other trees. It was also the name of a water nymph in Greek mythology, which seemed appropriate for the name of a lake house. But most surprisingly, it was a town in Asia Minor, best known for the saints who had lived there: Gregory of Nyssa…and his sister *Macrina*. I had no idea why my parents had named me for an early Turkish saint who lived fifteen hundred years ago, given that we weren't Turkish or even Christian, much less saints. But maybe it was somehow meant to be for me to come live in this house.

Before I turned my light out, for the first time I said, "Good night, Nyssa." And from the foot of my bed, Merlin answered, "Mreowp!"

***

The next morning, I made waffles. I had the batter ready to go when Meg came out of her room and into the kitchen – I figured, if she didn't like waffles, I could always put the batter away and have them for dinner. Then again, who doesn't like waffles?

She looked more cheerful this morning than she had last night, but I had no idea what to say. I mean, "Hi, are you over your grandfather's death yet? And do you still want to let me bond with your sort-of-aunt?" just didn't seem like quite the right thing.

So I settled on a neutral, "Good morning! Would you like waffles for breakfast? I have butter, maple syrup, blackberry preserves and powdered sugar to put on them in whatever combo you prefer."

She said, "Thanks, waffles sound great! And," she paused, took a deep breath and asked, "Are you all right?"

"Me? Why wouldn't I be?"

"Well, it's a lot to dump on you. This was just supposed to be a friendly visit, to say hi and see how you're settling in. Then you got landed with my family stories, and you find out the house you're living in is alive somehow… It's not like you're not familiar with magic, but I can see how you might be uncomfortable with all this."

"It's really kind of a relief, though – it explains so much of what was happening with the house. Also, I'm kind of excited to see what happens next. You think she can clean herself?"

"Maybe! You said she already blew dust out that one time."

"And why do you suppose she's a she?"

"Oh, I think that's just Grandpa. He was always referring to anything he worked on as 'she' – engines, projects, anything he was putting together."

"If she does decide to talk, we can always ask her!"

***

After breakfast, we lingered over our coffee. Meg said, "I suppose I'd better head back up to Portland after we do the ritual, but I'm in no hurry – it's been nice hanging out with you, and I loved hearing the stories Grandpa told your friend Genna. This house still feels like home in a way, even though it's so much more yours than my grandparents' now – I suppose that's all due to Nyssa."

I stood up and put our plates into the sink, and said, "It's a beautiful morning and you'll be spending a couple of hours sitting in a car – want to take a quick walk before we do the ritual?"

She looked at me curiously, and said "Sure – let me go put my shoes on."

Once we were out of the house and a block away, she looked hard at me and said, "OK, spill."

"Spill what?"

"There was something you wanted to talk about, wasn't there? And you didn't want to talk inside Nyssa's walls."

"OK, you're right. I was so excited to be bonded to the house and see what happens next that I wasn't thinking, but there are a few potential problems I didn't even think about until this morning."

I told her about the discussions Gil and I had been having about him moving up here, and how we couldn't even decide among the three possible options for how that could work. Then my questions all burst out at once. "So what if we remodeled it – I mean, her – would she hate that? Would it hurt her? If another person came to live here, would she be OK with that? And what if we decided to move somewhere else? I'd hate to do that even now, and it would probably be a lot more painful if I'm bonded to her. And would she feel abandoned?" I sighed. "I guess it would fix all those problems if he just moved up here and bought a separate house, but then why bother? That's not exactly living together."

"You sound like a panicky bride," she said, smiling. "I guess that's valid, since we are talking about a bonding ceremony."

"I'm not sure how many panicking brides are panicking about their boyfriends coming into the relationship!"

"You never know these days!" she deadpanned. "People have all kinds of complicated relationships. But no, you know I just mean your general tone. Anyway, it's OK, I can actually answer all those questions."

She held up one finger. "First, I don't think the house's spirit and body are really connected, like a person's or animal's. Don't think of remodeling like surgery. More like a new hairstyle, though maybe that's a bad analogy since that's on a body too. Whatever. Anyway, Grandpa Ray was always changing or rebuilding something, and I never saw any evidence that the house minded."

"Second," she held up another finger. "She won't mind if Gil comes to live there, either – remember, my Grandma Rose lived in her too. And Mom grew up here. You should definitely introduce him and tell her what's happening – like Grandpa wrote in his letter, think of it like telling the bees about a wedding. If you want, you can even haul out the candles and mead again, and see if you can bond him to the house too. I think she'd like that."

"Third," she said, "I do think she'd be unhappy if you moved away, especially so soon. So maybe don't do that one if there's any way to avoid it. But if you do, you can break the bond again, like I'll be doing today, and more or less put her into hibernation, or else sell it to someone else who can bond with her."

She stopped walking. "But I think even if you do that, and she's OK, it will make you unhappy. The bond goes both ways. I never lived here full time, but you have been, and you've been here as an adult, not just as a kid. I think moving away will hurt you, and at the very least you'll feel guilty. So yeah, that's probably not the best option. But it's still possible.

She sighed. "I'm sorry. It sort of feels like, in being so careful to give me my freedom, Grandpa accidentally trapped you."

"Don't be sorry," I said. "This just means I can have an incredible adventure without even going anywhere. You think any magic user would give up a chance to live in a magic *house*? Gil and I will work something out, and I already didn't want to leave Nyssa, even before I knew her name. So you've just given me an excuse to stay here, not to mention an easy way to cut three options down to two."

***

I felt a lot better after that discussion with Meg, and ready to go on with the ritual. If, as I suspected, I was already somehow partly bonded to Nyssa, then if I were to move out we'd already have all of the disadvantages of leaving, on both her side and mine. In fact, if I really needed to break the bond, it might be easier to break a bond that had been formally and ritually made than one that had just grown. On the other hand, I really didn't want to do that anyway. Even aside from my feelings living here, the office and lab suited my work so perfectly, and I thought it would be hard to be 'dry-docked' after spending a year looking out at the lake.

If I was honest with myself, I was excited about the bond itself. I wanted to see what would happen next! Maybe it would have been better to talk it all over with Gil, but we needed to do this while Meg was here. So I took a deep breath and said, "OK, let's do it."

Meg said, "Where?"

"I'd say in the kitchen – aren't kitchens usually the heart of a house? I get the feeling from your grandfather's letter that brúnaidh magic is less formal and more intuitive than the methods I'm used to, so if the kitchen feels right, it probably is."

"That makes sense. Do we need a bottle opener for the mead?"

"Yeah, here's one, and here are the matches." I grabbed the candlesticks and chalice from the mantle and brought them to the kitchen counter, while Meg pulled the candles I'd bought yesterday out of their bag.

We got the candles lit and the mead poured, then I looked over at Meg, for her to begin. Her voice was shaky at first, but grew firmer as she spoke.

"Nyssa. Thank you for all you did for my grandparents, Ray and Rose, and also for making their house so warm and welcoming all the times I visited them. I thank you also for providing a home to my friend Macrina and her cats, and for your welcome to me on this visit. My grandfather bonded us when he left this house to me."

She stopped and took a breath, and I knew this would be the difficult part for her – who wants to hurt a house's feelings? Especially while you are inside said house?

"But my life isn't here. My home and my love are three thousand miles away, and I need to live there, not here. So I am going to break our bonds now." The air felt as if everything was on edge, balanced on a knife blade now, but Meg went on, sounding stronger now, "But Macrina will be living here. She is the new owner of the physical house. We are breaking your bond with me, and bonding you with her instead. Please be good to her and those she welcomes to her home; keep them all safe and comfortable."

She took a sip of mead, then nodded to me and passed me the chalice. I said, "Nyssa. I have loved living here for the past year, and I hope to stay here for years to come. Life may bring change and challenges to both of us; let's face them together. I wish to be bonded to you." I sipped the mead, put the chalice down, and then blew the candles out.

There was a loud *ping!* I couldn't figure out where it came from for a moment, because as far as I knew there weren't any bells in the house. Then I looked down and realized all the mead was gone and the chalice was empty.

Meg looked over at me. "I guess she accepts the bond."

"I guess she does. Too bad the chalice is metal and not glass; I feel like I ought to stomp on a glass now, though I'm not sure if I'd be the groom or the bride in this scenario."

She was confused for a moment, then said, "Oh, right, you're Jewish, aren't you. I remember about that tradition now. Anyway, it's 2022; you can *both* be brides!"

"Gil might have something to say about that!" Then I thought a bit. "Well, he might have something to say anyway. I hope he's not mad that I didn't talk to him before bonding to the house."

***

After Meg left, I sat in the living room, reaching out with all my senses, trying to feel if the ritual had made any difference to anything. I remembered that the connection had felt stable but incomplete after I did the Solstice ritual; now I knew we'd only had a partial bond then, so that made sense. It did feel different now: the bond felt complete. I'd used a jigsaw metaphor before; now it felt like I had all the pieces and the puzzle showed the full picture. The next question was, what could I do with this new bond? I'd already seen that the house could augment my own power; I thought it would probably be more controlled and precise now.

Nyssa still had her mysteries, and I still had a lot to learn. How could I communicate with her? *Could* I communicate with her? In the spirit of experimentation, I said, "Nyssa, could you please sweep this floor?"

Nothing happened. Drat. But I knew it was within her capabilities; she'd collected all that dust in the house and then blown it out, when I'd left her at Christmas. There was no way to know if she hadn't heard me or if she had but just didn't want to sweep the floor.

Just in case she was listening, I said, "Nyssa, when Laxmi – the little girl – comes over, please, please, don't augment her power as you do mine. She is just beginning to learn, and she needs to go slowly to be safe. Thank you!" I wouldn't know if that had worked until Laxmi came over, and maybe not then, but I'd figured it couldn't hurt to ask.

Back to my own issue, though, I now had this bond with the house and no idea what it could do, other than make me feel safe and at home here. That was no small thing, but from the stories Rob, Leo and Meg had told me, Nyssa and Grandpa Ray had been able to do a lot more than that. Was the lack in me because I wasn't a brúnaidh, or was it just that she liked to reveal her secrets in her own time?

CHAPTER TWENTY-EIGHT: COMING OUT TO THE COMMUNITY

Gil was only a little mad.

"I wish we could have talked it over first, Macrina-Meli," he said. "But I know you had to do it while Meg was there, and honestly, I suspect we'd have come to the same conclusion anyway. You already didn't want to move, you were only talking about that as an option for the sake of completeness. I know theoretically you still *could* move, but we both know that's not happening."

Yup, he got me.

He went on, "So that still leaves us with the options of remodeling or living in two separate houses."

I answered, "And you don't really want two separate houses, and it looks like remodeling would depend on whether we can get a variance to the local building codes. Dammit. I thought us living together would be the complicated part and the rest would be easy!"

"At least we don't have strict time limits for all of this. I can go month to month once my lease is up."

"At least I got confirmation that the house wouldn't mind a remodel"

"Bet that's not a sentence you ever imagined yourself saying! Can you start looking for recommendations for good contractors around there? Though I think we need a better idea of exactly what we want before we talk to them. I mean, I think we agreed that we want at least one more room and a garage, right? But where would we put them and how would the existing rooms open onto them?"

"Oh, ouch. I have no idea. Well, that's not true, I have some ideas but no conclusions. You have to be able to drive into the garage, so that limits where it can be. The room for your office has to be on the lake side because there's no other space for it, but then how do we keep it from blocking the views from other rooms?"

"Could we go up instead of back?"

"You mean, add another story? I'm not sure if the house could support that."

"Maybe, but I was thinking more about adding on to the second story. I know the rooms you have take up most of the attic level, but what if we built out in back over the deck? We might have to increase the size of your covered deck, but that wouldn't be a bad thing. Or we could even extend the back wall of the house, making the dining room and kitchen a little bigger, and then build over the deck."

"Maybe. Can you sketch it up and send it to me? We can get something we agree on before I talk to any contractors. "

"Yeah, sure. I can draw it up a couple different ways, and you can see what you think. I'll bring the drawings with me when I come to visit you next week." He changed topics, "But meanwhile, how do you feel after the ritual? Any different? Has the house done anything new? Does it have, like, new powers?"

I laughed. "It does! Meg had to leave right after we did the ritual to drive back up to Portland. She went into the guest room to get her stuff, and when she came back out she was trying not to giggle. She nodded for me to come over to see what the house had done…want to guess?"

"Thrown a fit and scattered her things all over the room?"

"Oh, no, apparently it has a much tidier soul than that. All of the sheets had been taken off the bed and folded neatly! She told me it was like that when she went into the room, and she wasn't in there long enough to do it herself."

"So instead of a brownie housekeeper, you have a brownie house that keeps itself? Very handy." He chuckled too. "But was it trying to kick her out, or to help you?"

"I think it was trying to help, and to give her a nice sendoff, not kick her out. Because once she had her overnight bag, she went to get her purse, which was sitting on the kitchen counter, and found the second bottle of mead there next to it." I lowered my voice to a confidential murmur. "With a bow on it!"

***

Genna was now on crutches and able to manage most things by herself or with a little help. Charli and Oliver still came to play with the dogs most days, mostly because they all enjoyed it, and I still took them for longer walks a few times a week because it's hard to manage leashes and crutches simultaneously. And because I enjoyed it.

The next time I was over there after Meg's visit, I told her the whole story about finding the letter and doing the ritual that bound me to Nyssa, and asked whether Grandpa Ray had told her anything about his house. "Well, yes," she said, "but mostly mundane things – about how he was redoing cabinets, and that sort of thing. Even though he'd told me he was a brúnaidh, it was never really clear to me if he was using magic or not when he worked on the house – it was a hobby for him. The only time he mentioned anything was the very last time I saw him. He was very old by then, and getting frail, and he told me that he wouldn't have been able to keep living on his own but for the good care his house took of him. He was very grateful, because he'd have hated to have to live anywhere else, but he didn't really go into any details."

We talked a bit more about whether I was going to make any more changes to the house, and about gardens. She hoped to be able to at least plant some containers when she was able to move around more easily. And like everyone else, she passed on her horror stories about dealing with contractors, though at least she'd had a few experiences where things went smoothly and work was done on time. She gave me the name of her contractors, but later on when I called them, they told me they were booked out until October.

She also asked if I'd thought more about having Laxmi do an independent project. I hadn't, but when I got home I called her parents, Leo and Deepthi, and they and Laxmi all loved the idea – provided, of course, that she was supervised whenever she was doing spells. I also texted Menzy to see if she would be interested in being a guinea pig.

Why is it that no one ever likes to ask for help, but everyone loves being asked? However that is, Menzy willingly agreed to help. She seemed excited at the idea of helping Laxmi learn magic, and had only one question:

> **Menzy:** Can we try it with a really *fun* spell?"

> **Macrina:** …What do you mean by fun? Remember, it needs to be something unrelated to your own forest magic, and it should be something that won't get Laxmi in trouble.

> **Menzy:** Hmmm… How about mustaches?

> **Macrina:** Mustaches?

> **Menzy:** Yeah, you know, like you prank someone when they're asleep by drawing mustache on their face? We could make it one that would fade in ten minutes or so, so that she wouldn't get into trouble. Or rather, I wouldn't. Though it could be fun at work!

I had a moment of feeling sorry for her coworkers. A brief moment.

> **Macrina:** I'm sure Laxmi would love a mustache-drawing spell!

After some more texting back and forth with Menzy and Leo, we agreed that Menzy, Laxmi and one of her parents would come over for lunch next Friday, when she had a half-day at school, to talk about Genna's project idea.

***

That done, I got back to gardening. This was really my first garden, and so far, the work I'd done in it had convinced me that I was never going to be the sort of obsessed gardener so many people in this rural area seemed to be. However, the container plantings I'd put in a few weeks ago were doing well, and the plants in my house were still alive, so I was very interested when Brigid posted in our group:

> **Brigid:** All, I have a few extra heritage tomato starts I really don't have room for. Anybody want them?

> **Macrina:** Me, please!!! Want me to come over and get them?

> **Brigid:** That's all right, I can bring them to you if you'll be home this afternoon.

I was excited because homegrown tomatoes are barely even the same species as store-bought ones. My dad had been into growing them and we all loved eating his tomatoes every summer, but he was always experimenting with different types, different cages, soil amendments, whatever, and he made it seem so involved that I was scared to try growing my own. Still, by now I'd heard enough of my friends talking about growing tomatoes without making it seem like so much of a production, that I was ready to take a shot at it. I was growing other things anyway, so I already had to do weeding and watering and such. I still had enough soil left to fill another container, too.

Brigid showed up that afternoon with a six-pack of plants that she'd been growing in her kitchen window, and gave them to me with some planting instructions.

I asked, "Hey, while you're here, can you help me

bring another half barrel around to the deck? I can manage it on my own but it's easier with two people."

"Sure, no problem!"

We walked around the side of the house, where the last two half barrels remained where I'd found them, and I pointed out the one we wanted. As soon as we moved it away from the house, though, Brigid froze.

"Macrina? What's that thing behind the barrels?"

I took another look at the wood-and-metal gate or grate or whatever it was. "I have no idea. It was there when I moved in. There's another just like it in the attic. They both seem to be attached, and they don't open or anything, so I've left them where they are."

Her eyes got big. "I think they're one of our things."

"Our things?"

"Yeah, I think they're Sasquatch things."

"Really? How do you know? What do they do? And why are they here?"

"It's mostly the look of them. And see that symbol in the middle that looks sort of like a tree? That's one we tend to use. I have a very vague memory that I've heard of something like these, but I can't remember anything else about them."

We grabbed the half barrel from both sides and kept lugging it toward the deck while she went on, "As for what it does and why it's here, I have no idea."

"Did you know that a brúnaidh used to live here?"

"A what?"

"A brownie, but apparently he preferred the Gaelic name. He was the grandfather of my friend Meg, who sold me the house. I just found out."

I told her about the whole bonding ritual thing, too, just in case Nyssa had anything to do with the Sasquatch gate thingy.

"Do you mind if I pass this story on to my family? I'll be having dinner with them tomorrow."

"No, I don't think there's anything secret about any of it. How's that going, with your family?"

She took a photo of the gate to show her family.

"Good, I think. It still feels a little like we're all on our best behavior, but it's getting easier, and they haven't tried to matchmake once."

"Oh, glad to hear it."

"And tonight," she said, eyes dancing, "I'm going out drinking with a big hairy guy."

"Wait, the same one you told me about? I thought you said you'd never date him."

"I did, but it's not a date. We're just going as friends."

"Uh-huh."

She purposely pushed on the barrel we were still carrying so that I stumbled a few steps, but I was still laughing. That was not the expression of a woman going out with a friend. Friend with benefits, maybe.

***

A couple of days later, Brigid texted me.

Brigid: I told my family about those grate things at your house and now my uncle wants to come see them. He's sort of the family storyteller and thinks he might know something.

Macrina: Sure, I'd be happy to have him come take a look.

Brigid: Is tomorrow night OK, after 9? It needs to be after it gets fully dark. Bigfoot, remember.

Macrina: Yes, that's fine. But…I haven't met an older Sasquatch before. Like, is it OK to offer him a beer?

Brigid: Oh yeah, you don't have to do anything special for Uncle Bocephus!! It'll be just like meeting a human friend's big ugly uncle <grin>

Brigid: But don't turn an outside light on when we get there – almost forgot to say that. I know your neighbors aren't that close and there are trees, but… still.

Uncle…Bocephus? Sure, I'd just pretend I was meeting any human's Uncle Larry. In the dark. Right. (Why did half the humans I knew seem to have an Uncle Larry, anyway? It must have been a very popular name for that generation!) I resolved to stock up on beer, just in case.

I spent most of the next couple days working, but was ready the next night. Honestly, I'd been ready since I knocked off work at 4 because I couldn't concentrate. I'm not sure why; after all, I met dryads and naiads all the time and that felt completely normal. I didn't get twitchy when Sulis or Menzy or Brigid came over. Well, that's not true: I did, a little, if they were picking me up to go somewhere and I was waiting for the agreed time to arrive.

So that was part of this – just that I hated the waiting period, when it was too soon for something to happen, but you couldn't start doing anything else either. But the rest of it really was about Uncle Bocephus. (Did she really call him that or was she messing with me?) It wasn't that he was a Sasquatch but that he was older, and a story-keeper, and most of all that he might be able to tell me something about my house.

Finally it was 9:00, and a big pickup pulled up in front of my house. It was a cloudy night and I'd left all the outside lights off at Brigid's request, so I couldn't see much about the people who got out until they got right up to my door. I stepped toward the door, meaning to open it as they walked up, but Nyssa anticipated me. The door didn't swing wide open, but it did unlatch and open a few inches before I could get there and open it the rest of the way. Did Nyssa know Uncle Bocephus? She'd only opened up for Meg before, and Meg had been bonded to her at the time. I hoped she did know him; I didn't like the idea that my house might just open up to any passing stranger!

I stepped out onto the front stoop as they got there, and said "Hi, thanks for coming over. Would you like to come inside first?"

They came in and Brigid did the introductions: "Bo, this is my friend Macrina. Macrina, this is my Uncle Larry." She grinned. "But we call him Bocephus."

What did I say about Uncle Larrys? Another one!

Her uncle was probably the tallest person I'd ever met. I reached up to shake his hand (yes, things seemed to be more or less returning to normal, as far as touching other people went – and he was already in my house, anyway). And he was definitely on the hairy side, but he could easily have passed for human, other than being nearly seven feet tall. Honestly, what he looked like was an oversized Hank Williams Junior, circa the mid-1980s, and I suddenly understood the "Bocephus" nickname.

"Glad to meet you, Macrina," he said, in a resonant voice that had me wondering if he was a singer. (Had Hank Williams Sr. ever gotten lost in the forest out in this area? Also, were there Bigfoot bands?) I pulled my wandering mind back on duty just as he went on, "Please call me Bo."

"Thank you for coming over, Bo. Can I offer you two anything? Beer, water, Coke?"

"I don't drink any more. A Coke would be great." He hooked a thumb at Brigid. "And she's driving."

She sighed. "I'll have a Coke too, but could there maybe be a little rum in it, if you have any? One drink will be fine."

"One Coke, one rum and Coke, coming up." He gave her a look that made me suddenly sure he was older than the fifty-ish he looked (and I resolved to check the dates of Hank's musical career) and made me think that he might be prone to lecturing wayward nieces. Well, I wouldn't offer a second drink.

I got the drinks, including a rum and Coke for myself to provide Brigid moral support, and ushered them to the kitchen table. I put out a plate of cookies too.

"So, did Brigid tell you about this house and that I'm bonded to her?"

"Oh, yes," he said. "But I've met Nyssa before. I knew Ray Hobb."

Brigid looked at him. "You didn't tell me that! How did you meet him? You never come out of the woods."

"Ah, but a hundred years ago this house was at the edge of the woods." (I upped my estimate of his age and regretfully abandoned my fanciful theories about the late great Hank.) He went on, "There wasn't a lake then – that came later, when they decided to add the dams to control flooding and make electricity. So the whole area was forest, and then later they made it into orchards."

CHAPTERTWENTY-NINE: IDENTIFYING THE SEALS

"A hundred years or so ago, I was a half-grown kid. We lived mostly on farming, fishing and forestry around here, and they put us to work as soon as we were big enough, but after my work was done, I liked to wander the forests. You know, most people know about some of the other groups that look completely human, but they're not as open to us because we don't blend in. So we tend to keep to ourselves, and the women take care of any needful business in the town, since they can pass as human. But in this town back then, it was more open, because so many of the people who lived here were oak and pine dryads, or naiads from the lake."

"So when I saw Ray working on his house here, I went over to say hi. He was young too, not married yet, an' he liked the company. Next thing I knew, he put me to work. Working with trees 'n' wood is a Squatch thing so I was already pretty good, but nobody builds houses like a brownie. I learned a lot from him."

He turned to look at me. "I know Ray made a lot of changes over all the years, but you still got boards and beams in this house that I put in."

He leaned back and looked around. "I should have said hello when I first walked in. Hello, Nyssa. Good to see you again." He focused on me again. "I remember when he named her. I think he was more or less expecting the house to wake up and respond to him, but he wasn't real sure until it happened. And then he named her for the big willow that used to be out front – not the one that's there now but maybe its grandmother."

"Can you tell me anything about his relationship with Nyssa? He wrote a letter to his granddaughter Meg – she sold me the house – and said she'd have to work it out with Nyssa on her own, because it would be different with her."

"If that's what he said, then you'll probably need to figure it out too. I don't know much, because when I was in the house most, he was still building it. After it was first done, I still used to come over and talk with him, but we'd usually sit outside. We Squatch like to stay outside mostly, except some of the young girls like Brigid here who live more on the human side. All I know is that he used to talk to Nyssa all the time, like you would to your best dog."

Brigid said to me, "I told him about those wood and metal panels you found, and he thinks he might know what they are, or at least how they got here."

"That would be great, I'd love to know anything you can tell me about them. There are two, one in the attic and one attached to the foundation outside. You want to see the attic one first? That way you can see it in the light."

"Sure, let's go see it."

I took them to the attic stairs, which fortunately were a real staircase, sturdy enough to hold his weight, and then over to the storage niche. I moved the boards that had been stored there out of the way and stood aside to let him take a look. As I stepped back, I looked over at Brigid, behind Uncle Bo and out of his sightline, and mouthed "*Squatch?*"

She pulled me back another step and murmured into my ear, "It's one of those words you shouldn't use unless you are one. Sasquatch is the polite word."

I moved toward her Uncle Bo again, and watched him run a hairy finger over the grate-thingy. "Yep, this is Squatch work. My cousin did the wood and we got a guy from one of the clans north of here to do the ironwork. There's iron ore up there, so they're good with it – that's where Brigid learned to weld, in fact." He looked at her fondly. "She didn't like working with wood. Kind of strange for a Squatch kid."

Brigid rolled her eyes at him. "All right, old man, my friend doesn't need to hear about me being a weird kid. Can you tell her anything else about that thing?"

"Maybe not a lot, but at least I can tell her the story. Lemme take a look at the other one, then we can talk."

We headed back downstairs, then I grabbed a couple of flashlights, since I still had all the outside lights off, and walked around to the side of the house. "There it is, by that barrel. That's the one Brigid recognized as maybe being something to do with your family."

"Yup, it is, and she's heard about it many times, even if she didn't realize it was the same man who built your house – you know how families retell their favorite stories."

We headed back to the kitchen and sat down by our unfinished Cokes. Or rum and Cokes, for two of us, and I offered the plate of cookies around again.

***

"This was a few years after Ray finished building his house. I was grown up by then, and I didn't go over every day anymore because I had plenty of my own work to do, but I still went by now and then to see him. My cousin Lars was a couple years older than I was, but we'd always been good friends, and I'd introduced him to Ray too. He was already married and had two little kids – the older one, Henrik, was a boy, about three."

Brigid broke in. "Sasquatches live longer than humans, but we grow up at about the same rate. But our boys are bigger than human kids, so they're a lot faster than human toddlers. Just as ornery at that age, though."

"One day, Lars was out working in the forest, and the baby was fussy. His wife thought Henny was playing quietly. But then she realized it was too quiet, went looking, and couldn't find him anywhere."

"She looked everywhere she could think of, with no luck. So she told all the other adults, and everybody looked for him. After half an hour, they still couldn't find Henny, and his parents were starting to panic. So a few of us went out to tell the others – the dryads and naiads nearby. If it had been a girl, we might have sent one of our women to tell the human police in town, but we couldn't do that for a boy – he already didn't look quite human. Your toddlers don't tend to have facial hair. But I did think of one more person to tell, and I headed out to Ray's house."

"I don't know if his granddaughter mentioned it to you, but she must have grown up being spoiled rotten, because Ray just loved kids. Loved them. So he was upset when he heard little Henny was lost, and he came back out with me to help with the search."

"Thing is, Henny'd still only been gone less than two hours, and he was *little*. And it wasn't like he'd have been heading out in a straight line. So we knew he couldn't have been too far away, but it's not easy to find a little kid in a forest. He could have been hiding under a bush, for all we knew. But one thing we knew was, he was probably scared by now."

"Nobody can make a home like a brownie. So when we got back to our village and heard that Henny still hadn't been found yet, Ray asked for some wood, and he made a little playhouse, in about ten minutes, just outside the village. He put Henny's little pillow and blanket in there, and his favorite toy, and had his mom sit in there and sing the lullaby she always sang to him – anything that might spell 'home' to a little kid. And he put his brownie magic into it of course – it wasn't just having a home that was important or the kid would have come back to his real home. But that little playhouse kind of broadcasted that home feeling like it was a radio – I swear, I could have found my way to it from five miles away even if I'd never seen it before, and Ray said that little kids of any species are even more sensitive to that kind of magic."

"And it worked! Twenty minutes later, Henny came right up to that little playhouse, walked inside, stuck his thumb in his mouth, laid down with his head in his mama's lap, and went straight to sleep. He was a bit scratched up, but not harmed otherwise."

"The whole village was thankful to Ray after that. He was always our friend, but he mostly came to visit us, until he got too old. I don't think anyone but me ever went to his house much, and I stopped going once the town grew out to where he was. That's why Brigid here didn't recognize the house – plus, of course, this was all about fifty years before she was born."

Brigid was fifty? I'd thought she was younger than me, maybe mid-30s at most. I wondered if there were special anti-aging Sasquatch beauty products – but no, probably not. And anyway, I needed to keep my attention on Uncle Bo's story.

"Lars asked Ray if there was anything he could possibly do for him – not in return because you can't pay for saving a child, but to show his thanks. Ray asked us for just one little thing, these two panels made of iron and wood, imbued with our magic."

***

I looked at him then, because I didn't know anything about Bigfoot magic, and Brigid looked at him in shock. She said, "But that's –"

He said, "I'm going to tell her. She's Ray's heir, in a way, and I don't think Nyssa would have bonded to her if she weren't trustworthy. But please," He looked at me sternly, "This goes no further.'

"I can keep a secret," I said. Brigid nodded. "She can."

"Well then. We can warp space – just a little, but that's how we keep from being seen. If we're ever spotted and don't want to be, we *bend* the place to move elsewhere. So that's what's built into those panels. But then Ray built them into his house, and he put his own magic into the link between the panels and the house. And his magic was very strong. So even knowing how they're built, I'm still not rightly sure what they do. I'm sorry I can't tell you more."

"Wow. So they're definitely magic," I said.

"Yup. What kind of magic they are now, or if they'll even do anything at all for you since you're not a brownie, that I don't know."

"Bo, thank you so much. I really do appreciate you coming over and telling me more about Grandpa Ray. I wish I'd known him, but I kind of feel like I do."

"You might, at that. He put a lot of himself into this house." He looked thoughtful. (I think; it was hard to tell under all that facial hair!) "He might have magicked the house to govern what kind of person could come to live here after him; I don't know, but his magic was strong, and I think he loved Nyssa *almost* as much as his own daughter."

We finished our (rum and) Cokes, talking about Grandpa Ray. I think Bo enjoyed the chance to reminisce about his old friend and see his house again.

They drove off, and half an hour later, I got a text from Brigid:

Brigid: Uncle Bocephus approves of you. You should feel honored – that doesn't happen too often!

***

I didn't talk to Gil after they left, since it was after midnight in Austin by then. I wrote him a note on the WiFi message board to say that big news was afoot, and told him about my house's latest mystery the next night instead, leaving only a few of the most confidential details fuzzy.

His response was, "OK, I officially give up on Option 3: Big House. That house of yours is just too bloody interesting to leave! I know the contractor thing is being difficult, but I still think adding to your house is our best option – if the town's Planning Committee will let us! And maybe we could start brainstorming other options."

"Like what?"

"Like…I could rent office space to work in. I might have to go to Eugene for it, because I doubt you have anything like that in Percival. Or maybe you do, because all I really need is space with a desk and good internet. Maybe I could rent a room in someone else's house. No, scratch that, I don't really want to have to deal with other people every time I need to do some work. But maybe someone local has a detached building, a garage apartment or something I could rent. Or I could rent a small apartment in Eugene, that I could work in and also use if we need some space from each other, but live in your house otherwise. We could…get an RV and leave it parked out front and that could be my space. We could get one of those clear plastic bubble tents that you can put a heater in, and I could work out there. I could get a houseboat and park it at your dock. Oh, or a sailboat!"

"OK, OK, I get the idea. You're coming to live here."

He sounded a little hurt. "Only if you really do want me to."

I thought about it, because I owed him something more than a reflex, unthinking answer, and then said softly, "I really, really do." Then I thought some more and said, "We probably can't fit all your furniture here, though. We should go through item by item and decide, like, do we want to keep your couch or my couch? Your bed or my bed in our room? And whichever bed we don't use for us, is it nicer than the one in my spare room now? And so on. And depending on what we do, you might want to get a storage unit here, for anything that doesn't fit in your small apartment or igloo or houseboat or –"

"All right, all right, I get it, but why store it?"

"Just wanted to prove I was listening! And store it, because that way the RV or whatever buys us time to keep looking into contractors and variances, if that's our ideal solution."

"Good thinking. I'll be there in a couple of days; maybe we can spend the weekend looking around to figure out prices on all of those options. So, back to your new house mystery, are you going to try to figure it out? Or just ignore those things, or even get rid of them?"

"Well, I definitely won't get rid of them. Ray wanted them for some reason, and I can only think it was to make the house better in some way, or at least better for him. If it was a brúnaidh magic thing, I might never figure it out, but I'm definitely curious."

"So what are you going to do to work it out?"

"Research and experiment, I guess. Whatever I can think of, that doesn't feel like it will blow up the house."

"Or yourself!! Be careful, please. I'll be there in a few days, and I don't want to show up at your doorstep and find that the house isn't there anymore!"

CHAPTER THIRTY: UNSEALING THE SEALS

I didn't get to do any experiments until late the next afternoon; I figured I'd better get my work out of the way first, and by then it was a beautiful warm day, so I went kayaking to get some water time in before it started raining again. But after that, I started trying to figure out the Bigfoot panels in the attic and outside on the foundation. After hearing their story, I found myself thinking of them as the Henrik panels.

I started with some research, but so little was known about Sasquatches that I couldn't find anything relevant on the topic. Not too surprising, after Bo and Brigid told me that their people kept their magic a secret.

Without any history to fall back on, I resorted to experimentation. It made sense to start simple; of course I'd already tried pulling out the panels, but I hadn't pulled very hard once I figured out that they were attached. Now I grabbed a crowbar and tried applying a little force, but nothing happened. I didn't want to pull too hard and yank out a chunk of drywall along with the panel.

Next, I ran my hands all over both panels, to see if there might be a secret button or spring, like the priests' holes I used to read about in older English novels. If there was one, though, it successfully eluded me. I tried tapping on them in different rhythms, and tapping around the one in the attic to see if the space behind it sounded hollow (it did, but might just be a ceiling truss).

Then I got back to work since I did have orders to fulfill, though it was hard to focus with such a tantalizing mystery haggling right there. I forced myself to work, though; in three days I had lunch with Laxmi and Meg, and Gil would arrive the day after for two weeks' visit. I didn't know how long the lunch would take, and I wanted to be able to take some time off if Gil could, though we'd both need to do some work during his visit. I was hoping, now that it was warmer, to talk him into going out in a kayak with me – I had a double 'yak as well as the single one I normally used by myself.

Once I had my spells created, stored and ready to be sent out the next day, I went back to researching. This could take a while, since I had no idea what the panels were for. The only things I was sure of was that they were indeed magic; that they were important to Grandpa Ray, since they'd been his only request from a village of grateful Sasquatches; and that they had something to do with the idea of bending space, since that was the magic they'd been created with.

From those slender clues, I assumed the panels were some kind of doors, that were meant to open to…where? Somewhere in the house, or out of it? I might be wrong, but that idea was at least a place to start. The problem was that opening spells were a whole genre of magic on their own.

It was a good thing I had no deadline on this, other than an itching curiosity to find out what secrets Nyssa was still hiding from me!

I dug out my old schoolbooks on the subject, figuring I'd end up doing research online but the books might give me some starting places. They did, sort of; the problem was that they didn't narrow anything down much. There were magic keys and locks, as well as spells to open boxes, chests, doors, rooms, caves… I decided to avoid the subject of keys and locks, since there were no obvious keys or keyholes anywhere on those panels. Of course it was possible that they were there and had been magically camouflaged somehow, but I'd come back to that idea if other avenues didn't lead anywhere.

I decided to start by researching spells to open doors, since that seemed most relevant here – if my assumptions were even correct. This looked like it might be a long haul.

***

That set the pattern for my next couple of days – work, research, work, research, varied with the occasional internet search or actual trial of some spell I'd found, to no effect. By Thursday evening, I realized that I was supposed to have three people over for lunch the next day and I had nothing to feed them. Fortunately, although we couldn't get meals delivered out here, we were able to get groceries delivered to our door, so I placed an order to be delivered the next morning. It was early May by now but still a bit cool until later afternoon, so I decided on a baked potato bar. That would be fun for Laxmi and relatively easy. Menzy didn't eat meat, and Laxmi was coming with her mom today, who was also vegetarian, so this could work for everyone. (Thank goodness neither of them were vegans, or I'd have had to be more creative!) I also grabbed a container of leftover chili I'd frozen – if that didn't get eaten at lunch, I could have it at dinner.

When I got up the next morning, I set a bunch of alarms for myself: one to put the potatoes in the oven mid-morning – somehow they taste better when they're really baked than when they're microwaved – and one for a little before lunchtime, to get everything set up. I'd cheated and bought shredded cheese instead of grating it myself, as well as some pre-made bacon bits so the whole house didn't smell of cooking bacon, but I did make a quick cheese sauce. I heated the chili and cut up some broccoli and scallions and put those out, along with the shredded cheese, plus butter, and sour cream. Hopefully that would be enough options to please everyone. I baked some cookies for dessert, too – I knew Laxmi would appreciate those!

Laxmi and her mom arrived right on time. When they walked in, Laxmi said, "Hello, house!" as usual, then her eyes got big. "It felt like the house said hello back to me!"

"Nyssa," I told her. "Her name is Nyssa. Nyssa, this

is Laxmi, the young magic user I told you about, and her mother Deepthi."

"Nice to meet you, Nyssa," Laxmi and Deepthi chorused. Laxmi whispered to me, "She seems a *lot* more awake now!" and I made a mental note to ask her more about her perceptions about houses in one of our future visits.

Menzy was late as usual, so I took advantage of the extra time with the two of them to broach the idea of training Laxmi to kayak this summer. (And to make sure she could swim!) It turned out she'd gone canoeing with her dad a few times; though he'd done more of the paddling for the two of them, she'd at least gotten to try it, so hopefully that experience would give her a head start.

Deepthi said, "I'm OK with her learning to paddle, as long as you both solemnly swear she will wear a life jacket at all times!"

"I always wear one myself in cooler weather, and I take it along in the boat when it's hot out. But we can promise that she'll wear hers at all times – and I will wear mine, in solidarity."

"Good. We do have one her size that she can bring with her. It will be good to get her used to small boats – and then you can make her paddle you around the lake while you work on your spells!" She winked at me over Laxmi's head.

"Mo-om! I promise, she makes me work, not just play. You saw how tired I was last time."

"I know. That's why I like you having lessons with Macrina," she said, in a mock-stern voice.

"But, Macrina, we won't only paddle fast, will we? I don't think I can paddle very fast or very far."

"No, I think the whole point of kayaking is to enjoy being out on the lake. And don't worry, we'll start out in the double kayak with both of us paddling. We won't put you in a single by yourself until you feel ready. Even then, I'll be right beside you, because I can paddle the double by myself while you're in the single.

When Menzy showed up, we sat down to talk about

Laxmi's project first, before lunch. I gave them a quick overview of how I thought this would work: we could try it in two stages, with Laxmi first teaching Menzy how to invoke a stored pre-prepared spell (which I would provide, though Laxmi could help make it). Next, Laxmi would learn to do the spell herself, hopefully learning it well enough that I wouldn't need to guide her or provide extra energy as I'd done before. Finally, she'd teach the spell to Menzy. I'd spoken to Menzy before when we were first discussing this project idea and had learned, to my surprise, that she never had done any human-style magic at all, even to the extent of using a pre-made stored spell ("Never needed to," she shrugged) so she was a perfect test subject.

When Menzy told Laxmi about her mustache-spell idea, they dissolved into matching sets of giggles. Deepthi gave me a look that said, clearly and with no words needed, "We're in trouble, aren't we?" I nodded an agreement.

I estimated that it would take a day to prepare the stored spell and maybe 2-3 weeks for Laxmi to learn the mustache spell well enough, with lessons from me and practice on her own, for her to start teaching Menzy, so we agreed to meet again in about a month.

After that, I pulled the potatoes out of the oven where they'd been keeping warm and set out all of the topics I'd prepared. Once we'd all loaded our spuds to our satisfaction (and Laxmi had a heap of toppings bigger than her actual potato) we sat down to eat and talk. The cats lurked under the table, just in case someone might accidentally drop a bit of cheese.

Laxmi and Menzy had clearly bonded already. They'd moved on from the discussion of exactly what style of mustache they should magically draw on people, and were now involved in a discussion that ranged from hairstyles to K-pop stars to comic books I'd never heard of. Still, they started listening with more interest when I told Deepthi about my house's latest magical mystery. When I said that I thought I might be researching for weeks yet, they looked at each other and both faces acquired smirks that were almost creepy in their perfect mirroring.

"What??" I demanded.

Menzy nodded to Laxmi to answer for the pair of them. In a clear but clumsy attempt at tact, Laxmi said, "Macrina... Have you tried just *asking* Nyssa to open her panels?"

I hadn't. But in an attempt to defend myself from a charge of obvious idiocy, I said, "Well, no...but I did ask politely if she would clean the house last week, and nothing happened."

This time Menzy answered. "You said she's kind of at the level of a pet dog, right? She can't really talk to you, but she understands some words and can help you if she wants? Well, maybe she's more like a pet cat – you know, only does what she really wants to do."

Laxmi chimed in. "And she should want to open those panels, if they really are doors, because Grandpa Ray made them and gave them to her, and you said they loved each other."

I put my face in my hands. They were right. I was an idiot.

Then Deepthi added, "If you want to try it, it might be good to do while we're all here. After all, if they are doors, it wouldn't be really safe to explore what's behind them on your own."

I gave her a look. "Oh, now you're on their side?"

I looked around at my guests and smiled sweetly. "Are you all done? Anybody want seconds? Anything else I can get you?"

Menzy said, "Now you're just trying to torture us. You know you want to try if it works, even more than we do!"

I gave up. She was right.

"Come on, everyone, up to the attic."

***

We walked up the stairs to the attic, past the office,

through the lab, to the storage niche — with the four of us plus the cats following us, it felt like a very small indoor parade. I said, "It's over here, behind these boards," and Menzy helped me move them out of the way and lean them against another wall.

Menzy looked at the panel and said, "Oh, yeah, can't see what it does but I can definitely see it's magic. Can you tell, Laxmi?"

Laxmi bit her lip and stared at it, then said, "No. I can't see anything special about it. How can you tell?"

I told her, "Don't worry, neither can I. I didn't know it was magic at all until a Sasquatch told me."

Menzy looked surprised. "You had a Sasquatch here to look at it? They hardly ever come out of the woods."

"Yeah, long story." I didn't want to reveal Brigid's secret – Menzy might know about her, but Laxmi and Deepthi probably didn't – or talk about Uncle Bo. I went on, "But dryads and Sasquatches have a lot in common, right? I mean, you're nothing alike but you're both linked to trees and forests. That would explain why you can see it and we can't."

Menzy answered, "Could be. It's not just Sasquatch magic though. There's something else there – it must be the brúnaidh contribution Rob added."

By now, Laxmi was bouncing up and down. I asked her, "Too much talking and not enough opening for you?"

She answered very politely and with complete falsehood, "Oh, no, Macrina, I'm just curious."

I looked over her head at her mom and said, "Impressive manners."

She looked proud, but I decided it was time to put Laxmi out of her misery. My turn to be polite. I called out, "Hello, Nyssa? If Grandpa Ray made this panel to open, could you please open it for us? I know he was OK with letting a new person be bonded with you, so I think he'd be happy to let us in."

There was a creak that sounded like an answer, but nothing happened for a moment, so I wasn't sure what kind of an answer it was meant to be. And then one side of the panel moved just a little away from the wall.

We all looked at each other with wide eyes, and Menzy said, "Go on, Macrina. It's your house and your bond."

I took hold of the open side of the panel and pulled it farther away from the wall – it was stiff at first, then seemed to move more smoothly.

And then I looked inside.

CHAPTER THIRTY-ONE: WHAT WE FOUND

It couldn't have been more exciting. Dear Reader, if someone came to you and asked, "If your house had a secret room, what kind of room would you want it to be?", what would you say?

Yep, me too. And that's what it was: a *library*.

It wasn't huge; we're not talking the library from Beauty and the Beast here. In fact, it was a duplicate of the lab in shape, an ordinary biggish room with an annex on the far side that was fitted with a desk, just as the lab had an alcove for storage space. You entered it from the lab's storage alcove, of course, but the door was just barely inside the alcove so that the space could still be used for storage without blocking the door – those boards must have been left there as deliberate camouflage.

But though the library wasn't enormous, it was covered with bookshelves from floor to almost to the ceiling, with a proper library ladder on each side to access books on the higher shelves. Just as in the lab, there was a row of thin windows the whole length of both long walls over the bookshelves, that would look like roof vents from the ground, and another big window in the alcove on the left side of the desk where it would provide plenty of working light. The whole space was either camouflaged from outside with more magic or existed somewhere else entirely. There wasn't another window on the outside of the house, nor was there space for the library to be there on the second floor next to the lab. However, the view from the windows was exactly what you'd expect given the room's seeming location next to the lab.

Grandpa Ray's collection of books was larger than my own, and I spotted some familiar magical texts and many new to me, as well as classics and newer books, both children's and adult books. But there were also empty shelves – I thought there might be enough space for whatever books of Gil's were left over, after the two of us went through our respective libraries and got rid of our duplicates. (My books were already in my own bookcases in various rooms, of course.)

That was the point when I made up my mind: Gil was out of luck. Well, no, he wasn't, this library and its office area solved a lot of the problems we'd had with the idea of him moving in, but this office just off the library was going to be MINE. He could have the one I'd been using. Anyway, this library opened off my lab, while the other office had a separate entrance from the hallway at the top of the stairs. And that office was bigger than this nook, anyway. If he was lucky, I might let him use the library; it was big enough that he wouldn't bother me if I was in the office area.

At that point I became aware I had just spent several minutes standing in the doorway of the room with my mouth gaping open. The others were trying to see over my shoulders into the room. They'd been remarkably polite to let me stare at the library for that long, but now Menzy tapped my shoulder and said, "Macrina? Do you think we'd better do some tests to make sure no one is going to get locked in there?"

She was right again, and I also needed to stop being rude, so I said, "Yes, but first let me step out of the way so you can all take a look."

I did that and they all took turns staring at the room and making appreciative comments. Even Laxmi seemed impressed, and said, "Look, it's got all three of the Percy Jackson series over there!"

I smiled and said, "Do you have them too?"

"No, I read them from the library."

"Well, it looks like now I have duplicate sets. I'm not sure yet if I can take things out of the library, but if I can, maybe you can have the extra set."

She grinned wide. "Thanks, Macrina!"

***

Next, we did testing. First, I asked Nyssa to seal the library. We all tried the panel and found that we couldn't open it. I asked her, "Can you please open the library again, and leave it open? Please, don't ever lock someone in there unless I ask you to."

There were no creaks or other noises this time, but suddenly I smelled the scent of the cookies I'd baked that morning. I took that as agreement.

"Can you all please wait outside, while I step in, close the door and try to open it again?"

Deepthi asked, "Not to steal your new toy, but would it be better for one of us to try it? We don't know if she'd open the door again if any of the rest of us ask her to."

I said, "Problem is, she doesn't really know any of you well except Laxmi, and I don't think we should let her go in first until we test it."

Laxmi protested, of course, but I stopped that by simply entering the library. I stood in the middle of the room and looked all around. I was going to have to spend time exploring this room and everything in it, but for now I moved back to the door, closed it (it looked like a regular wooden door from this side, with a lock) and reopened it, to see their relieved faces on the other side.

I called out, "Anyone want to join me in here?" and Laxmi popped in, before Deepthi or Menzy could stop her. Nothing happened.

She stood in the center of the room and revolved, looking around her just as I had. "What are those other doors?" she asked, pointing to two on the far side of the room.

"Don't know. Let's finish our tests before we check them out. Come on, let's make sure we can both leave."

I put my hand on her shoulder and nudged her out first, then stepped back out myself. Once again, I shut the panel and reopened it, relieved to still be able to move the panel and to see the library beyond it looking just the same. "Menzy and Deepthi, do you want to try it too? That way we can make sure it works for humans and magical people – though you are both MCs, even if you, Deepthi, don't do much magic."

Deepthi said, nearly as enthralled as her daughter by our discovery, "Sure, what should we do?"

"One at a time, just what I did first: step in, close the door, open it, and come back out."

They did, with no issues. I called out, "Thank you, Nyssa," hoping she'd appreciate the recognition.

I tried one more thing: "Hey, everyone, can you step back into the lab? I'm going to ask Nyssa to seal the door with me inside; when I knock twice, try to open it."

They left, and I closed the door, then said, "Nyssa, can you please reseal the door?"

I heard a click, then tried to open it. It opened normally. I was a little confused – and so were the faces of the other three – then I realized what might have happened. I closed it again and knocked twice. Nothing happened. I waited a moment, then opened the door. "Did you try to open it?"

"We did," said Menzy. "The panel was sealed to the wall just like before." I guessed my earlier request to Nyssa to avoid sealing anyone inside had given her some clue to what I wanted, even when I'd asked her to reseal it. Cool. I had a panic room!

***

After that, I felt fairly safe letting everyone into the library, so we all went in and looked around. There were a couple of comfortable chairs with footrests and a floor lamp and small table between them; I wondered if this was where Ray and his Rose spent their evenings.

Looking at the books, I noted a few I thought might be antiquarian books of some value; was that why Ray had hidden the library, or had he simply not wanted to be disturbed? Or had he hidden it for the sheer fun of having a secret library? I wondered if I'd ever find out.

Laxmi had taken a quick look at the shelves of children's books, but then made a beeline for the two doors on the other side of the room. These proved not to be locked; she opened the one on the left to find a powder room, just a toilet and small pedestal sink, with rosy red walls and an oval mirror over the sink.

I realized their plumbing was just on the back of the wall where the lab sink stood; very sensible. Because of that I was sure the toilet and sink would work, but I flushed the one and turned on the other, just to make sure. They did. This was going to be convenient!

I stepped out of the powder room, then Laxmi poked her head in, looked at the mirror, and started laughing. I turned to see why, and realized that her reflection was sticking its tongue out at her! Well, house spirits like brownies and gruagach were also known for their pranks; this seemed like a harmless one Grandpa Ray had kept in his private space.

Laxmi said, "You said all magic uses energy. Is this hidden room and that mirror going to take energy from everyone who comes in here?"

I reassured her. "I don't feel any drain. The spells would have taken a lot of energy to create, but I think Grandpa Ray would have built them over years, and they can probably keep running indefinitely on the magic they were built with."

She looked relieved for about a microsecond, then headed over and opened the other door. That's when things got weirder.

***

We'd entered this library from my lab, on the attic floor. But when Laxmi opened the second of the two identical doors on the far side of the room, we found ourselves looking into a garage.

I didn't feel the need to do the thorough testing we'd done with the library in this second hidden room, but just to be extra careful, I asked, "Nyssa, can you please keep us safe and make sure no one gets trapped in any of these rooms?" There was another whiff of cookies, so I felt relatively safe stepping into the garage.

It was fairly dark in there, but I felt the wall to the left of the door and found a couple of light switches. I turned them both on and saw… Yep, a garage. There was a small vehicle with a cover over it, a workbench, a couple of tool chests, and a garage door on the far side of the room. There was room for a pickup on one side, and a small car could fit in behind the covered vehicle. Looking around, I saw a button beside the light switches, so I pushed it, and the door began to open.

I said sharply, "Everyone stay back on this side of the room," and held my breath to see if we had a door opening in midair on the second floor of the house. But nope, it opened right out to ground level. It took me a minute, but I realized I was looking out from the left side of the house.

I began to suspect how this worked, walked outside, and realized the garage door opening was right where the mystery panel had connected to the foundation – though it was a lot larger. This was seriously powerful, and I began to develop even more respect for brúnaidh house magic.

I thought of one possible pitfall before doing any further testing, and said, "Can you folks please wait here a moment? Leave the door open, but don't let the cats run out." They were still sniffing around the library, but I didn't want to take the chance of having to chase them down.

I went back through the library, back through the lab, back down the stairs, grabbed my housekeys, then retraced my steps. As I re-entered the garage, I brandished the keys. "I had a sudden realization that, depending how much Nyssa can hear and respond when we're outside the house, we could've gotten locked out. Ready for the next test? I think this one is going to be really strange."

We walked out of the garage door, and I called out, "Nyssa, can you please close the garage door?"

The door stayed open, so I walked back inside. I was going to ask her to close the door from inside, wondering what use a garage was that you could only enter after opening it from the attic. Before I could speak, though, I noticed something glowing red on the inside wall, beside the door. I walked over to it, and realized it was a normal-looking automatic garage door opener. Huh. I reached out to touch it and realized it was hooked onto a big nail in the wall, so I grabbed it off and stepped outside
.

"Everybody out?" They were, so I pressed the button. It was odd to watch a garage door closing, there on the side of my house where normally all I'd see were a few windows. Then just as it finished closing, the whole door disappeared – and there was the original Henny panel, stuck to the foundation.

I tried calling again, "Nyssa, can you please open the garage door?" But again, nothing happened. I pressed the button, and the panel transformed back into a garage door, in the process of opening. This was house magic on a scale I'd never seen before, but then I'd never been in a brúnaidh's home before. Certainly I'd seen any number of major spells done: I'd seen people flying, transformations, translocations, and so on, but it usually took many people to execute one of those. Then again, I'd seen Sulis step out of the lake and Menzy disappear into a tree; I guess a house is equally a brúnaidh's natural habitat, and this one had clearly been Ray Hobb's life work. I wondered if Nyssa might still be hiding other secrets.

I had other, more practical questions as well. "Nyssa, what happens if I want to be able to store two cars in the garage, say if I have a visitor?"

The same red glow peeked out of a drawer in the smaller tool chest. I opened it and found one more opener plus an envelope labeled, "Instructions for making more garage door openers." I recognized the writing – it was the same I'd seen on the letter to Meg. Ray Hobb really had thought of everything.

CHAPTER THIRTY-TWO: EVERYTHING WE NEED

By that time, Menzy had to leave, and Deepthi was telling Laxmi that it was past time to start on her homework for the weekend. Laxmi said, "But can't we help Macrina take inven – inventing –"

"You mean inventory?" her mother said. "I think Macrina deserves a little time to explore her own house without anyone else intruding."

I was suddenly conscious that she was right. I wanted, more than anything else, to be alone in the house. Or even better, to be here with Gil, but that would have to wait until tomorrow. I did owe them all for giving me the key to Nyssa's mystery panels, though, so I smiled at Laxmi.

"Thank you so much, you and Menzy. Without the two of you I might have been researching for months, and still never figured out how to open those panels. I promise I'll let you look around more next time you come over."

"What I still don't understand," Deepthi mused, "is, why keep a garage secret? It didn't look like there was anything special in there. A secret library somehow seems more likely."

"No idea," I told her. "Maybe it was something he was working on in there. Maybe he just did it because he could?"

Deepthi added one more possibility. "Maybe he wanted to keep his property taxes down? I think we just added a few hundred square feet to the floorplan of your house, not to mention a two-car garage."

Laxmi looked disgusted. "I bet he had a better

reason for it than boring taxes!"

I sort of hoped she was right, and wondered what else I might learn from Nyssa. She'd been more responsive today than ever before; was it the bond growing, or were there just certain things she would do and some she wouldn't? I still had a lot to learn about her.

And I definitely wasn't going to tell Gil tonight. That might make for a very short phone call, since I'd be biting my tongue the whole time, but it would be better to surprise him when he arrived tomorrow.

As they were leaving, I managed to pull Deepthi aside to reassure her that I'd be preparing a mustache-removal spell, just in case. I wasn't going to tell either Laxmi OR Menzy about that though! Let them have their fun; I'd be ready if cleanup was needed.

Once they were gone, I went back to the library. As she'd done in the rest of the house, Nyssa had kept the dust from building up here – nobody would have been in here for more than a year, but thanks to her, I wouldn't need to spend hours cleaning up the library or garage before they could be used.

My initial impression had been almost correct – there were lots of books on magic, but most of them weren't college textbooks. They were a wide range, from books for MC kids to scholarly works, including a few that I suspected were rare, maybe valuable. I hastily revised my impressions of Grandpa Ray, or was Grandma Rose the scholar? These weren't the books of someone who only did the instinctive magic they were born to, but of a voracious reader who loved to learn. They'd all been read; none of the oldest books were uncut, and some of the children's books were bedraggled very well-loved. Next time I talked to Meg, I'd tell her that her vague childhood memories of a library in this house really were true, and I'd check to see if any of these little books had been favorites she might want for sentiment, or in case she ever had children of her own.

The books on other topics were less scholarly – magic had clearly been the main topic of serious study for whoever built this library – but just as wide-ranging. There were plenty of books on home architecture and design, from treatises on post-and-beam building to photo books of everything from tiny homes to extravagant log cabins. I recognized some of my own favorite books on the subject, like Sarah Susanka's Not So Big House and How Buildings Learn, by Stewart Brand. Whichever hand had built the rest of the library, I was positive all of these "home" books had been Grandpa Ray's.

And then there were the books of people who just loved to read, everything from the kind of history and science books that were aimed at laypeople but required serious attention, to adults and kids' fantasy series. Ray had kept some books in the living room's library area, maybe for convenience, but his main collection was here. I could see that he'd continued collecting throughout his long life, and had apparently always loved fantasy – the juveniles included everything from what looked like early editions of L.M. Montgomery's Anne books on up to Carlos Hernandez's Sal and Gabi books, and the adult books ranged from Tolkien and Dunsany to the likes of Jodi Taylor, Mark Hayden and Ben Aaronovitch. The latest books I saw were from a year or less before Ray's death, and all showed signs of having been read.

I also had to laugh, noticing a special section that held only books whose stories included sentient houses. I saw more of my favorites here, from Howl's Moving Castle to Matteson Wynn's Housekeeper series to Ilona Andrews' Innkeeper Chronicles. I most often read on my Kindle these days, but I'd need to buy physical copies of the most recent books in those series, plus Linzi Day's Gretna Green books, to add to this section.

I'd need to examine the books closely with help from Google – I suspected some of these were first editions. I'd honor Ray's memory by reading them, not keeping them as a sterile collection for collecting's sake, but I'd be careful with the unreplaceable ones!

It was looking to me like this had been where Ray and Rose spent their time, more than in the living room downstairs. There had been nothing *but* books in the downstairs bookcases when I first saw them. The house hadn't been cleaned out before I moved in; since we were deep in the middle of pandemic quarantine, Meg had simply mailed me a key. The house had been as Ray left it, though now I suspected that Nyssa had quietly kept it from getting too dusty before my arrival. There were more treasures on the shelves up here, though; the living room had been neat, with some art on the walls but not many knickknacks or trinkets anywhere. Here there were items that were clearly treasured memories in front of the books, from a photo of small Meg with her mother to an enormous pinecone and a few chunks of Oregon sunstone and beach glass – Ray and his Rose must have left their home sometimes, at least to travel within the state.

I had visions of myself and Gil sitting up here, just as they had. Gil would probably be on his table, researching or scrolling or even watching a movie (we'd probably have to put a TV in the living room but I didn't want one up here!) and I'd be reading a book – probably on my e-reader, to be fair, but I'd enjoy the feeling of being surrounded by all of these physical books.

***

After spending some time gloating over the new library, I went to check out the garage. This wasn't my native heath as the library had been, or as my lab was, but clearly it had been Grandpa Ray's. The tools were lovingly kept and neatly stored. There were hand tools enough to open a hardware store: hammers and mallets, screwdrivers and bit drivers, ratchet wrenches and socket wrenches and Allen wrenches, plus tackle boxes full of nails and screws, nuts and bolts. There were also a few power tools I wasn't so sure of, though I recognized a table saw and a router.

I took the cover off the small vehicle stored there, and found it was a golf cart – presumably Ray had found it useful for getting around town as he grew older.

It was undeniably strange to have a garage that could only be accessed inside the house from the attic. Of course you could get into it on the ground level from outside if you had the opener – but if you'd parked the car in there, you'd have been likely to leave the opener in the car. There had to be another way, for the sake of unloading groceries if nothing else.

If there was another entrance, it was likely to be from the kitchen, or perhaps the laundry room. I could probably ask Nyssa to show it to me, but I decided to wait and let Gil have the fun of finding it with me.

Our conversation that night was short; hopefully, he thought that was just because we'd see each other soon. I'd be picking him up from the airport. Once again, he'd decided not to rent a car because he gotten along fine without one last time; either we'd gone out together, or he'd gone somewhere while I was working at home and could borrow mine.

I thought about different ways to show off Nyssa's new features; I could give him the tour right away – but on his previous visits he'd swept me off to the bedroom right away, and it might be awkward if I pushed him away and said, "Wait, let's tour the house first!" I didn't want to damage his frail male ego, after all. (I am joking; Gil's male ego was quite secure and not at all frail!) I could wait until after dinner and just say, "Let's go sit in the library," but it had been hard enough not to mention the new rooms on our brief phone call, and I didn't really think I could do it for hours and hours.

Besides, it was always fun watching someone's jaw drop; I didn't want to be subtle about this!

I decided to just take the opener along and drive directly into the garage with him. We'd have to carry his bag downstairs after that, or walk around outside, but it was worth it.

***

When I picked Gil up at the airport, he seemed a bit gloomy. Of course this was meant to be work time for him, not a vacation, but still I'd have thought being with me, in the town he'd said he wanted to move to, would have resulted in a better mood.

I waited to see if he'd say anything as we hugged and walked out of the airport to the car, but he still hadn't said anything more than basic greetings by the time we pulled out of the airport parking lot. So finally, I said, "What's wrong? Are you having cold feet about moving here?"

His head came right up at that. "No, NO! It's just all being so damn difficult – I mean, I knew it would be hard, but I was expecting the difficulties to be the usual moving-in-together stuff. Moving is always a pain in the ass, and so is remodeling, and if you're buying a house there's always the issue of timing, making sure the new place is ready by the time you need to leave the old one. And I know that, as much as I want to live with you, there will be shakedown issues – we're both probably set in our ways after all these years in a long-distance relationship."

He stopped talking and took a deep breath. "I was prepared for all those things. But what I wasn't expecting was for it to be so difficult to figure out where we're going to live. I really don't want to move all the way up here just to keep living separately. You really don't want to leave your current house, and Nyssa, and I understand why. And it doesn't seem like there are many houses on the market that would work either way, anyway. So adding on to your house is the obvious solution, but we don't even know if we'll be able to get the variance to allow us to do that. I know I said they do that all the time, and it's true, but some cities are more willing to grant variances than others."

He took another breath and spoke more softly. "And all of this has made me realize that I do really, really want to live with you. Meli, I want to hold you as you fall asleep every night, and watch you wake up every morning, tell you about my day and hear about yours. We're old enough now to feel our bodies changing a little bit and I don't want to get any older without doing it together. I guess I'm just torn; on the one hand, I trust us to be able to find solutions to almost any problem, and on the other hand, I'm terrified about that "almost" part. What if this is the one problem we can't solve?"

Well, that put me in a difficult situation. I don't like to lie, most especially not to Gil, and I'm a terrible actress anyway. On the other hand, flippancy would be flat-out cruel; I couldn't just wave my hand blithely and tell him everything would work out, without offering any evidence. He'd think I didn't care as much about living together as he did – and I realized in a burst of joy that I did care, even more than I'd realized. We'd known each other so well for so many years that we didn't talk that much about our feelings anymore. I knew how much he loved me but after so many years when he seemed content to love me from a distance, his words moved me deeply.

And that, I realized, was how I could keep my secret. I said, laughingly, "Oh, Gil, you do like me!" but instead of just blinking hard to clear my eyes inconspicuously, I let him see me wipe away tears, and then said, "I want to live with you every day just as much. But if we can't find a perfect solution, we'll find an imperfect one, like you said – rent an office somewhere for you, or get you a houseboat to be your office and man cave. I promise this is not the one we can't solve. If there ever is one where we'll have to separate again, like if one of us is in the hospital, I hope it won't be for decades and decades. Besides, we have a tradition to uphold."

As he turned to me with a lecherous look replacing the depressed expression, I held up the hand that wasn't on the steering wheel. "No, not that one. Well, that one too, but what I meant was, Nyssa is used to having a happy family living there. From everything I've heard, Ray and Rose stayed very much in love all their lives, and they lived together there for a very long time. That's the tradition we need to continue."

For the rest of the drive, we talked about living on the lake – did we want to get a boat? Should we get a kayak for Gil, or maybe a paddle board? I had my own single kayak and a double that we could paddle together, but it would be nice to have more options. He'd lived in an apartment most of his life, and thought he might like to start a garden; I told him how my container plants were doing, and that I'd be happy for him to grow even more food.

Finally, we were on the dead-end street that the curving gravel driveway to my house led from, so I said, as casually as I could, "I know I said we'd live with an imperfect solution if we had to, but luckily, we don't have to. Let's just put the car in the garage and I'll tell you about it."

He looked surprised at my first sentence, but I was watching and I could see the exact minute the ramifications of my second sentence hit him. "Put the...in the what?"

CHAPTER THIRTY-THREE: IT ALL COMES TOGETHER

Instead of pulling into the carport, I drove right onto the scraggly grass that went around the left side of the house and pulled up facing the blank wall, perpendicular to the small panel. He'd seen that before and I'd told him about what Uncle Bo had said, but I hadn't told him any of the latest developments, of course. I slyly reached into the leg pocket of the cargo pants I was wearing, where I'd stashed the garage opener so he couldn't see it, and hit the button to open the door.

If he'd looked shocked before, he was now completely flabbergasted as the small panel instantly changed into an opening door that was almost as tall as the whole ground floor of the house. I drove in and used the remote to close the door behind us – normally, I'd probably have walked outside and around to the front door, since the bedrooms were on ground level, but I wanted him to get the full experience.

He'd said a few words since the door started opening but none of them had made any sense – mostly variants on "What the hell?" Now he stopped speaking, closed his mouth, shut his eyes, took a few slow, controlled breaths, and then said, "You jerk. You didn't tell me about all of this!" His smile was huge and happy as he got out of the car, walked around to the driver's side, pulled me out, and hugged me fiercely.

"How long have you known about this? Are there any other secrets you haven't told me? A magic entrance to Oz, maybe?"

"Come and see!" He grabbed his bag, and I led him

to the door into the house, flung it open, and waved him on into the library. His jaw dropped again, and he said, faintly, "Oh. Not Oz, Discworld. The Unseen University Library, clearly. Should there be a Beware the Orangutan sign?"

I laughed and said, "Not nearly that big. But isn't it beautiful?"

"It really is."

"I do have one bit of bad news for you, though."

"What's that? The library turns into a pumpkin at midnight? I can't enter it unless you're with me to open the door? The magic takes a year off our lives every time we come in here?"

"Nope, none of those. The bad news is, that desk over there is *mine*. You can use my old office, and if you ask very prettily, I will let you put your books in the library and keep your cars in the garage."

"Please, beauteous Macrina, may I humbly put my lowly books on your sacred shelves?" Changing to a normal tone, he said, "Don't you want to put your car in the garage?"

"Nah. You can keep your cars in the garage. Mine is fine in the carport. I frowned, thinking. "We may want to pave that driveway, though, or at least put gravel in, or it'll turn to muck when you drive over it in the rainy season. We'll have to think of a way to make it not look weird when it stops at a blank wall."

"We'll figure it out. We're back to easy problems now, thanks to your magic house!"

"Nyssa. Her name is Nyssa. I think she likes it when you talk to her."

"Thank you, Nyssa," he called. "You've solved some of our problems beautifully, and I hope you're OK with me living here with Macrina."

A cooking smell drifted by, and I started laughing again. Not cookies this time!

"What did I say?" He looked puzzled.

"It's not what you said, it's what she said."

"What she said? Does she talk to you? You didn't

any anything about -"

"No, take a sniff."

"Is that – is someone nearby cooking steaks?"

"No, apparently she remembers you, and clearly she approves!"

"Wow, this is going to be an adjustment," he muttered, then said louder, "Thank you! Glad to be here!"

He turned to me and lowered his volume again. "You don't think she watches us *all* the time, do you?"

"I doubt it. We're not that exciting! But also, remember Ray and Rose spent their whole married life here and had their daughter here. I'm sure people have had sex in this house before. Besides, who would she tell about us? If you're squeamish, you could ask her not to watch when you're in bed or in the bathroom – but I wouldn't. She might be literal about it, and I'd rather have her let us know if the house catches fire or whatever."

"If you say so." He wandered over to the window, appreciating the view of the lake, and once again I could see the realization hit him. He turned back to me.

"Wait a minute, didn't we come in here from the garage?"

"That's right," I said demurely.

"But this view looks a lot higher up."

"Yup."

"Hmmm, clearly I need to finish exploring."

He wandered over and opened the door on the left and poked his head through. "Another bathroom! That's handy!"

Next, he opened the other door and walked through. "Wait, this is your lab." His eyes narrowed. "Your *attic* lab. So we drove into your garage, which is on a fairly level plot, and walked straight into the upstairs library without ever going up stairs? That's like -"

"Magic, yes," I said, struggling to keep my face straight.

"But I don't do magic. Did you do some spell to make this work?"

"No, it's all Nyssa."

He looked elated now. "OK, I really don't
understand the concept of a garage whose only direct
entry to the house is on the upper floor, but I cannot *wait* to
move in here!"

He thought for a moment, then said, "Revelations
are done, right? So it's time for tradition. Come to think of
it, this has been a very short-lived tradition – spending the
whole afternoon and evening in bed when I arrive for a
visit at your house. We won't be able to do that anymore if
I live here."

He took me in his arms, nuzzled into my neck until
I shivered, and said into my ear in his deepest, softest
voice, "But don't worry; I'm sure we'll come up with a new
tradition to replace it."

***

The next day we talked about bonding Gil to Nyssa
– it seemed like something we ought to do if he was going
to live here. We checked the supplies I had left. Nyssa had
put a bow on my remaining bottle of mead and given it to
Meg – I'm pretty sure Meg didn't actually want it, but she
took it to avoid hurting Nyssa's feelings. I'd thrown away
the rest of the bottle we'd opened; it wouldn't have kept
this long after opening, anyway. So we would have to go
get another bottle of that, but fortunately I still had
beeswax candles. There were other factors to consider
about the bonding as well; although Gil was MC, like
Laxmi's parents he only had enough magic to do low-
powered spells bought from other people (or cadged from
me). Even so, I wasn't sure how well bonding him to
Nyssa would work, since his name wasn't on the deed to
the house (not yet, anyway – another thing we had to do). I
didn't know if she'd care about legal ownership.

We decided to hold off on getting more mead, and
to wait on the bonding ceremony until the day he arrived
back here without a return ticket to Austin – that way, he
didn't have to bond to Nyssa and then traumatize her by
leaving right away. More correctly, we'd wait until the day

we arrived back here. We decided we'd both take time off and drive his sleek little BMW convertible roadster from Austin, Texas to Percival, Oregon.

And believe me, it wasn't an easy decision, for either of us. Gil had to convince himself to let me take turns driving his baby, because making a 2000-mile drive with one driver wasn't a safe option. It wasn't personal; he didn't let *anyone* else drive that car! The factor that convinced him was that, if he didn't let me drive, he'd have had to let the movers transport the BMW, and that was apparently even more painful than letting me drive it. (He did have a practical vehicle as well, a compact SUV, but decided to sell it before leaving Texas and replace it once he got to Oregon.)

The hard part of the decision for me was how to pack for a road trip in a 2-seater with a trunk that was just about big enough for a backpack each and a small cooler. It turns out there are innumerable articles online about packing light and "capsule wardrobes" – the trick is to find the ones that aren't trying to lure you into buying an entirely new set of clothing for said capsule! The most difficult choice, as always, was which knitting project to bring with me – I'd have lots of knitting time when Gil was driving.

Gil spent his visit with me lining up movers to pack and move his stuff; arranging storage for the items that wouldn't fit in Nyssa, and buying me a plane ticket to Austin. He scheduled his vacation time. Since I worked for myself, I only had to warn customers I'd be away for a week. Genna's husband Duncan was home from Scotland, so I no longer had dog-walking commitments, though I still occasionally borrowed them for company when I was in the mood for a hike or long walk. Sulis volunteered to watch the cats again. (She occasionally dropped by just to snuggle with Merlin and Morgana; I think she viewed us as her own personal cat cafe.) This time I asked her to come over again before I left and reintroduced her to Nyssa by name, to make sure there was no trouble while we were gone.

In an amazingly short time, just around three weeks, it was early June, and we were flying to Austin. We almost ended up with extra baggage despite my dedication to packing light; when I picked up my backpack to take it to the car, it was considerably heavier than it ought to have been. Somehow, in the little bit of space that was left in the bag, Morgana had not only wormed her way in but somehow managed to zip the bag behind her. Or did Merlin help with that? Magic users' pets could be decidedly odd, but this was the first time mine had done anything quite that dramatic. I got her out, and warned Sulis to be careful about escapees.

Finally, we were in Austin sans cats, checking Gil's almost-empty apartment to see if there was anything else we needed to ship or pack. Gil had decided to put a few pieces of furniture in storage for a while "just in case" (I think he was hoping more magical rooms would materialize). We would keep his bed because it was bigger, relegating mine to the spare room and donating the bed that had been in there. We'd also move his dresser into our bedroom, since there wasn't much extra space in mine.

That was about it, though – other than the pieces we kept and the ones he cared enough about to pay for storage, Gil sold the rest of his furniture and just brought his clothes, books, electronics, guitar, and so on. He'd sold his SUV to a friend for somewhat less than its actual value, with the promise that he could borrow it when he visited Austin. Gil's friends Jimmy and Deepak and their partners had five kids between the two families, and Gil was an adopted uncle to all of them. He took that role seriously and had promised to come back and visit them at least a couple times a year.

We'd spent the flight to Texas brainstorming topics we needed to discuss on the drive, like how we'd split up expenses and chores and even whether we should get married, as well as all the decisions we needed to make for the trip itself – what route we'd take, audiobooks vs. music, what snacks to bring, and so on. The trip decisions were easy to make: we'd start on I-40 rather than I-10 because we'd lived in Phoenix and had driven I-10 way too many times – and also because Phoenix held some bad memories for us. That was where we'd lived together last time, when it hadn't worked out. It wasn't that we were scared to go back there, but choosing another route to Oregon felt symbolic of our new path together.

The driver got to choose what we listened to, since they were the one who had to stay awake. We had no back seat so we wouldn't load up on snacks, just whatever we bought at each fuel stop, with sandwiches or whatever we could find for lunch in the cooler.

The decisions for life after our trip were more momentous, but we had plenty of time to hash them all out and it kept us occupied along the way. Really, it turned out to be the perfect bridge to our new lives; spending 33 hours in a tiny car and small hotel rooms together is actually a pretty good preparation for living together. We made decision after decision, and whoever wasn't driving wrote them down for posterity – we'd split all our joint expenses down the middle for the first year, then re-evaluate whether to combine our bank accounts. We each got to pick a couple of chores we absolutely hated, ranked them in terms of effort, and let the other person handle those, or we'd alternate the ones we both hated. And whoever cooked, the other one would do dishes. And we'd go through our decision list every month or so for that first year, and change whatever didn't work for us, and keep talking until we found solutions that did work. And we agreed to combine our libraries – his, mine and Grandpa Ray's. We'd go through them, find which books we had multiples of, and decide which copy we wanted to keep. It all felt oddly like building a house – no, it felt like building a home. Because we were. I hoped Nyssa would approve.

***

The drive took us nine days – it would have been eight, but we decided to spend an extra day in Las Vegas, since we hadn't been there for a while. Neither of us were big gamblers, but we saw the sights, ate in fancy restaurants, and even rode the zipline over Fremont Street, in what felt like another metaphor for this change in our lives – a headlong rush, but with guidelines to keep us safe and steady.

When we got to Eugene, it was mid-afternoon and we were starving, so instead of heading directly to Percival, I navigated us to one of my favorite casual restaurants, the Bier Stein, on the theory that as a new Eugene-area resident, Gil needed to try the place out. After we ate, we could pick up mead there and do the bonding ceremony to Nyssa that night.

We didn't need any dinner after that meal, and the movers wouldn't deliver Gil's stuff until the next day, so we just brought our packs in, dumped them in the bedroom, texted Sulis to let her know we were home, and looked at each other.

"Ready to get bonded to Nyssa?"

"Remind me again why we decided to wait on deciding whether to get married? It seems a bit silly to more or less get married to a house before I get married to you."

"This one is easier – no licenses needed, no witnesses but ourselves, no societal expectations, no special dress…"

He sighed. "All right. Let's take a quick bio-break, then go for it."

On my way back into the living room, I grabbed the candles, matches, and mead. I looked at Gil and raised my eyebrows. He nodded back that he was ready, so I motioned for him to get the chalice and candlesticks from the mantlepiece. We set the candles up and each lit one, and I poured the mead into the brass chalice.

I said, "Nyssa. Gil is back here now for good – we might travel away from here now and then, but we'll always come back to you. I reaffirm my bond to you." I drank a sip. (Nope, still not a mead fan.) "We'd like to bond Gil to you as well." I handed him the chalice.

He held it and said, "Nyssa, I want to be bonded to

you, together with Macrina here. I hope to live here for many years, and I will do my best to treat you well." He sipped.

As with my previous bonding, there was the loud *ping!* of a nonexistent bell, and the rest of the mead disappeared from the chalice. He looked at me in shock. "Macrina, I think I feel her!"

"You feel her? How?"

"I don't know how to say it. I mean, not like telepathy or anything, just a presence. Like – well, you know how you can enter a dark room and know if someone is there, even if they're being quiet? Like that, but in my head."

I thought about it. "Strange. The same thing happened when I bonded with her, with the ringing sound and the mead disappearing, but I don't remember feeling anything different. But then I always feel the magic around me, so maybe she's part of that. You don't, do you? Or at least you didn't, 'til now."

He shook his head dazedly. "Maybe that's what it is."

"Well, tell me if anything else changes. We should have you do a spell, or even try to create one, and see what happens. But not now, not after driving all day. I'm tired, and I'm sure you are.

"I am. But not too tired for one last run-through of our old tradition, before we start a new one!" he said, putting an arm around me and pulling me gently to him.

EPILOGUE

Moving Gil in wasn't any more fun than you'd think it would be, but at least we got to do it together – and there wasn't that much stuff to move in, after all. The movers not only brought Gil's big bed in, they helped us move my bed into the spare room and took the old one away.

There was room on the library shelves for the books Gil had brought, so we could take our time to winnow out duplicate books. We put Grandpa Ray's small desk and desk chair in storage with Gil's furniture – reluctantly, but we both had desks and chairs that suited us better, and since we'd be working from home, we really did need workspaces that fit us. We'd bring ourselves to sell or donate his one of these days, or ship it to Meg if she wanted it. It still took us more time and work than I could possibly have imagined to unpack everything, find a place for it and get rid of the boxes (except the ones still full of books).

After a few labor-intensive weeks we'd done it, with occasional breaks for a quick hike or a short wine-tasting trip, and we decided to throw a party – a combination house-warming and introduction of both Gil and Nyssa to the whole George group.

> **Macrina:** Would you all be available for a July 4 party at my house? Though it would really be on the 6th, since that's Saturday.

> **Macrina:** Most of you have met my boyfriend Gil, but he's here for good now, so it's to welcome him and to introduce you to Nyssa – my house. If

any of you haven't heard that story yet, I'll tell you at the party!

Genna: We don't have any plans, and I am completely off crutches now! What time on Saturday?

Macrina: We'll start at 5. We can stay in the house until it cools off a bit, and then go outside once it's dark and set fireworks off from the dock.

Andrew: Are kids welcome or adults only?

Macrina: Please do bring Charli and Oliver – I'm going to invite my young apprentice Laxmi and her parents, and they'll be good company for her. And it's not like you could put them to bed early that night anyway, right? I'm sure there will be fireworks all over the neighborhood keeping them awake.

Rob: And at least yours will be safe – your dock is metal, right?

Macrina: Yes, and I've only got the small legal fireworks anyway.

Cayden: I can fix that ;-)

Rob: Cayden! I'm a firefighter!

Cayden: Oh, good. You can make sure I'm practicing safe methods.

Sulis: Get a room, you guys.

***

Everyone was able to make it to the party – yay! They showed up with even more food and drinks than Gil and I had already provided, and both Rob and Cayden were carrying bags of fireworks. So two things were immediately apparent: they'd resolved that argument...and I was going to have to make sure everyone took some leftover food, because there was no way we could even fit all this in the fridge and pantry. Make that three apparent things: I had generous friends.

Once everyone arrived, we all milled around chatting for a while; I noticed that everyone was making an effort to say hi to Gil, and I heard him telling more than one person about our long drive up from Texas. Morgana and Merlin weren't people-shy at all; they went around head-bumping legs and charming people into picking them up. I think Morgana, especially, spent almost the whole party being carried around by one person or another. This would be their first Independence Day, I realized – I hoped both our neighbors' houses and our own dock were far enough away that they wouldn't be too scared by fireworks.

Just in case, I slipped into the bedroom and muttered, "Nyssa, there will probably be fireworks everywhere tonight for July 4ᵗʰ – if you have any way to soundproof the house a bit so the cats don't get scared, can you do that?" I wasn't sure if she'd heard, but I thought the party chatter in the other rooms seemed more muted from here.

It was time to introduce her, anyway. I went back out, grabbed a bottle of champagne and two of the plastic flutes I'd bought, poured the champagne, and said, loudly, "Hey, everybody!"

The room grew quieter. I went on, "You've all met Gil by now – please welcome him as our newest resident of Percival!" Several people clapped, and Nell said, "As town mayor, I say you are *officially* welcome!"

Gil took one of the flutes from me, and held it up. "Thank you all for the welcome! We have champagne for everyone – well, kids, it's up to your parents if you can have a sip. But we do have sparkling cider for you, or for any adults who don't do champagne. Please all get yourselves a glass, so we can make an introduction and a toast."

Everyone grabbed a bubbly drink of one kind or the other, and I took back over as mistress of ceremonies. "This is not an ordinary house, and she's had some surprises for us – we'll give you all a tour of our new spaces and tell you the whole story later, if you haven't heard it yet. We don't know if she's got more surprises up her nonexistent sleeves, but we're looking forward to living in her space for as long as we're able, and we know she loves us too. Please let me introduce our home: Nyssa!"

There was more clapping. A lot more. And of course they'd all heard the story by now, because this was a small town and also most people here were on the George forum – I'd even seen that Leo and Deepthi had joined us there.

A bit later, Rob and Cayden pulled out a second bottle of champagne I hadn't seen them bring in, and Rob said, "Hello, everyone? We have an announcement too – and I'm glad Macrina has champagne flutes, because Cayden here totally forgot about them."

Cayden rolled his eyes and said, "Yeah, it's not like we went shopping together or anything." Rob winked at him, then got more serious and put an arm around him.

"Macrina once told me that we haven't been as subtle as we thought we were. So maybe this is no surprise to anyone, but we wanted to tell you all anyway. We're officially moving in together too, and –"

He looked at Cayden, who said, "And we're engaged. And since you were all there from the beginning, we want you all to come to our wedding."

Rob put in, "At least, once we decide when and where it will be!"

There were congratulations all around, and the air felt like it was buzzing with happiness over the double celebrations. I thought some of that might be from Nyssa, who seemed to like having happy people in her.

We gave tours through the house to anyone who hadn't seen the new rooms already, and Genna pointed out something I should have thought of: if we were ever ill or injured while living in this house and couldn't manage stairs, we now had another way to get to the office, lab and library in the attic, by going through the garage. It still seemed weird to me not to be able to get to the garage directly from the ground floor of the house, but I sensed that Nyssa still had some secrets. We'd been too busy ever since she revealed the library and garage to do any more investigating, but we had the rest of our lives here to learn more about her.

Later that evening, I didn't protest when Rob and Cayden more or less took over the fireworks lighting. We were all on the dock, sitting on chairs or blankets. Gil had one of the chairs, so I sat at his feet and leaned back on his legs, while he played with my hair. I thought back to our very first party, before Samhain, when I'd first gotten a taste of how much these people could mean to me, mulling over the past not-quite-a-year, and how much had changed in that time. I hadn't really gone anywhere much, and I'd still spent most of my time at home – though, thankfully, not quite as much as in the first year of the pandemic. Things had opened up, and I only wore a mask now in very public indoor areas, like airports or supermarkets, but I felt comfortable having this group of people inside my home. In this short time, I'd gained good friends, a self-aware house, an apprentice, and most important, the man I'd loved for so many years to be by my side every day instead of thousands of miles away.

Plus, right now, I had champagne, fireworks and a warm man to curl up against. No complaints here!

ACKNOWLEDGEMENTS

I have a lot of people to thank, without whom this book would have been nothing but a short-lived writing hobby for me. First, thanks to you for reading this book! If you liked it, please leave a review on Amazon or Goodreads – Indie authors depend heavily on reviews to get their books made visible, and reviews are also a favor to other readers to help them find books they might enjoy.

This book both takes place in a village, and took a village to create. Foremost among those are the book's three godmothers / alpha readers: Maria Elmvang, who read the first few pages and told me this book was worth doing, and then reinforced that as one of my alpha readers. My other two incredible alpha readers, Lore Deus and Allison Aldrich Smith, gave me extremely useful feedback both general and specific. The three of them together also exemplified in my mind the people I was writing for, as I was writing the first draft.

I also owe a lot to seasoned writers Mark Hayden and Alma Alexander, who reached back their hands to help me begin to walk the path they've traveled successfully. They're very different writers, from me and from each other, and both well worth checking out if you haven't already.

Next, to the Ravelry FLFT writing group, who provided support and useful information along the way (with special thanks for Elaine Fuller and Diana Bolsinger for starting the discussion thread). I'd also like to thank Ravelry friend Vesna Gronosky who gave me permission to borrow her cats' names for Merlin and Morgana, and as a memorial to her Merlin, may he always hunt in summer fields.

Thank you to my beta readers, especially the always Quality-minded Martha Jones; Kiwi Carlisle; Peggy O'Kane; and Kim Finch, for letting me know what worked for them and what didn't, and to my editor Phyllis Irene Radford, who came in and caught whatever mistakes no one else had found. (Any errors left in are my own fault entirely.)

To the Moai group: Sharon who started it all, Kim, Kerry, Sherrill, and Lori, who were there for sisterhood as well as the real-world version of some of the events that inspired Macrina's life in post-pandemic small-town Oregon.

And more than anyone else, to Ted: husband, best friend and life partner, who took this project seriously from its beginning, encouraged and supported this book as well as my previous (nonfiction) one, gave me his unerring eye in spotting wording issues. Without him, my life would be altogether different and almost certainly not as good. I'm still sorry I never got to put a dedication in the first book!

ABOUT THE AUTHOR

A Home in Percival is Paula Berman's first novel; her previous publication is Successful Business Process Management: What You Need to Know (AMACOM, 2014), but you should only read that one if it's relevant to your job.

Paula lives in a small lakeside town in Oregon that is rather like Percival, with her husband and two cats who bear an even stronger resemblance to Merlin and Morgana (the cats, not the husband). Her house is not self-aware, unfortunately. When not working on a sequel to A Home in Percival, she reads, rows, reads, knits, reads, kayaks, reads, and hangs out with friends who bear no resemblance at all to any of her characters.